WENDY ALEC

END OF DAYS

INSP:RE

Harper*Inspire*, an imprint of
HarperCollins Christian Publishing
1 London Bridge Street
London SE1 9GF

www.harpercollins.co.uk

First published by HarperCollins Publishers 2018
4

A catalogue record for this book is available from the British Library

ISBN: 9780310091011 (TPB)
ISBN: 9780310096238 (ebook)

This novel is entirely a work of fiction.
The names, characters and incidents portrayed in it are
the work of the author's imagination. Any resemblance to
actual persons, living or dead, events or localities is
entirely coincidental.

Set in Sabon Lt Std by Palimpsest Book Production Limited,
Falkirk, Stirlingshire

Printed and bound in the UK by CPI Group (UK) Ltd, Croydon CR0 4YY

MIX
Paper from
responsible sources
FSC
www.fsc.org
FSC™ C007454

This book is produced from independently certified FSC™ paper to ensure
responsible forest management.

For more information visit: www.harpercollins.co.uk/green

PROLOGUE

Large Hadron Collider
574 Feet below Earth's Surface
CERN
North-West Suburbs of Geneva
Franco-Swiss Border
2026

Professor Alessio Bernoulli, Chief Physicist of CERN, removed his glasses and rubbed his eyes for the fifth time in ten minutes.

They were still there. The apparitions.

Except that they were no longer apparitions.

The forms directly in front of him were rapidly materializing from a fine ethereal substance into something resembling what, up until a minute ago, he would have characterized as flesh and blood.

Bernoulli took two steps backward.

With trembling fingers, he pushed his hands through his long dark hair and placed his glasses back on the end of his nose.

He couldn't accurately count the creatures.

More of them were materializing with every passing second.

They were at least eighteen feet in height, some far taller, their heads gigantic in circumference. Each figure was at least three times the size of a human.

He stumbled back towards the hidden alarm system as his decades of scientific training imprinted every grotesque detail of the monsters in his mind.

Yellow hair, matted and coarse. On each hand and foot, an extra digit. On each wrist and ankle, a broad copper manacle.

Monstrous grey wings springing from massive shoulders.

Eyes glimmering with the lilac pallor characteristic of all Nephilim.

'You have summoned us, the Fallen, from our sleep beneath the Earth in the lowest levels of hell, the bottomless pits of darkness until the time of the Great Judgement.' The monster was now speaking – in perfect Italian. 'Why do you summon us? Is it time?'

'Wh-who . . . *what* . . . are you?' Bernoulli managed to stammer, still edging his way toward the alarm.

His eyes locked on to the underside of the far-left console. Perspiration broke out over his brow.

'Is it time?' the monster rasped. 'We left our First Estate and lay with the daughters of Earth. We are the Fallen, the Nephilim, who sodomized the race of men. We are the Fallen, who conducted genetic experiments and created hybrids and chimeras – beasts and monsters. Is it time? Is it time?'

Perspiration drenched Bernoulli's crisp white shirt.

He was not a religious man, far from it, but the whispered myth of Genesis 6 was manifesting right in front of his eyes. The monstrous hybrid fallen giants, spawned from the co-habitation of fallen angels and human women.

His eyes fixed on the enormous copper shackles around the monsters' ankles. With each step, the creatures' chains ripped up the smooth marble tiling of the laboratory floor.

Bernoulli was now only a foot and a half from salvation.

Suddenly, the hideous monsters all parted as one. Bernoulli stared, rooted to the ground in terror, at the grotesque apparition lumbering slowly towards him out of the collider.

A creature thirty feet in height materialized in the tunnel. It had the body of a colossus, a huge lashing tail of seven poisonous serpents, six muscular arms growing from the sides of its ribcage, and three enormous heads. One head was of a lion with six eyes. Another was of a monstrous leviathan with black, rubbery skin and fire billowing from its nostrils. A goat's head rose from the creature's back.

The last living vision that Alessio Bernoulli saw was six rows of grotesque yellowed teeth, the instant before they ripped into his neck.

'We have opened the gates of hell,' he gurgled, suffocating, as the blood from his carotid artery drained from his neck.

His lifeless, glassy eyes stared up at the Large Hadron Collider, where he lay drowned in his own blood.

No one noticed the slight, petrified girl, with long dark hair and big glasses, peering through the glass doors . . . then running for her life.

Castel Gandolfo, Italy
Seven Days Earlier

Raffaelle Ricci, 19-year-old assistant to Father d'Angelis, walked swiftly through the cloisters' ancient winding corridors, his long dark hair falling across his beatific features.

He whistled softly as he did a cartwheel through the vast observatory library housing the priceless antique works of Copernicus, Galileo, Newton, and Kepler – euphoric in the fact that he was finally alone . . . king of the castle.

Apart from his adored mentor.

And the stranger.

The Italian *carabinieri* who on a normal day would be on alert, their sub-machine-guns at the ready, were glaringly absent from their posts. Raffaele grinned, making a beeline for the chestnut doors towering eighteen foot high at the east side of the *castello*.

Pushing them open, he entered the Palace wing that now housed the headquarters of the Vatican Observatory. Raffaele paced through the newly renovated corridors and stopped at a set of doors exquisitely carved with interlacing leaves. Here lived Father d'Angelis, who was not only the Chief Astronomer but also a personal confidant and mentor to the Pope himself.

He stared down at the two trays of food that lay untouched on the antique Aubusson rug. He shook his head in disapproval.

Four days previously, Father d'Angelis had dismissed all the ecclesiastical staff, apart from Raffaelle.

And the stranger.

The stranger who had arrived at Castel Gandolfo on a bicycle, precisely seventy-two hours and twenty-two minutes earlier, dressed in the humble garb of an Italian farmer, his features almost completely hidden beneath a straw hat.

Father D'Angelis himself had welcomed him. Minutes later, they had disappeared into the father's private cloister.

For three days, Raffalle's meticulously laid silver trays – laden with the finest preserves, freshly baked wholegrain bread, lean and tender bresaola flown in on a private jet from Valtellina, festooned with pressed white linen napkins, silver cutlery, and the Limoges Chine Petit Panier Chinois china that the Chief Astronomer currently favoured – had been left outside the huge mahogany doors. Untouched.

This was the fourth day that the men had been locked

within the confines of the ancient chamber. Raffaelle knelt down and gathered the trays, sighing, resigned to the fact that his meticulously crafted handiwork had once again gone unappreciated.

Only he and one other in the entire Vatican even knew that the two men were meeting. And only the two men themselves would ever know the unspeakable horror of the things discussed within the ancient stone walls.

The Third Secret of Fatima.

The sophisticated, maleficent magic of fallen angelic entities.

Interdimensional portals.

CERN.

The young intern was about to retreat to the palace kitchens, having been given strict instructions that he was not to disturb the father and his guest under any circumstance.

But Father d'Angelis refusing his favourite food? The aged salted beef that was his favourite delicacy?

He frowned deeply, then taking his life in his hands, moved toward the door, took a deep breath, and knocked.

There came the faintest tread of slippered feet, then the key turned in the lock. The door edged open a few inches.

The stranger lifted his head. His eyes met Raffaele's.

It was the head of the Roman Catholic Church, the ruler of the Vatican, his Holy Eminence, Pope Boniface XI.

The Pope looked up from the towers of papers, his normally tranquil countenance clouded in righteous anger.

'Iniquitous!' He slammed the papers down onto the table. 'It is consummate evil. Even in all my days as a humble priest in Malta – in all my days as an exorcist – never *ever* . . .'

His right hand trembled.

Father d'Angelis laid a gentle hand on his friend's shoulder.

'Nikola,' he pleaded, his pale blue eyes shining with affection. 'Beloved Nikola,' he said, almost in an undertone. 'We exist in the time of the very end. The Great Tribulation. We stand at the very edge of all things.'

'But *this* . . .' Pope Boniface, once known as Nikola Cassar-Desain, removed his spectacles with trembling fingers. 'Francois, old friend, this is consummate evil. Their doomsday machine. It is an attempt to open the interdimensional gateways; the wormholes that will allow evil beings, dark spiritual forces, fallen angels, demons, freely into our dimension.' He paced the room. 'It is Nimrod reborn; a twenty-first-century Tower of Babel!'

'Ah, Nikola,' Francois d'Angelis gazed as if into remote distances. 'It has been the quest of corrupt men for centuries: to open up a portal to the other side.'

'Their attempt . . .'

'This is no mere attempt.' Francois d'Angelis's voice was very soft. 'That CERN will open up the hyperdimensional stargates is beyond question.'

The Chief Astronomer stood and stared out over the lake glimmering in the sunset. His voice quavered. 'Over four hundred years ago, John Dee, Adviser to Queen Elizabeth I, attempted to open a stargate – a literal stairway to the heavens.' He turned to the Pope. 'It was one of the first recorded attempts at opening a portal to another dimension. The spiritual entities he summoned called themselves the Enochian Angels; evil angelic forces that communicated their dark magic to Dee. He discovered through his interactions with the Enochians that there were watchtowers where stargates exist on the Earth. Stargates or wormholes that could be accessed by performing dark apocalyptic spells. According to his writings, the Enochian entities, however, refused to allow Dee to initiate the apocalypse. They told him that a specific time had been set.'

6

The Pope stood perfectly still. 'And you believe that time is now?'

'I believe it is so. Yes.'

'The apocalypse working,' the Pope murmured. 'I remember this from my early years as an exorcist. In the twentieth century, Aleister Crowley tried to complete it.'

Father d'Angelis removed his pince-nez and placed them carefully on his antique writing desk.

'Crowley.' The Pope's voice took on a tone that Father d'Angelis had never before heard from the Holy Father. 'Aleister Crowley, British occultist, known by some as the wickedest man in the world. Years ago, my old mentor, Brother Amartini met him one stormy night in St Ives, Cornwall. Crowley was much older by then but Brother Amartini was a very young and inexperienced exorcist and thought Crowley was without doubt the most evil man that ever existed.' The Pope's voice was barely audible. 'It was his eyes apparently.'

He raised his face to Father d'Angelis.

'He never forgot his eyes. It was as though he was looking directly into the eyes of the *diabolus*. It was the day that Brother Amartini discovered that consummate evil truly existed amongst us.'

He hesitated. 'Even Crowley failed to open the portal.'

'Yes. He failed. For the past 4,500 years,' Father d'Angelis continued, still *sotto voce*, 'Lucifer and his cohorts have been waiting for an opportunity to open the gate. Finally, man's science has caught up with the knowledge of the Fallen Watchers. This time using sophisticated scientific methods, they have found a high-powered dimensional device that can bend space-time, open dimensional portals – stargates. That device is the Large Hadron Collider at CERN.'

'Open the portals to where?' the Pope breathed. 'Or to *what*?'

7

Father d'Angelis gazed in silence at the full moon, suspended above the lapping waters of Lake Albano.

'*That,* old friend, is what we are here to uncover.'

Large Hadron Collider
CERN

The slender dark-haired girl locked herself in a small glass anteroom, hyperventilating. She scrabbled on the floor for her heavy black-rimmed glasses, grasped them in her left hand and held her eye to the scanner. The metal door in front of her swung open.

Putting on her glasses, she studied the meticulously numbered files of the secret archive. The sinister apocalyptic files, hidden far away from public scrutiny, stretched forty feet high, from floor to ceiling – some twelve miles of shelving.

She rushed inside, willing herself to concentrate. She had done this every day for the past two weeks, delivering the strange black files with the crest of golden vipers into the professor's hands each night at 2 a.m., returning them before dawn.

Professor Bernoulli had sworn her to secrecy.

She walked swiftly to archive number 1006666 and sifted through the catalogued files until she found the slim gold box with the ornate embossed crest.

She brought her gaze to the strange carving of an eye on the box. It clicked open. Removing the ten black files, each marked 'BABEL', she tucked them into her rucksack, then quickly entered a ten-digit code. The pulsating red light in the box turned green and a hidden compartment clicked open.

Inside was a box the size of a matchbox, carved from crystal. Lifting off the lid, she took out a computer chip no bigger than a pinhead. Popping open the back of her digital watch, she dropped the chip into a tiny cubical space in the watch and replaced the cover.

She had one more mission.

Hidden in Alessio Bernoulli's private archives were her secret papers.

She ran down the aisle, turned right, then a sharp left down three flights of wooden stairs until she reached the small musty private archive and stopped.

She and Alessio Bernoulli had the only access to Archive 33. She reached for an unmarked black box on the fifth shelf and entered a digital code.

The box snapped open.

There was the plain beige file belonging to her great-uncle Professor Hamish Mackenzie: Number 112, marked 'AVELINE. 1981. Restricted access for 50 years'.

She removed the file from the box and placed it in her rucksack.

Then raced at breakneck speed out of the room, through the deserted corridors.

Hurtling down the modern steel emergency staircase, until she reached a rusted metal stairway in the tunnel.

Running for her life.

Down . . .

Down . . .

Down . . .

Seventy-two Hours Later

'We are sure, then?'

Francois d'Angelis nodded. 'It is everything we feared and worse. They will bend the timeline and open the wormhole that has been closed for all eternity in the heart of our Milky Way galaxy. They have discovered what holds back the veil between two spiritual realms. Antimatter.'

The Pope rubbed his forehead, scowling. 'Antimatter?'

Father d'Angelis nodded. 'Antimatter is always connected to its source: chaos, from which all antimatter emanates.'

They exchanged foreboding glances.

'Lucifer's realm,' Father d'Angelis said. 'Call it a different frequency or a different realm. Antimatter is so powerful that when released, it cannot be contained.'

'So CERN is trying to manipulate the darkness for their own ends,' the Pope replied.

Father d'Angelis sighed deeply. 'Yes. Manipulating frequencies and polarities. The orchestrators, the Black Jesuits . . . The Brotherhood.'

'They answer to no one,' the Pope said, swinging around, pale. 'They have only one master.'

Father d'Angelis, looking grimly at his old friend, said, 'Lorcan De Molay himself.'

'Francois, what is their endgame?'

Father d'Angelis said, '"For if God spared not the angels that sinned, but cast them down to Tartarus and delivered them into chains of darkness, to be reserved unto judgment." Second letter of Peter, chapter two, verse four. Nikola, they intend to release the two hundred.'

'The two hundred?'

Father d'Angelis nodded. 'The holy Scriptures reveal that these fallen angels – sons of God – of Genesis 6 are confined in Tartarus. CERN is erected above the temple of the Greek god Apollyon.'

'Abbadon.'

'The same. The Brotherhood's intention is to release the reprobate Watchers from where they lie shackled in darkness. The world of the occult knows exactly the hour that the imprisoned ones will be released, as the energy released by CERN causes the prison gates of the devils to open.'

Father d'Angelis's voice caught. 'Nikola, their diabolical

intention is in no doubt. Abaddon and the fallen angelic entities imprisoned in Tartarus.'

He turned to stare out at the calm waters of the volcanic crater lake that shimmered in the falling Italian dusk.

'They intend to release the supercriminals of the universe.' His veined hands trembled. 'They are opening the Abyss.'

CHAPTER ONE

Jerusalem

December 2026

Jason De Vere lay on his side, the steel handcuffs chafing his wrists, gasping for breath under the suffocating material of the burlap. His heart was hammering in his chest like a proverbial drum.

Tears, mucus and congealed blood ran down his cheeks. The blood.

Oh god, he screamed noiselessly. *Adrian's blood.*

He had just murdered his own brother.

Assassinated Adrian De Vere, the President of most of the Western World.

One shot through his neck. The second, straight through the temple.

Shivers ran down his spine. The unrelenting thudding of his heart accelerated to fever pitch.

Blood. He could still taste Adrian's blood on his parched swollen lips.

He retched violently under the burlap. Gasping desperately for breath, choking. Breathing in his own vomit.

Unrelenting image after image bombarded his brain.

Adrian's blood spurting from his carotid artery onto his face . . . onto his hands . . . staining his shirt.

He could feel the sweat running down his spine.

Voices. There were voices shouting in Hebrew. In German. Doors slamming. The sound of van doors opening above him.

He was being dragged unceremoniously out of the van and onto his feet. Someone shoved him forward. He stumbled to his knees. The black burlap was pulled roughly from his head.

He was staring straight into the squat black barrel of a sig Sauer P22 semi-automatic pistol.

Oh god. This was it.

They were going to shoot him. In cold blood. He steeled himself. He was beyond caring. Julia was dead.

Suddenly he realised his face was wet with tears.

Julia. He had never got to tell her how desperately he still loved her.

Images of her long blonde hair, her London rock-chick charm, her feisty passion for life, intersected with vivid memories of them arguing passionately . . . his storming out . . . the brutal divorce. Whisky had become his saviour, his mind-numbing narcotic.

But *Lily*.

What would happen to Lily?

His adored, intrepid, raven-haired, green-eyed daughter.

Lily. He had to stay alive for Lily.

He raised his head by degrees as his entire body shuddered violently.

Looming over him was a tall, bony man with a grey complexion, humourless eyes and badly dyed jet-black cropped hair. He wore his trademark thin round spectacles and poorly fitting black suit. Kurt Guber. 'The Butcher'. Director of EU Special Service Operations. Adrian's ruthless Nazi sidekick and exotic-weapons specialist.

14

'My, my. If it isn't Jason De Vere. Cold-blooded murderer. Puts Lee Harvey Oswald – how do you English phrase it? – in the shade.'

His expressionless pale eyes bored into Jason's dispassionately.

Guber made a slow circle around him, caressing the semi-automatic pistol in his black leather gloved hands.

'Guber,' Jason uttered.

Guber kicked him viciously in the stomach with his iron-tipped boots.

Jason collapsed onto the snow-covered ground, screaming in agony, his knees drawn up to his chest. Saliva ran down his chin.

'I *could* shoot you now in cold blood,' Guber stated in his guttural, clipped German accent. He took a swig of brandy from his ever-present hip flask. 'But that would spoil *all* the surprises I have in store for you. No, Herr De Vere. This is just . . . a little taster; an aperitif.

'They are preparing your cell as we converse. I am assured it is the worst prison this miserable tract of dust has to offer. Black site.' He punched Jason savagely in the face with his gloved fist. 'Undisclosed location.' He twisted Jason's arm back till he groaned in agony.

'My intelligence assures me its guards are handpicked; the most barbaric torturers on the planet.'

He raised his eyebrows.

'One can't put a price on the marvels of efficient waterboarding.'

Jason's breathing was hard and fast.

'You *bastard*, Guber.'

'*Ich kann ein Bastard sein.*' Guber stared at Jason with humourless eyes. 'But you, Jason De Vere, are the *walking dead.*'

Guber walked back towards his sleek black electric

Mercedes Model X and clicked the remote. The door opened.

Guber settled himself casually into the cream leather driver's seat. The door shut automatically.

The tinted window rolled down.

'Travis!' Guber addressed a tall lean man with cropped brown hair. 'Escort the prisoner to hell.'

Guber accelerated away at speed, disappearing down the narrow Mount of Olives Road towards Jerusalem.

Neil Travis, ex-SAS man, head of Adrian De Vere's security services, cupped his hand over his earpiece.

'Copy that,' he nodded.

'Code Red. Jerusalem Precinct 7!' he shouted to the Special Forces unit guarding the van.

'Code Red! *Yallah!* Resisters!' he yelled. 'I'll deal with De Vere.'

Six militia in black saluted Travis, sprinted towards a second van, revved the engine and roared off in the direction of the Old City.

Travis looked around, every muscle in his body taut. Wired. He laid his sub-machine-gun on the front seat of the van, then holstered his revolver.

He reached out his hand to Jason.

Jason stared up at him, dazed, his mind swimming.

'Get up, Jason De Vere,' Travis said urgently. 'Time's not on our side.'

Jason stared in confusion at Travis. He staggered clumsily to his feet. He glanced back towards the sub-machine-gun.

'I . . . I don't understand.'

Travis turned to a tall figure standing in the shadows outside a massive iron gate.

'He's all yours,' he said to the figure. 'Part of my debt repaid.'

Feeling as though he was part of a voyeuristic audience at a surreal movie premiere, Jason watched the two men embrace.

16

He rubbed his eyes. He must be hallucinating. The second man was Liam Mercer, Jason's personal bodyguard and former Navy Seal.

There was no mistaking it. Six foot two, lean and muscular, cropped blond hair, close-fitting black suit.

Incredulous, Jason looked from Mercer to Travis. They could almost be brothers.

'Mer– Mercer?' Jason stammered. Travis placed his hand on Jason's shoulder.

'You're in safe hands now, Mr De Vere, sir.'

'I don't understand.'

'There'll be time to explain later. You have an appointment.'

Mercer pushed open the gate and led Jason, who was leaning on him heavily, through the tourists' Gethsemane to a second smaller garden.

Jason collapsed in agony onto the ground underneath an ancient, gnarled olive tree, barely conscious.

Mercer pulled out a small hypodermic pack, removed a small syringe, inserted it into a phial, drew the plunger and jabbed it into Jason's thigh.

'Painkiller,' he said. 'It'll take the edge off, sir, until Lane-Fox picks you up.'

Leaving Jason, Mercer swiftly retraced his steps back to the gate, slamming it shut behind him, to rejoin Travis.

'We have three hours before Guber discovers the package has not been delivered to the black site,' Travis said tersely.

Mercer nodded.

Both Mercer's and Travis's bodies started to transform until they stood facing each other – towering, lean, imperial angelic forms with vast wings outstretched.

Mercer, now Michael, stood nine foot tall. He removed his silver battle helmet. Travis, now the equally tall Astaroth, did the same, shaking his long brown hair free from its bands.

'Astaroth, once my close and trusted companion, commander of my armies, return with me,' Michael pleaded. 'Lucifer's fury against you will be unrestrained.'

'Of this I am well aware.'

'He will send you to the Abyss.'

Astaroth shook his head. 'No. He will force me to battle against you in the coming war. He will take great delight in seeing me forced to fight my former comrades, and my revered compatriot and commander.'

'It will not go well with you, Astaroth,' Michael urged.

'I told you, Michael. I made my choice. There is no way back for me. I have paid some of my debt. But I can never repay enough.'

Astaroth stood before Michael, his once-noble features fierce. 'The next time we meet' – Astaroth bowed in deference to Michael – 'it shall be in battle.'

'Astaroth!'

Astaroth vanished before his eyes.

Gates of Gethsemane
Jerusalem
Dawn

The battered green 1971 Morris Minor came to a halt outside the old gates of the ancient garden, just as the sun started to rise over the walls of Jerusalem. Alex Lane-Fox, twenty-five-year-old investigative journalist, got out of the car and limped through the half-opened gates.

A few yards away, under one of the ancient olive trees, he caught sight of Jason. Alex walked over to where Jason lay facedown in the dirt and half-melted snow. He knelt beside him.

'Uncle Jas!' He shook Jason's shoulder. '*Uncle Jas!* Thank god you're okay. We got a cryptic message you were here.

They're looking for you. It's a manhunt. Guber caught me, but I escaped. Everything's still in chaos. There are military search parties all over the city hunting for you. You have to come with me.'

Jason curled in on himself.

Alex turned Jason's face and, with a light touch, brushed the dirt from his cheeks. Jason pried open his groggy eyelids.

'Julia . . . Julia, is that you?' His arms flailed in panic.

Alarmed, Alex got him upright. 'No, Uncle Jas. It's Alex. Alex Lane-Fox.'

'Julia . . . Where is she? I need to see Julia.'

Alex grasped Jason by the shoulders. 'Uncle Jas, We have to leave. They're looking for you.'

'Who?' Jason mumbled. 'Who is looking for me?'

As fast as he could, wincing from the pain in his right leg, Alex led the disorientated Jason out through the garden gates and into the back seat of the ancient Morris Minor.

Then he put the car into gear and drove like a bat out of hell toward the old city.

Abbey
Outer Hebrides
11.15 a.m.

A lone priest in his black cassock, a rucksack slung over his back, moved swiftly through the strangely deserted corridors of the red-granite medieval abbey, his footsteps echoing on the polished stone floor.

He frowned.

There were no signs of the normal hustle and bustle of the usual thriving abbey community.

It was Friday. The priest popped his head around the kitchen where Brother Diarmait should without doubt be castigating two novices as he meticulously prepared the

19

customary Friday dinner menu. It had never deviated in two decades – the favourite dish of their beloved abbot, Father Columba: steak and kidney pie, mounds of fresh steamed kale and Brother Diarmait's herbed mashed potato, a recipe he guarded as zealously as Colonel Sanders had protected his eleven secret herbs and spices.

The kitchen was deserted.

The priest walked swiftly to the laundry, always a place of frenetic activity. A mountain of linen lay abandoned next to the sink. The washing machine and tumble drier were silent. He peered out of the small window overlooking the farmyard and workshops. Deserted. He made a beeline for the library where Brother Aidan would be quietly archiving theological and classical texts, and his beloved books of antiquities. The room was empty, the computer still running.

He softly closed the library door, then walked in the direction of the chapel where the monks held their matins at 11 o'clock precisely, every morning of their lives. It was empty.

Where *was* everyone? In fact, where was *any*one?

A strange spine-tingling foreboding crept through every fibre of the priest's being.

There was no sign of life anywhere.

He retraced his steps to the atrium, noting that the hands on the antique grandfather clock there were stopped at 3.07 then climbed the wide mahogany stairs two at a time to the living quarters on the second floor, a strange mixture of dread and euphoria in his heart.

He pushed opened the first dormitory door and caught his breath, surveying the room. Each bed had been slept in, the sheets and blankets and pillows awry. The first rule of Father Columba was never broken: precisely made beds with hospital corners.

Father Columba was generous by nature and progressive.

Next to each bed, an iPhone was still plugged in. The priest checked the time on the first iPhone: 3.07 a.m. He swiftly checked each device in the dormitory. Every iPhone clock had stopped at precisely the same time.

He slammed the door and moved immediately to the second dormitory. And the third.

Empty. The clocks had all stopped at exactly the same time.

He knew exactly where he must head next.

He climbed the narrow creaking wooden stairs to the Abbot's attic bedroom and pushed open the old teak door.

Father Columba's bed was in apple-pie order. His night habit lay discarded on the floor next to the bed. The hands of the Abbot's deep-blue antique alarm clock were stopped at 3.07 a.m.

There it lay – the familiar, well-worn, black leather-bound Holy Bible, still open at the place where Father Columba had stopped in the reading he had conducted for vespers from two to four in the morning every night of his life.

The priest picked it up and held it to his lips in remembrance of the softly spoken, gentle Abbot; his mentor for over thirty-five years.

A small brown envelope fell out of the bible.

In the Abbot's elegant italic hand, his own name was scrawled on it.

He placed the bible back on the side table, pushed the envelope into the rucksack, retraced his steps back down the stairs into the atrium, turned right at the end of the corridor and stopped outside a small wooden door.

He removed a cluster of iron keys from the belt of his cassock and, with trembling hands, tried them one by one.

Finally, the door to Father Columba's private study and library opened.

Pushing past the Abbot's mahogany desk, he took a smaller set of keys from a deep pocket in his robes and moved straight towards a rusted filing cabinet that lay underneath the unending rows of musty books.

He tried the first, second, then third key in frustration, then fished one more key from a rosary around his neck.

He inserted it in the lock, turned it. The cabinet door sprang open.

The priest knelt and sifted through the sixty meticulously ordered files, finally stopping on one. He took it out and opened it, shaking the contents out onto the floor.

Birth certificates; death certificates; postmortem results; X-rays; black-and-white photographs; three passports.

He scrambled for his iPhone and methodically photographed the X-rays, then eight documents. He stuffed the passports and the remaining documents and photographs into the rucksack, rushed out of the room . . . then hesitated.

Turning a quick right into a large kitchen, he opened the 1940s Hotpoint refrigerator and stared at the rotting food.

He slammed the fridge door in disgust, then left by the kitchen door.

The priest sprinted through the deserted kitchen gardens, hiked up his cassock, vaulted over the crumbling stone wall of the monastery, and ran out into the isolated windswept wilds. He kept running through a broad expanse of peat bog and didn't slow down until he had disappeared into the sprawling, heather-clad mountains.

Boardroom
One World Bank
Forty-Fourth Floor
Manhattan, New York City

Lorcan De Molay sat at the head of the enormous boardroom table. Charles Xavier Chessler sat to his right, Kurt Guber to his left.

De Molay's face, although strangely scarred, was imperious. The wide brow and straight patrician nose framed sapphire eyes that held a haunting, mesmerizing beauty. His raven hair was pulled back fastidiously from his high cheekbones, into a single braid.

Drawing heavily on his cigar, he surveyed the twelve men around the table.

'The clone Adrian De Vere lies in state as we speak,' he said. 'In precisely three days, the second resurrection in the history of the Western world shall occur. This time, however, unlike his unfortunate predecessor's, in an inconsequential tomb, witnessed by a lone ex-prostitute . . .' He gave a condescending smile and let the silence hang in the room. Finally, he continued. 'Unlike that of his unfortunate prede-cessor, the resurrection of Adrian De Vere will be witnessed by six billion global viewers in real time. The Nazarene's pathetic resurrection pales by comparison. Seventy-two hours later, he will be crowned King Alexander VIII, named for his great-great-grandfather of Julius De Vere's ancestral line. We will introduce Darsoc and the Grey Magus as ascended gods.' With heavy emphasis, he stubbed out his cigar in the marble ashtray, then rose and circled the room. 'And announce that *we,* as ascended gods, were the creators of the race of men. Then our coup d'état: we break our covenant with Israel – the Concordat of Solomon is annulled. Jerusalem is finally ours.'

He smiled. 'To business, then, gentlemen.'

He nodded to Guber, who flicked a switch, and the entire right wall of the room became a screen.

'The Mark of Alexander is ready, Your Excellency,' Guber said in his heavy German accent. He stood up.

'Pale Horse was our first test run. It exceeded all our expectations. The Mark of Alexander is now perfected. As we meet, four billion chips are being shipped to designated

23

precincts all across the territories of our ten-kingdom axis. Every human being on this planet will be gagging for it.'

He nodded to Xavier Chessler.

'The chip of immortality, the elixir of youth,' Chessler said with a self-satisfied smile. 'The chip that repairs any malfunction in DNA. Healings of cancer, multiple sclerosis, Alzheimer's, and a hundred other deadly maladies will occur instantaneously upon inoculation.'

Images appeared on the screen.

'Once the chip is inserted in the right arm,' Guber said, 'as we are aware, the DNA codes will interact with the recipient's genome instantly. A masked genetic marker will be activated by a second chip in the forehead. It will not only quite literally destroy any malfunction or damage in the recipient's personal DNA, but will simultaneously add a non-human gene. Inserted DNA originating from a non-human species will rewrite the human genetic code. Nephilim DNA; the source code of the Fallen.'

'Every human recipient on the planet will have its human source code quietly mutated forever,' Dieter Von Hallstein murmured.

'Our greatest triumph in the history of the Fallen to date,' Chessler continued. 'Four billion humans implanted with the DNA of the Fallen. Four billion mind-controlled mutant super-soldiers. Every chip monitored from our underground laboratories in Babel.'

De Molay gave a malevolent smile. 'These resisters,' he murmured. 'This *Ghost* . . .'

'Rumours, Your Excellency,' Chessler said dismissively.

De Molay walked nearer to Chessler, who began to tremble.

'*Rumours*,' De Molay hissed. 'A hundred and fifty thousand nameless, faceless elite mercenaries wiped out our Axis Ten forces in the Eastern Bloc. Germany, Russia, Norway, Sweden. And you dare to call them *rumours*?' he screamed.

24

His hand pressed hard on the base of Chessler's neck.

'Who – are – they?'

His fingers continued to press.

'All – all we know, Your Excellency, is that they are . . .' Chessler gasped for breath. 'Israelis, Your Excellency.' Chessler clicked the remote.

'Israelis.' De Molay stared at the screen in undisguised hatred. 'Sayeret Matkal,' he whispered. 'Shayetet Thirteen: elite naval unit, counterguerrillas. Ferocious, highly trained, deadly mercenaries.'

He released his hold on Chessler.

Still gasping, Chessler croaked, 'They are registered on no databases, Your Excellency. But all under twenty-five years of age.'

'Who,' Lorcan De Molay's voice was like ice, 'who is this Ghost?'

'We don't . . . we don't know, Your Excellency.' Chessler gulped. 'He moves three hundred and sixty-five days a year. Never sleeps twice in the same place. No one has ever seen his face. No one knows his identity. Rumour . . . rumour has it that he bears a supernatural seal – that he cannot be killed.'

De Molay surveyed the room, then lit up another cigar. 'Babel.'

Guber flicked a switch, and the entire side wall of the boardroom became a virtual map of Babel, the new Iraq.

Guber nodded to Dieter Von Hallstein.

'Gentlemen, to recap,' Von Hallstein said. 'Iraq, now known as Babel, has been declared uninhabitable due to our false reports of the greatest nuclear spill ever recorded. Since February, no human has been allowed access for a radius of a 120 miles, enabling the implementation of our master plan: the erection of the City of Babel, headquarters of the Fallen.

'Before the evacuation of over forty thousand, we incarcerated a human workforce. They have all received the Mark of Alexander, and are mind-controlled from our underground laboratories. Our mind-control programmers make MKUltra look like kindergarten.

'The crème de la crème of the world's top astrophysicists, particle physicists, astronomers, clinical geneticists, cytogeneticists, genetic engineers, laboratory geneticists, molecular geneticists, population geneticists, research geneticists, nanotechnologists, neutron scientists, architects, antimatter theorists – all working day and night. And, of course, our worker bees.'

The images on the screen changed.

'Babel's supercollider: 55 miles of the most sophisticated underground laboratories, underneath the new Babylon. The supercollider lies in a massive underground ring measuring more than 50 kilometres in circumference, linked under the Euphrates and the Mediterranean to CERN.'

'The Tower?' De Molay smoothed his Black Jesuit robes.

Von Hallstein continued. 'The twelve palaces and Your Excellency's Tower of Alexander are nearing completion and are now habitable for the Fallen in this dimension. Twelve palaces for your twelve Satanic Princes, Your Excellency, surrounding your own palace in the centre of the tower.'

'And De Vere?' De Molay said, blowing a chain of blue-grey smoke rings.

Jason De Vere's face appeared on the screen.

'His live execution will be broadcast as a deterrent to any resisters,' Von Hallstein said, smiling. 'We have implemented the largest manhunt in the history of the world.'

'The bounty?'

'Set at $50 million, Your Excellency. Alive. The execution details are on your desk, Your Excellency.'

'The meeting is adjourned then.' De Molay stood at the floor-length windows overlooking the Atlantic Ocean.

'Oh, and find this Ghost,' he murmured. *'And bring him to me.'*

CHAPTER TWO

Armenian Quarter

Old City
Jerusalem

Jason leaned heavily on Alex as they walked through a maze of narrow, winding cobbled streets, past a hookah bar and the local souk where middle-aged, heavy-jowled men with pot bellies were playing cards. The intense aroma of freshly roasted coffee and recently baked bread, mingling with the scent of incense and spices, wafted through the streets, invading their nostrils.

'Where are we going?' Jason rasped.

'Armenian Compound. My grandparents are hiding out with old family friends, the Petrosians. Guber will scour the whole of Jerusalem before searching there.'

The two men continued past the cacophony of vendors displaying their wares and old women and tourists haggling over the prices of silks, Caucasian rugs, and spices. They narrowly missed a group of young children running towards them, screaming in glee.

'How far?' rasped Jason.

'Nearly there.'

Alex led Jason past the Gulbenkian Library and the Convent of Holy Archangels, turned right down a narrow alleyway, then sharp left, then ducked into an alcove. Alex knocked four times on a tiny door like the entry to a crypt.

Silence. Then the sound of multiple locks turning.

'Come in, come in. *Macht schnell*!'

Alex's feisty and silver-haired grandmother, eighty-three-year-old Rebekah Weiss, grasped Jason swiftly by the arm, looked up and down the deserted alleyway, and then hustled him and Alex into the cramped quarters of the old Armenian city apartment.

'Search parties are combing Jerusalem, looking for Jason. The last place they will look is the Armenian Quarter.'

She turned to a tall elderly man with thick white hair. '*Bubelah*, take them to the secret quarters. I will tell the Petrosians we are all accounted for.'

Alex pushed the *shashuska* round on his plate. He surveyed the sparsely furnished room.

Antique Caucasian rugs and kilims covered every inch of the stone floors. There was one threadbare sofa, two wooden chairs, an antique chest of drawers. A large flat-screen TV from the previous decade sat in centre place in front of the sofa.

He studied the tall, regal, white-haired man intensely who was reviewing papers at the solitary desk next to the fireplace – his grandfather, former head of NASA's astrophysics division. It seemed strange that this genial, softly spoken man had overseen the agency's covert UFO programme for over thirty years.

'Uncle Jas just sits there, *Zayde*. Not talking, not eating; completely out of sync with reality. Something terrible has happened to him.'

David Weiss rubbed his eyes, laid his papers aside and

walked over to Alex. He laid his hand on his grandson's shoulder. 'Your grandmother has seen to his wounds. It is the dark night of the soul, Alex. He murdered his own brother in cold blood. It is Jason De Vere's valley of the shadow.'

Firmly but gently, his grandfather removed the hip flask from Alex's hands. 'Enough, Alex,' he said. 'Take him his food.'

'He thinks Aunt Jules is dead. He won't bathe, won't eat.'

Rebekah Weiss walked in. 'Julia hangs between life and death,' she said quietly. 'She is stable but still in critical condition. She needs complete quiet. Jason cannot under any circumstance be told she is here. Or that she is alive. Promise me!'

She cupped Alex's face in her hands, her expression softening.

'Oh, you are so like your beloved mother, God bless her soul.'

Her light touch explored the deep bruising on his neck. 'What those thugs did to you, Alex.'

'Uncle Jason won't eat, *Bubbe*.'

'He will bathe, and he will eat,' Rebekah declared, 'when it is time.'

'Tell him he has a visitor coming later tonight.'

'A visitor?'

His grandfather nodded.

'Who?'

His grandmother smiled and patted Alex's cheek.

'Be a good grandson and take him his food, *boychik*.'

A lex knocked, then entered the tiny bedroom to find Jason sitting on the iron-framed single bed, still in his bloodied shirt, staring blankly at the wall. Alex laid the tray down beside him on the bed. Jason continued to gaze straight ahead.

'Uncle Jas,' Alex said, sitting down beside him.

'Get out,' Jason growled.

Alex touched his uncle's arm and instantly felt an intense burning sensation fill his own ribcage. He clutched his sides in pain as a liquid fire surged through his chest.

Stunned, he stepped back and stared, gasping at the searing pain still coursing through him.

'Who did you meet, Uncle Jas? In the garden? Tell me who you met!'

'I don't know!' Jason shouted.

Alex stood at the door.

'Get out!' Jason yelled. 'Get *out!*'

He flailed blindly and flung the tray to the floor.

Alex stood silently another moment, then left the room, shutting the door quietly behind him.

David Weiss clasped Professor Lawrence St Cartier in his arms and kissed him on both cheeks.

'Ah! I smell freshly roasted coffee!'

David helped Lawrence out of his houndstooth coat just as Rebekah came out of the small kitchen holding a steaming mug of coffee. She handed it to Lawrence.

'She is still beautiful,' Lawrence said, kissing Rebekah in affection on both cheeks.

David looked lovingly at his petite, silver-haired wife, with her exquisitely formed bone structure.

'Ah, Professor, she is indeed – and still feisty as ever.'

Rebekah blushed and slapped his arm. 'Dry the dishes, David. The dishes!'

'How is she doing?' asked Lawrence.

'Stable.'

'And Jason?'

'Slowly recovering.' Tears of anger welled in Rebekah's eyes. 'That barbarian, Guber. Jason was terribly bruised, badly beaten. I've seen to his wounds but he refuses to take off his shirt.'

She raised her hands in despair. 'He's still covered in Adrian's blood.'

She beckoned to Lawrence to follow her. Through a hidden door they reached a large white chamber that looked like a spacious hospital room.

'You have everything you need?' he asked.

'Thanks to your generosity, we have everything.'

Lawrence followed Rebekah to the far side of the chamber, where a frail white figure lay with tubes coming out of her nose and throat.

'Julia,' Lawrence whispered.

'It's touch and go, Lawrence,' Rebekah said, compassion thickening her voice. She looked down. 'I asked *Adonai* to give these old hands the nimbleness they used to have, just one last time. She's in an induced coma.'

Lawrence nodded. He laid his hand on her forehead. Then he bent down and kissed her. And removing a small vial of liquid from his inner pocket, he anointed her with frankincense.

'And Jason – he cannot know she is still alive. She is still too frail.'

Lawrence nodded. 'He won't hear it from me.'

Rebekah peeled off her sterile gloves and walked Lawrence back through the door. 'His face is plastered all over the news. It is a manhunt.'

'He's not sleeping. Not bathing. Not eating.' Rebekah sighed. 'He just sits there, caked in Adrian's blood. He's lost touch with reality, Lawrence.'

'When he was in the Garden,' Lawrence murmured.

Tears filled Rebekah's eyes. 'Gethsemane,' she whispered.

'Something . . . or someone,' he said. 'You of all people surely know the answer to that.'

Rebekah's wrinkled features softened. 'Yes,' she murmured. 'As do you.' She pointed to the door of the small room. 'Jason is in there. Your dinner is on the desk.'

Lawrence stood in the doorway, surveying the room. Jason lay facedown across the bed, breathing loudly. A tray's worth of food was strewn on the floor.

Lawrence walked over and quietly started to clean up the mess.

Jason stirred. 'Alex, I told you to get out,' he muttered groggily.

'Young Alex you can tell to get out, Jason De Vere – you must have terrified the poor boy. But Lawrence St Cartier you do not scare,' he said crisply, adjusting his cravat. 'Now, I will sit on this bed for days if I have to.'

Jason looked stonily in the direction of Lawrence's voice. Lawrence got out his pipe, lit it, and gazed calmly out the tiny window. 'For days.'

Jason shook his head. 'Julia . . . Julia's dead.'

Lawrence stared ahead impassively.

'I . . . I shot Adrian. Twice.' Jason shook uncontrollably. 'Once through the neck. Then . . . then . . .'

'Through the temple,' Lawrence said, no trace of recrimination in his voice.

'I murdered my own brother.'

'Yes, I know.'

Jason closed his eyes, still shaking violently.

'You remember being in a garden?'

He looked up blindly in the direction of Lawrence's voice. 'I remember a . . . a garden.'

Lawrence crossed himself quietly, then got up, walked over to the desk, and uncovered the tray of food. 'One cup of *shaneeneh*, two poached eggs medium, wholegrain toast, marmalade, and Earl Grey tea.'

He licked his lips and closed his eyes in bliss. He drank down the aged goat's-milk yogurt in three gulps, then tucked his napkin into his shirt collar.

'Ah! It's good to be back. Rebekah's cooking – unbeatable!'

He cut the poached eggs neatly in half and took the first mouthful. They were gone in short order, and he wiped his mouth with the napkin then started to butter a piece of toast.

'You remember the book *The Robe,* Jason? Lloyd C. Douglas? You used to watch the film with your mother every Christmas when you were a precocious six year old.'

He studied Jason out of the corner of his eye, then dipped a silver teaspoon into the marmalade.

'Marcellus, the Roman soldier, after the crucifixion, the robe came into his hands.' Lawrence spread the marmalade on his toast. 'Every time he came into contact with the robe, it induced in his soul almost a form of madness.'

He cut the slice of toast into four triangular pieces. 'You didn't come into contact with the robe.' Lawrence wiped his mouth gingerly with the linen napkin. 'But you came into contact with the one who *wore* the robe.' Lawrence stirred his Earl Grey tea twice.

Jason stood up. Pale.

Lawrence looked knowingly at him. 'You have to return, Jason De Vere,' he said. The tone was kindly but the words stern. 'You have to return to Gethsemane. To put an end to the same form of madness that Marcellus endured.'

Jason stared at Lawrence with a rage that bordered on hatred, then walked to the tiny shower room and slammed the door violently without a look back.

Lawrence walked out of the room and closed the door. Rebekah stood outside. She raised her eyebrows.

Lawrence shook his head. 'His physical body reacts to the bitterness of his soul. It is temporary, Rebekah.' He held her hand. 'He should regain his mental faculties overnight. It is his soul that will take time.'

He followed Rebekah through to the cramped living quarters.

He walked over to Alex, who was sipping gin from a hip flask, his gaze riveted to the television screen. With quiet authority he cocked an eye at the flask, and Alex slipped it back inside his jacket.

'You have much courage, my son.'

Rebekah dabbed her eyes with her apron. 'He woke in the night screaming, his sheets soaking with his sweat.'

They turned to look at Alex, who was rolling what must have been his tenth cigarette of the evening.

'He has post-traumatic stress. He was caught by Guber's thugs when he was searching for Jason. He was hung upside down, beaten senseless, and tortured before he escaped. Only he knows the full story.'

Lawrence clasped her hands.

'Your boy is strong, Rebekah. Like you.' Lawrence took both her wizened hands in his. 'First the loss of Polly, then the torture . . . It will be a process, but he will heal. Now, we have to get Jason out of Israel immediately. They will kill him the moment they get the chance. I must take my leave.'

'Not before you taste my *harissa*!' David Weiss shouted from the kitchen.

David walked towards Lawrence carrying a ceramic bowl filled with a thick porridge from Kolkata and fat rich meat.

Lawrence took a large spoonful and closed his eyes. 'Ah! Memories of when we slept under the stars at the Ararat Plain.'

'And of course washed down with mulberry *oghi*,' David laughed. 'Can I twist your arm to stay for dinner, Professor?'

Lawrence embraced David warmly. 'It would be my honour, but I am meeting with General Assad.'

A loud pealing of church bells resounded through the streets. Lawrence crossed himself, then checked his watch. 'Three p.m. precisely. The monastery of St James. Luckily some things never change.'

He kissed Rebekah tenderly on both cheeks.

'I shall be in touch. With the plans.'

'*B*ubbe, look. Look at this!'

Alex sat beside his grandmother, watching the old television.

'It's Adrian De Vere,' Rebekah said. 'He's lying in state. In *our* Temple. An abomination.'

No, *bubelah*,' said David Weiss. 'The abomination has not even begun.'

Alex grasped the television remote. 'His funeral is being broadcast in over two hundred nations, to six billion viewers. Live.'

'Turn it up, Alex.'

The newscaster's voice filled the small chamber. 'Adrian De Vere, President of the Axis Ten, lies in state in a casket placed on a catafalque – a decorated wooden frame – in the Third Temple in Jerusalem. Over one thousand leaders have flown in to pay their respects.'

'The state funeral is planned for the third day,' David muttered. 'Today is Wednesday, so Friday.' He scowled. 'Turn to the BBC. Turn it up.'

'Never has there been such a day,' the emotional BBC commentator reported. 'Today millions of people throughout the world are trying to find words adequate to express their overwhelming grief at the cold-blooded assassination of

36

President Adrian De Vere. The reaction to the deaths of John F. Kennedy or Princess Diana cannot come near the outpouring of grief we are seeing displayed on the streets of every major city in the world. Workplaces are closing as I speak. Friday has been designated an international day of mourning for the President. He will lie in state for three days. His state funeral will be broadcast across the whole world.'

The commentary was accompanied by images of streets across London, Berlin, Paris, Moscow, New York, lined with sleeping bags: thousands of men, women, and children clutching votive candles that illuminated saint-like pictures of Adrian De Vere. Then the commentator announced, 'We cross over to our BBC correspondent in Jerusalem.'

'The first three-and-a-half years of Adrian De Vere's presidency had felt like a new beginning,' the intense red-haired Irish reporter said, struggling to keep her composure. 'His negotiation of the Solomon Concordat, the groundbreaking Israeli – Palestinian Peace Agreement; his skillful peace negotiations ending the Third World War; his rejuvenation of the Western world's banking system and industrial military complex; and his removal of the threat of nuclear annihilation.'

The Weisses and Alex watched, riveted to the screen, as cameras zoomed in on the dead and embalmed Adrian De Vere, lying in the open coffin in Jerusalem with thousands of men, women, and children lined up behind ropes, waiting to pay homage to the beloved President who had beamed his glamour and charisma directly into people's living rooms across the globe.

His assassination had been the consistent and unrelenting fodder of every major newsfeed from London to New York, Berlin to Moscow, Beijing to Islamabad. Adrian De Vere, President of half of the Western world, was dead. Every other news story had been buried in obscurity for the past thirty-six hours.

The images of the dead President in his casket were plastered over every newspaper front page, broadcast on every internet outlet, beamed to every digital television. Network television channels were even cancelling commercials to capture the event.

Thousands of arrests had been made in the UK. Military police stationed at 10 Downing Street, where Adrian had served as British Prime Minister for ten years, were attempting to keep the enraged and grieving public calm. Mont St Michel in Normandy, Adrian's European Summer Palace, was surrounded by officers under the Commandement des Opérations Spéciales.

All flights to Ben Gurion Airport in Tel Aviv had been closed to the general public. Axis Ten special forces were stationed all across the perimeter of Jerusalem.

The volatile, half-demented public had only one thing on their minds. They were *baying* for the blood of Adrian De Vere's murderer.

Jason's face filled the screen.

'A manhunt is being conducted in all Axis Ten zones for Jason De Vere, the cold-blooded murderer of President Adrian De Vere. If anyone catches sight of him, do not approach. We repeat, do not approach. He is a killer and likely armed.'

Ten phone numbers for each Axis Ten zone appeared on the screen.

'There is a $50 million reward for him to be brought in alive.'

David clicked the remote, and the screen went black.

'Oh god,' Alex whispered. 'We *have* to get him out of Israel. *Now.*'

'It is in hand, Alex. All is in hand.' Alex looked up from

the television. His right hand started to shake, and he reached inside his leather jacket for the hip flask.

His grandfather placed a steady hand on his shoulder. 'Enough of the gin, *boychik*,' he said with gentle reproof.

Rebekah Weiss closed her eyes in pain. 'The things they did to you, Alex. I will get you something.'

'I don't want anything, *Bubbe*.'

Alex was shaking again.

His grandfather stood over him. 'Remember what the therapist said. Breathe in deeply. Count to three. And out.'

Rebekah hurried back in with a white pill.

'Take this,' she said. 'It will calm you.'

Alex swallowed the pill

Rebekah's eyes fell on the photograph standing on the television. She studied the picture of Rachel Lane-Fox. Supermodel. Her beloved feisty daughter. Alex's mother.

Killed on 9/11, the day Rachel had boarded the Boston–Los Angeles flight when Alex was only three months old.

She looked from the photograph of Rachel, back to Alex. He was so handsome that all the girls had chased after him since kindergarten. He had Rachel's perfectly carved features: the high cheekbones, aquiline nose, penetrating dark eyes, and thick, glossy dark-brown hair that fell below his collar. The girls never left him alone. But he also had his mother's spirit, her strength . . . her stubbornness.

Rebekah sighed. 'You're so like your mother, *boychik*. Especially when you're angry! May she rest in peace.'

She clutched David's hands tightly.

'It is time, my darling. He is old enough.' She looked back over at Alex. 'Show him our Rachel's papers. I go to sit with Julia.'

As the door closed, David walked over to the far side of the room and picked up a bulging old leather briefcase.

'It is time for you to know the truth about 11 September 2001. About your mother's death.'

Alex sighed. '*Zayde*, I've researched 9/11 for over six years. I know everything there is to know about it. The case is closed, *Zayde*. Closed.'

'No, Alex, it isn't,' David answered. He walked over to a tall antique chest of drawers and returned with a thick file of papers and a thumb drive. 'You've only scratched the surface. She was a truth-seeker. She wouldn't rest until she got to the truth. Neither will you.' He hesitated, then handed Alex the bulging file. 'Your mother's papers.'

'My mother's . . . what papers?'

David handed Alex a file labelled *Mossad*.

'You're not telling me she was Mossad?'

His grandfather nodded.

'You've always known this?'

He nodded again. 'You weren't ready. Now you are. This is what she was working on the two years before her death.'

He passed Alex the memory stick. 'And this is what your godfather was killed for.'

'Alex? Alex Jennings? *Zayde*, he died of a heart attack.'

'No, Alex. He was murdered.'

Alex cast his mind back to his godfather, the tall, fit former Naval Intelligence officer, who had died when Alex was just fourteen.

'Your investigation into 9/11 revealed only the tip of the iceberg.' David sighed. 'Alex, for forty years, your grand-mother and I have been members of a group known as the Illuminus. Your mother's investigation was connected with the events of 9/11. And your godfather was murdered because he linked the two. Never forget this one thing, Alex: they cast no shadows.'

It was 3 a.m., and Alex hadn't slept. He poured his sixth cup of coffee and rolled another cigarette. What his mother had uncovered was not merely revelatory, it was explosive. For two years before her death, Rachel Lane-Fox, supermodel, photographer, and Mossad agent, had been investigating a covert multi-billion-dollar operation.

He rifled one more time through the documents headed *Project Hammer*. It was a four-pronged attack. The stability of the rouble had been undermined. The treasury of the Soviet Union had been pilfered. Amid all this, money had been siphoned to a group of generals in the KGB to fund a coup against reformist premier Mikhail Gorbachev. And a massive grab had been made for the gigantic nation's most crucial industries – defence and energy.

That was just the tip of the iceberg.

The next piece of information had blown his mind.

His mother's major investigation had revolved around a covert war chest of gold worth trillions of dollars, *which had been completely concealed from Congress for over sixty years*. The elite and the shadowy masters of the military industrial complex called this hoard – a veritable war chest – the Black Eagle Trust.

Alex pushed his hair back from his face, incredulous.

But *what* was the link to 9/11?

He looked up to find his grandfather standing over him. 'Pack up, Alex,' he said. 'General Assad and the Professor are arriving in two hours. We're evacuating.' He nodded at the documents. 'Take them with you. They're yours now. Your mother would have wanted you to have them.'

Alex removed the thumb drive from his X-pad and placed it in a compartment in his rucksack. He gathered the documents, stacked them back in the grey Mossad file, and laid them on top of his computer. Then he limped past his grandfather and disappeared down the hall.

He reappeared minutes later, clutching his bulletproof vest, slinging a second rucksack and two cameras over his shoulder.

David Weiss stared at him in horror.

'I'll be back in good time, *Zayde*.'

'Where are you *going*?' he shouted after Alex. 'They'll shoot you in cold blood if they catch you this time.'

'I'm the proverbial cat with nine lives, *Zayde*,' Alex grinned.

'Alex, what do I tell your grandmother? *Alex*!'

But Alex had already disappeared.

CHAPTER THREE

Gabriel

Gabriel walked silently through Eden, deep in contemplation.

He frowned, then raised his exquisite features to the heavens. Far in the distance, he saw the monstrous black apparition winging its way towards him.

Soon the grotesque birdlike creature was hovering directly over Gabriel's head. It had the skeleton of a raven but was at least forty feet in length, with a curved beak, three heads with beady red eyes, and a long, violently swishing leathern tail.

'Deliver your master's missive!' Gabriel cried. 'Then be gone.'

Gabriel watched as the monster flew toward the Palace of Archangels until it vanished through the walls directly into Lucifer's old West Wing chambers.

West Wing
Palace of Archangels

Gabriel stared up at the soaring gold-columned palace that towered high above the western wall. The Palace of Archangels, where once he and his two elder brothers, Chief Prince Michael and Prince Regent Lucifer, had dwelt for thousands of moons in an unbreakable kinship, the walls of their inner sanctum resounding with camaraderie and laughter.

The realm of the First Heaven, in worlds long gone, never to be recaptured.

Aeons had passed since Lucifer, seraph, great archangel, light-bearer, had been banished. Now only the grand wings containing Michael's and Gabriel's chambers were occupied.

The majestic West Wing of Yehovah's Prince Regent, the Son of the Morning, had lain desolate since his defection. The soaring golden and jewel-studded doors engraved with the emblem of the Royal House, had stood barred and shackled since the dusk of his betrayal, when the darkening shadows of insurrection had fallen across the realm of the First Heaven.

Gabriel strode towards the West Wing, past Lucifer's abandoned orangeries.

He bowed to the six fiery seraphim guarding the entrance to Lucifer's chambers. They bowed in deep reverence to the Revelator.

Gabriel's beautiful features were still flawless: the perfectly carved cheekbones; the long, fine platinum locks; the regal, heart-shaped countenance. But aeons in his office as Yehovah's Revelator had transformed him into the fierce, holy, noble warrior he was today. The tender, vulnerable young Revelator that Lucifer had toyed with and manipulated emotionally was long gone. In the Royal House of Yehovah, Gabriel, Chief Prince and Archangel, was second only to his beloved brother Michael the Valiant.

He removed a large, ornate golden key from his belt and unlocked the heavy iron chains that shackled the heavy doors to the West Wing. He pushed them open and walked inside. As they closed behind him, his footsteps echoed through the marbled palace corridors, the walls adorned with frescoes and art.

Finally, he reached Lucifer's chambers.

He stood quietly outside, then gave a sigh of long regret and pushed open the doors.

Gabriel flung his deep-blue velvet cloak onto Lucifer's throne and walked over to the pools where the brothers used to swim and raise their goblets in merriment. They were now murky and tepid.

This was the only place in the First Heaven that manifested deterioration and decay.

He tugged the dust cover loose from the huge picture still lying against the wall, and stepped back. He stared, strangely transfixed by the painting, transported all those aeons ago . . . back to the time when he, Michael and Lucifer had been inseparable.

Before the shadows had fallen on their perfect world.

He closed his eyes.

Remembering that exact day.

'*Gabriel.*' *Lucifer kissed him on both cheeks. 'Beloved Gabriel, a great day dawns for you.' He had stepped back with the pride of an elder brother glinting in his sapphire eyes. This is a great honor, are you ready to receive this responsibility? Are you ready to join Michael and me in rank and in service of our Father?' One third of the angelic host wholly at your command. Are you ready to take on the mantle of power, the weight of accountability?*

With Lucifer's hand laid protectively on his shoulder and looking straight into Lucifer's eyes without fear or guile, 'I am,' was the firm reply.

Lucifer, with his brilliant smile, clapped his hands,

gesturing towards an enormous object covered in gold cloth, just inside the doorway. 'I have a gift for you, my beloved brother. The muslin fell to the floor, revealing an exquisite painting depicting himself before the Seat of Kings at his inauguration.

Gabriel replaced the dust cloth swiftly over the painting, to drown out the searing memories.

He walked in the direction of Lucifer's writing desk where his brother used to spend his evenings writing his missives in his elegant italic hand.

The missive lay there, exactly as he knew it would. Black smoke rose from the ominous black seal of Perdition.

Gabriel tore it open.

> *You continue to return my missives unopened, brother. Silence. Then more silence. You are afraid of my eternal influence over your soul.*
>
> *I know you still mourn for me.*
>
> *There are nights I still come to you unawares. Guarding your slumber. Watching as you toss and turn, your dreamings filled with Megiddo.*
>
> *The Final Great War. Lucifer versus the Nazarene. Armageddon.*

Gabriel crumpled the missive in his fist, then walked over to the soaring casement doors.

He unlocked them, flung them wide open, and stepped out onto the balcony.

He surveyed the First Heaven, staring out to the Labyrinths, a mammoth golden tower that peaked into seven spires, disappearing into the clouds, guarded by his white eagle revelators. He could see the Angelic Kings to the east gathered in council on the Tower of Winds, where the angelic

46

zephyrs of wisdom and revelation raged in eternal cyclones. His gaze fell to Yehovah's Eden. In the furthest corner of the lush hanging gardens stood two trees, their fruit glistening blue and gold in the lightning, almost wholly enveloped by swirling white mists. To the north of the two trees, a colossal golden, ruby-encrusted door, ablaze with light, was embedded into the jacinth walls of a palace – the entrance to the Throne Room. It was here where the One dwelt, whose hair and head were white like snow from the very radiance of his glory, whose eyes flashed like flames of living fire with the brilliance of his multitude of discernments, and great and infinitely tender compassions.

Yehovah.

The only one whose very name brought his brother Lucifer trembling to his knees.

Lucifer.

Gabriel moved his hand across the breathtaking vista.

A vision of Lorcan De Molay appeared, standing in the centre of an enormous valley. His thick raven hair fell loose past his shoulders, blowing in the icy Israeli wind. He stood in the centre of a vast plain, his Black Jesuit robes blowing tempestuously.

'Gabriel,' the priest murmured, his back to his brother. 'I knew you would come.'

'Megiddo,' Gabriel whispered. 'Armageddon.'

The priest turned slowly.

A voracious smile spread across his face. 'The Jezreel Valley. In the words of Napoleon Bonaparte, "the most natural battleground of the entire earth". Thutmose III versus the Canaanites; Deborah and Barak versus Sisera; Saul versus the Philistines; Solomon versus Pharaoh Shishak; Saladin versus the Crusaders; Napoleon versus the Ottomans; General Allenby versus the Ottomans.

'And now the greatest battle of all.' He raised his arms dramatically to the heavens. 'Armageddon! God versus the devil. *Moi*!'

He swung around with a Machiavellian grin.

'Megiddo. Study it well, my brother.' He gestured to a sprawling military complex on the plains under construction. 'My military headquarters for the battle of the ages are already well advanced. My greatest victory approaches.'

Gabriel stared at his brother, his grey eyes like steel.

De Molay added, 'Your greatest defeat . . . *brother*.'

He surveyed the vast expanse of the valley, then moved his hand across the scene.

Suddenly, the skies turned crimson. Gabriel watched as the priest's form roiled and grew, like a billowing thundercloud, into Lucifer, Prince of the Damned.

Before him was the very scene that had tormented his dreams these past aeons.

The exact details never changed.

The vision had become more frequent these past thirty-nine crimson moons.

Lucifer at Megiddo.

It was always the same, down to the very minute details.

Lucifer stood in his monstrous black war chariot, riding on the shafts of thunderbolts, the huge silver wheels sprung with the sharpest war blades, pulled by his dark-winged stallions, their manes intertwined with platinum, caparisoned as for war.

In the vision, his elder brother's scarred, misshapen features were always masked behind his battle helmet, but the soulless sapphire eyes were imperious, his bearing still kingly. He held his head high, his long raven hair gleaming and plaited with platinum and lightnings, his fist brandishing the cat-o'-nine-tails.

Gabriel watched as Lucifer surveyed the valley before

48

him. A thick red mist of human blood mingled with the reek of burning human flesh rose unendingly from the valley of slaughter. Millions of massacred soldiers – Chinese, European, American, Arab, Israeli – floated next to drowned horses and half-submerged tanks and other armoured vehicles in a vast quagmire of blood and mud 1,600 furlongs in length; all that was left after the assault of the massive 200-million-man army. Hundreds of thousands of griffon vultures, their wingspans over nine feet wide, blackened the crimson skies, circling the killing fields, where massive swarms of raptors gorged on human flesh. A holocaust. The eerie silence hung heavily over the valley. Nothing stirred. Nothing could be heard but the bloodcurdling screeching of the vultures.

Lucifer waded through the bloody quagmire, which reached up to the bridles of his dark stallions, toward higher ground.

'One for eternity, brothers!' Lucifer's cry echoed, tormenting. His steel-blue eyes glittered.

'I will annihilate the whole race of men before I am done, Gabriel.'

And as in every vision, Lucifer drove his whip of panther tails, embedded with sharp steel, violently onto the lead stallion's back, drawing blood. The horse's eyes flickered red, and he snorted in pain, sending flames and sulphurous smoke billowing from his nostrils.

'I will take my vengeance!' Lucifer cried.

Gabriel watched as Lucifer and his Mephistophelian stallions took off on the burning white crest of the black hurricanes and rode the thunderbolts, disappearing into the darkening crimson skies.

'You see Lucifer at Armageddon.' Jether's voice was very soft. 'The very End of Days.' Jether placed a strong hand on Gabriel's shoulder. 'Steady yourself.'

'It is the same vision,' Gabriel whispered. 'In exact detail. It has haunted my dreamings since his banishment, Jether. But it has intensified these past thirty-nine moons. It fills my dreaming every night.'

Jether walked over to where Lucifer's tabors and viols lay untouched. 'Yes, yours as mine. The weight of being a seer, beloved Gabriel. You see the future. It is nigh upon us. The thirty-ninth crimson moon rises this next dawn.'

He looked down at the crumpled missive.

Gabriel sat at Lucifer's desk.

'You are remembering.'

'Yes,' answered Gabriel, mingled regret and resignation in his voice. 'Before the shadows fell.'

'Michael awaits you, Gabriel. This place is infused with Lucifer's bewitchments. Come.'

Underground Cisterns
Jerusalem

Alex followed the underground watercourse beneath the Armenian Quarter, his secret path since he was a five-year-old adventurer.

He knew exactly where the slow-flowing stream would take him. Directly under the Holy of Holies of the newly erected Third Temple.

He needed solid evidence that Adrian De Vere was truly inert . . . dead. That there would be no resurrection.

He pushed his hair under a black cap, placed contact lenses in both eyes, and swiftly affixed a short goatee and round black glasses. Next, he removed a rumpled navy suit jacket from the rucksack and slung it on.

He took another swig from his hip flask, his hands trembling uncontrollably, and followed the stench of the tepid water.

'Ticket for the 15:30,' the dark-haired girl muttered to herself as she entered the information into the ticket vending machine.

She put her iris to the scanner. The transfer from her Bitcoin account was instantly approved. She snatched her ticket from the machine.

And ran for the last train to London.

Alex grinned in triumph.

'Bullseye.'

He joined the bustling gaggle of reporters, a camera slung over each shoulder.

'Credentials?' demanded the black-clad Israeli policeman.

Alex put his falsified press card forward. He was now Dominic Logan, TV reporter for Britain's Sky News.

Now time for Dylan Weaver's digital magic – the contact lenses.

'Step forward.'

Alex lined up his eye with the camera, willing his hands to stop trembling.

There was a hesitation.

'Again,' commanded the policeman.

C'mon, Weaver, he willed.

He placed his eye against the camera again.

It illuminated blue.

'Thought we had you there,' the officer deadpanned. 'Get in the press line.

51

Alex smiled politely and entered the soaring hundred-foot gold doors of the Temple.

He was in.

Outer Hebrides

The priest unlocked the wooden door of the dilapidated stone croft with its turfed roof perched on soaring cliffs over the churning Atlantic waters.

He stared up at the massive weather front coming in from the Atlantic, then ducked inside.

Third Temple
Temple Mount, Jerusalem

Alex could hardly believe his eyes. There were at least a thousand dignitaries lined up against the ropes paying homage to the figure in the casket. World-famous presidents and monarchs were openly weeping.

He was now so close to the coffin that he could see Adrian's pale, waxy countenance from where he stood.

He could be mistaken for a wax effigy.

Alex picked up his camera and took ten photographs in quick succession.

As he stood over Adrian's body, Dylan Weaver's thermal monitor came to life.

Three more seconds, and he would have the readings.

Three . . . two . . .

'Move it.'

One. A supersonic bleep went off from the thermal detector.

It registered no life readings whatsoever from Adrian De Vere's body.

He was definitely dead.

'Thank you, sir.'

Alex strode swiftly toward the Sky press box, then did a swift about-face and walked calmly out through the jostling crowd and into the nearest alleyway, towards what used to be the Arab Quarter.

A young Arab boy of not more than thirteen held out a freshly baked *shawarma* at him. 'Me your fixer.' He grinned broadly.

'Yes.' Alex bit hungrily into the lamb and pita bread. 'Starving. Take me to the old Bedouin. Your grandfather.'

'I take you.' The boy saluted.

They disappeared into the bustling streets of vibrantly coloured scarves and tourist prayer shawls.

'Ahem.'

Alex stopped dead in his tracks.

He would have known that voice anywhere.

'Guber,' he murmured.

He looked up at the man with the domed head and badly clipped black hair.

It was unmistakable. Kurt Guber, Adrian De Vere's loyal Nazi fixer and sycophant.

Guber smiled his thin, cold smile.

'Identification!'

Guber held out his hand.

Alex's heart was beating like a drum.

He handed over his press pass.

Guber smiled a smile that didn't reach his eyes.

'Your *papers*.'

He pulled Alex's cap off his head, then grasped his arm in a vice-like grip.

Alex struggled violently as Guber reached for his revolver.

Alex pushed his thumb down into Guber's solar plexus, Krav Maga style, rammed his good knee into the throat of the man known as 'the Butcher', then ran for his life.

53

Rebekah was crying silently in the kitchen. Jason entered, unshaven, his eyes swollen and red from crying.

Rebekah swiftly wiped her eyes with her apron.

'Show me Julia's body,' he demanded. 'It's here, isn't it?' He grasped Rebekah's arm so tightly that she gasped. 'I *have* to see her body. Where . . . is . . . she?'

David Weiss came out in his dressing gown and slippers. 'Jason.' He removed Jason's hand firmly from Rebekah's arm.

'Take me to Julia,' said Jason, staring at the couple with a wild look in his eyes. 'I know she's here.'

David and Rebekah exchanged an intense look.

'You are correct.' David sighed. 'Julia is here.'

'Well, *where* is she?' he demanded.

'Follow me, Jason,' Rebekah said.

Jason followed her through the hall until they reached a small room at the very rear of the apartment. She stopped outside it.

'There is something you need to know, Jason.' She spoke now in a husky whisper. 'Julia is alive.'

Jason reeled back in shock,

'*Alive*?'

'But not for long,' Rebekah whispered. Tears glimmered on her wrinkled cheeks. 'We've done everything possible, Jason, but she is very, very frail,' Rebekah said softly. 'She's fading fast. We are doing everything to keep her with us.'

Jason paled.

'What are you *talking* about?'

He stared in horror at Rebekah.

Rebekah unlocked the door to the tiny makeshift sanatorium.

"What do you mean, *fading fast?* Jason's voice rose in panic.

'Her condition deteriorated . . . around midnight. The bullet passed through a portion of her left ventricle. We operated, but she'd lost a lot of blood. We've done everything humanly possible.'

Jason pushed past Rebekah, into the room. He stopped in his tracks. There in a hospital bed surrounded by bleeping monitors, drips and tubes, her chest swathed in blood-stained bandages was his beloved Julia. Rebekah removed the oxygen mask from Julia's face and stood back.

Slowly Jason moved towards the bed, leaned over and gently took Julia's cold, tiny hand in his, his eyes riveted on her small, pale face.

Tears fell from his eyes onto her fingers. 'Julia,' he whispered. The hiss from the oxygen canister into the mask lying on the bed sheet, the relentless bleeping from the monitors were the only sounds in the quiet, dark room.

Sobs wracked his body. Finally he managed to speak.

'Julia, darling, can you hear me?'

Julia stirred. Slowly her eyes opened.

'Jason,' she managed to whisper, tears of joy and tenderness welling in her eyes.

'Jason . . .' Julia struggled to get the words out. 'Jason, I'm not going to pull through.'

'Of *course* you are.'

He turned, panic-stricken, to Rebekah and David.

'Of course she is . . .'

Rebekah looked long into Jason's eyes, then very gently shook her head.

Jason turned back to Julia in desperation.

'You have to *fight*, Jules. You've always been such a fighter. *Fight now.* Fight for me. Fight for Lily.'

'Lily . . .' Julia whispered, her eyes closing.

'Jules. I can't live without you.'

With supreme effort, she opened her eyes.

'Jason. You have to help the others.'

'Julia, you have to *fight*.'

Julia opened her mouth, struggling to talk.

'Stay with me, Julia. *Stay with me . . .*'

David stood at the door.

'Jason, we have to get you out of here. They're searching house to house.'

Julia's head fell back onto the pillow.

Comatose.

'I'm *not* leaving her' he raised his head.

'Jason . . .' Rebekah said softly. 'There are times in life, where you just have to trust. This is one of them.'

She grasped Jason's hand.

'Don't die needlessly because you are too stubborn to listen. . .'

Jason looked deeply into Rebekah's eyes, then turned to Julia.

'Darling, I don't know if you can hear me. I'm leaving now but Rebekah will take care of you. I'll be back as soon as I can.'

Jason took Julia's face in his hands and kissed her full on the lips his tears mingling with her own.

'Fight for us, Jules . . .'

He gently stroked Julia's head, then turned to Rebekah, his expression determined.

'OK. I'm ready. Let's get out of here.'

A small pile of rucksacks was stacked at the door of the apartment.

Alex burst in the front door, breathing heavily.

'You worried your grandmother sick,' David admonished Alex. Rebekah Weiss and Lawrence St Cartier stood talking in hushed voices.

Alex watched as his grandfather and grandmother embraced.

'*Ikh hab dir lib,* Rebekah.' David held his wife to him tightly. Long seconds passed before he let her go.

Alex frowned. 'I don't understand.'

'Your grandmother is staying. With Julia.' Lawrence picked up his silver cane. 'She'll be safe,' he continued. 'The Petrosians will look after them.'

Jason stood in the doorway, trembling, his phone clenched in his fist. 'Lily . . .' He managed to get the word out.

'Lily . . . . She doesn't know her mother is dying.' He slumped into the nearby chair.

'I couldn't tell Lily.'

CHAPTER FOUR

Military Plane

Lawrence St Cartier took out a bag of Maltesers and sucked at the chocolate in ecstasy. 'Ah, British chocolate. So much more delicious than Hershey's.' After a moment, he assumed his accustomed tone of civility and said, 'Alex, my dear, are you ready?'

Alex nodded, intent on his X-pad.

David Weiss, eyes closed, was praying in Hebrew.

Jason sat apart from the others, at the very rear of the plane, unshaven but in a fresh blue shirt, his head in his hands, incessantly moving the links of Julia's cameo on her silver chain, as if it were a rosary.

'Where are we heading?' David asked Lawrence.

'London.'

Basement Apartment
Earl's Court
Safe House
London

Dylan Weaver paced up and down, looking out surreptitiously from a corner of the faded patterned curtains. *No lights. Use torches*, General Assad had instructed.

He unlocked the door to a dank basement apartment.

Weaver, Nick De Vere's old schoolfriend and genius IT specialist, stood inside the doorway, wearing his signature grubby yellow canvas anorak, his beer belly hanging well over his creased, unwashed jeans.

'Welcome, welcome,' he muttered, his mouth filled with battered sausage.

'It looks like a nuclear waste dump,' Alex remarked drily, surveying the heaps of Weaver's unwashed clothes strewn unceremoniously on the threadbare sofa, on the kitchen table, and across the scuffed oak floorboards.

Weaver shrugged his shoulders sheepishly.

'It's a safe house. Nice to see you too, bud.' He grinned, removing a pile of dirty socks from the top of the digital television. He stared at Alex's bruised neck. 'You don't look too pretty yourself.'

'Long story.' Alex limped into the flat, followed by Jason and David Weiss.

The sound of screaming sirens drew nearer.

Six police vans came to a halt outside St Luke's Church on the opposite side of the square.

'What's that, Weaver?' Jason stood at the front door. At least thirty British military police in black, armed with sub-machine-guns, were raiding an apartment directly opposite them.

'Happens all the time.' Weaver shrugged.

An entire family was hauled out brutally at gunpoint, and bundled into the back of the police vans.

Police Alsatians barked ferociously.

Alex hauled Jason inside, then slammed and locked the door.

'What are they looking for?'

'Dissidents,' said Weaver. 'Resisters.'

59

'I thought you said we'd be safe in London,' protested Alex.

'We are. We have twenty-four hours. After that, we have no protection. Jason's face is plastered *everywhere*. He's the new Lee Harvey Oswald, who killed the people's President.' Weaver turned to Jason. 'Quite the celebrity, Mr De Vere.'

The security alarm sounded as General Assad opened the door and entered, followed by a soldier who dumped three black steel suitcases unceremoniously in the hallway.

Weaver rubbed his hands in glee.

'Ah, the babies have arrived. Alex, help me set up the computers. They're the only eyes we have.'

A second soldier entered, in full British armed-police regalia, including a sub-machine-gun. 'Checking in,' he said and threw a sack down on the table. 'Dried milk. Sugar. Chocolate. Canned beef. Coffee. Cigarettes?'

Alex nodded.

The soldier threw a pack of Marlboro Red cigarettes to Alex, who plucked them from the air with his left hand.

'I'm assigned to the Square. You're safe . . . for now.'

'Well, I would have thought we could find a place with more than two bedrooms for six of us,' Jason muttered, glaring up at the grimy peeling cerise-and-gold floral wallpaper in the cramped living room. 'Boy, the Brits like their florals.' He surveyed the rest of the room. 'This place can't have seen a Hoover in years.'

He glared at the grubby lime-green floral curtains hanging within an inch of their life from a wooden pole; at the single threadbare couch, in dire need of being reupholstered; at the two torn brown leather chairs and a scuffed wooden dining table surrounded by seven mismatched wooden chairs. Mattresses, grubby duvets and pillows were slung over the floor. A cheap picture of the goddess Medusa, minus its frame, hung at a strange angle over the old gas fireplace.

'It looks like a down-market brothel that hasn't been used since the sixties. There wouldn't be hot water, by any chance? Or is that a stretch?'

'It's a Resister safe house,' Weaver mumbled. 'What were you expecting, De Vere – the Waldorf Astoria? The water, actually, is lukewarm. And there's only one shower.'

Jason grunted.

There were five knocks on the door. Then a pause and five more.

Jason rose to his feet.

He walked to the door, peered at the security screen. His shoulders sagged as he swiftly unbolted the locks.

'You're late,' he growled as Lawrence St Cartier stepped into the apartment.

'Lily should be with us' – he checked his watch – 'in 45 minutes 30 seconds precisely.'

Jason frowned.

'Lily?'

'As intrinsically stubborn as her father. She insisted on being with you, Jason.' Lawrence was followed into the apartment by a figure in a bowler hat and tails, whose face was hidden by a huge number of green shopping bags bearing the Harrods logo.

'I picked up a . . . erm . . . friend on the way.'

Jason frowned. There was something incredibly familiar about the figure's stance.

The bowler-hatted man dumped all the Harrods bags unceremoniously on the kitchen table with a huge sigh.

'Maxim!' Jason couldn't hide the delight in his eyes.

'Master Jason, sir.'

He dabbed at his opaque blue eyes with an oversized lilac handkerchief.

'My deepest, *deepest* regrets about our beloved Madam Julia.'

Maxim picked up the bully beef with an expression of distaste, and was about to discard it in the bin when Weaver grabbed it.

'That'll be mine.'

Maxim studied Weaver's grubby anorak with equal distaste.

'Tut-tut. I bought your supplies, Master Jason.'

'Not hungry.'

Maxim removed his bowler hat, his wiry silver hair springing out in all directions, rubbed his hands, gingerly removed Weaver's underpants from the rickety kitchen table and eagerly pulled out three large jars of pâté, guinea fowl, boiled potatoes, champagne, Ladurée macarons, a cafetière, Harrods coffee, six loaves of milled bread, Irish butter, strong cheddar and Jarlsberg cheese.

He peered into the bottom of the last shopping bag.

'And especially for you, Master Jason.'

He looked distastefully at Jason's stubble.

'Deodorant, your soap, aftershave, razor. You know how Madam Julia hates stubble. She likes you clean-shaven – and in a freshly pressed *white* shirt.'

'You haven't?'

Maxim held out a perfectly folded white shirt and tie.

'Forget the tie, Maxim,' Jason growled, but he grudgingly took the white shirt.

Maxim fished out a small bottle of Isle of Islay and a cut whisky glass.

'I thought your spirits might need a bit of a lift, sir.'

He hesitated.

'My profound regrets about Madam Julia,' he repeated. 'Never was there a more courageous woman, Master Jason, who loves only you.'

Jason's eyes welled up with tears.

Maxim handed Jason the whisky.

Jason held it up. 'To Julia,' he whispered. And slugged it down. 'You've done us proud, Maxim.'

Maxim beamed. 'Thank you, Master Jason, sir. And I have Miss Lily's teddy bear and favourite reading matter of late. And her slippers.'

He walked stiffly over to David.

'And for you and Dr Weiss, Professor, I have a small, shall I call it, *surprise*.'

He fished in the last Harrods bag and brought out chicken, lamb, pita bread, and fattoush salad.

'I shall do the honours, dear Maxim,' Lawrence announced.

Maxim laid out a crisp white tablecloth, removed silver cutlery from his carpetbag, and proceeded to set the table.

David, Alex, and Jason sat watching the BBC.

Lawrence was cooking lamb and chicken avidly, apron on, stirring the mismatched saucepans vigorously on the old black Aga stove.

The TV cameras zoomed in on Adrian's embalmed body in the coffin.

'Grub's up.'

Lawrence shooed Alex away from the stove.

'Sit, sit. Make your plans. There is not much time.'

He placed two large bowls of fattoush salad on the scuffed wooden table.

'Shish taouk. Lamb. Rice. Garlic sauce,' he announced. Halloumi cheese and your falafels, Alex.'

'What do you mean, *there's not much time*?'

Alex dipped pita bread into the hummus and lamb and stuffed it into his hungry mouth, while David dished chicken-rice tabbouleh onto his plate.

Meanwhile, Maxim dished up guinea fowl, pâté, dauphinoise potatoes, and grilled asparagus onto Jason's plate.

Weaver stared at the food suspiciously. 'You couldn't have got some fish and chips, mate?'

Maxim gave him an icy glare.

'Uncle Jas, you killed Adrian at point-blank range,' Alex said, devouring a falafel.

Jason nodded.

Maxim stood over him sternly.

'Not hungry,' Jason muttered.

Maxim glared at him. Jason clenched his jaw, reluctantly unclenched it, and picked at his guinea fowl without enthusiasm. 'Point-blank,' he muttered. 'He was dead.'

'I verified it,' interjected Alex. 'The readings from Weaver's scanner are here. Dead. No life force at all.'

'Well, that's as may be, but not for long,' Lawrence interjected.

Jason stared at him in disbelief.

'What do you mean, *not for long*?' he said suspiciously.

'Bring the Holy Scriptures, David,' Lawrence said.

Jason rolled his eyes. 'Oh, here we go. Well, *that's* going to really convince me.'

Picking up the remote, Jason switched from the BBC to Sky News. 'Look, it's the second day Adrian's been lying in state. Dead for over forty-eight hours.'

Lawrence paced the room.

Jason looked from one to the other. 'Look, guys, I'm really trying to follow here. Give me a *break*. If you're suggesting that some bizarre kind of alien resurrection is about to take place, you've been watching too many reruns of *The X-Files*. Let me assure you, Adrian is dead. He's *dead*.'

He stood up, impassioned, pointing at the television screen.

'There, dead, in front of four billion television households.' He slammed the whisky bottle onto the table. 'Are you guys on crack, or something?'

Lawrence stood and paced the chamber.

'Adrian will come to life, Jason. He will literally be resurrected in full view of six billion live viewers, who will immediately hail him as a god. He will gain the allegiance of the entire world in a matter of minutes. It will be the first time since Christ's resurrection that such a thing has occurred.'

'You mean if there *was* a first resurrection.' Jason glared at Lawrence in disbelief. 'God, Lawrence, this is utter insanity, even for *you*. I *killed* him.' He took a long slug of whisky. 'I shot him right through his neck. Straight through the head. There!' He flung the television remote control on the table. 'The fact is facing you on live TV. Adrian De Vere is *dead.*'

He strode to the far bedroom.

'*He's dead*!' Jason yelled, and slammed the door violently behind him.

The lock turned. Lily pushed past General Assad. 'Daddy? Where's Dad? Where's Mum?'

The room quieted. Lawrence took Lily gently by the arm. 'Your father's waiting for you, Lily.'

It's . . . it's Lily. She won't come out of the bedroom.' Jason ran his fingers through his cropped hair. 'She's inconsolable.'

'I've just given her a strong herbal sedative,' Lawrence said. 'She'll sleep for at least eight hours.'

The interior alarm shrilled deafeningly, followed by a loud, insistent banging on the apartment door.

Jason picked up the revolver, gesturing to the others to stay back. He studied the surveillance security camera screen in the hallway. 'It's a girl.'

'No,' Weaver stated emphatically. 'We're to let no one in. Probably a scavenger.'

Jason looked again. Alex pushed past him and viewed the screen.

With trembling hands, the girl with dark hair and glasses pushed up her sleeve, revealing the resistance tattoo.

'She's one of ours,' said Alex. 'She wears the resistance tattoo.'

'Nope,' Jason stated emphatically.

The girl scribbled something frenziedly on a piece of paper, then held it up to the camera.

'CERN,' Alex muttered. 'She's from CERN.'

'I don't like it, Alex,' Jason shook his head.

The girl held up her right arm.

'Weaver,' Lawrence said calmly, 'would your scanner work remotely through the surveillance camera?'

'This little baby can see through walls,' replied Weaver. 'It's a stretch but I might just be able to pick her barcode up.'

Weaver grabbed a small black flashing piece of hardware with a small screen.

Jason hesitated. 'Keep your arm extended,' he instructed the girl.

Weaver scanned her invisible barcode through the screen. Instantly her photograph and profile appeared on the screen.

'She's clean,' he said.

'How on *earth* do you know she's clean?' demanded Jason.

Weaver patted the scanner smugly. 'I plugged the Resister Global Database into this baby. Nicked it from my informant in Cheltenham's GCHQ. She's a Resister.'

'That contraption had *better* be reliable,' said Jason, then grudgingly pulled the waiflike figure inside and slammed the door, bolting it.

He grabbed the scanner from Weaver and studied it closely.'

Storm Mackenzie. Astrophysicist. CERN.

'Storm,' she rasped in a soft Scottish accent. 'Stormie. My family call me Stormie.' She stared at Jason with a hunted look.

Alex's attention was now riveted on her.

'You were there? You worked at CERN?'

Storm nodded, unable to stop shaking. 'Astrophysicist.' She held out more papers.

Alex scanned them. 'She's a top scientist at the Large Hadron Collider.'

She nodded, then abruptly she put her face in her hands and started to sob. 'I saw things – evil, evil things.'

'When was the last time you ate?' Jason asked.

Her shoulders shook.

'They – they're dead,' she stammered. 'They – they killed them all. In cold blood. The mon– monsters.'

'She's not making any sense.' There was a mixture of chagrin and incredulity in Jason's voice.

'Maxim,' Lawrence instructed. 'Go through Lily's bag. They're roughly the same size. Get her a change of clothes. Run her a hot bath.'

'God damn it, Lawrence,' Jason growled, 'What she needs is a stiff drink.'

'Let her clean up,' Lawrence said firmly. 'Get some food in her stomach.'

'But how did you find us?' Alex grasped her shoulders. 'Why did you come *here*?'

Storm shook her head vehemently. She turned and pointed directly at Jason De Vere.

'*Him,*' she said with conviction.

Then fainted.

The priest undid the buttons of his cassock with precision. He walked to the tiny bedroom and opened the makeshift wardrobe. He pulled a long-sleeved T-shirt and a cream Arran knit jumper over his head and slung on a pair of faded Levi's jeans.

He walked over to a tiny basin, undid a canvas bag, turned on the taps, and shampooed his hair as black dye flushed down the sink. He towelled his hair until he was sure it had reverted to its original color, removed the green contact lenses, and studied his reflection in the tarnished mirror.

High cheekbones. Aquiline nose. Piercing grey eyes.

If not for the strong jawline with a two-inch scar splayed across his chin, he could almost have passed for pretty.

He ran his fingers through his cropped dirty-blond hair, repacked the canvas bag, then walked through to the sparsely furnished living room.

He opened the small croft door, walked outside into the ferocious wind and dragged in a sack of coal, shovelled it into the fire grate, and lit it with matches, then walked over to a cupboard, unlocked it, and took out a half-drunk bottle of Isle of Islay and poured some into a small glass tumbler.

He rubbed his hands together to warm himself from the freezing cold. Next, he emptied the entire contents of his rucksack onto the table in front of him and sank into the torn leather armchair.

He took a slug of the whisky, staring hard at the unopened brown envelope from Father Columba, breathed deeply, and with trembling fingers tore it open.

Charsoc bowed deeply to Lucifer. Aeons past, in the First Heaven, he had served Yehovah as Angelic Monarch and elder, second in rank only to Jether the Just, once his closest, most trusted compatriot.

Jether. He dug his long sharpened nails into his palms almost until they bled. Jether the Just, now his sworn enemy. After the Fallen's banishment, Charsoc had swiftly become the most depraved of Lucifer's Necromancer Kings, Governor of the dreaded Warlock Kings of the West and the Dark Cabal Grand Wizards.

Iniquitous, cold-blooded, and scheming, he now ruled with a rod of iron, second-in-command only to Lucifer.

'Your missive shall be delivered, Your Excellency,' Charsoc said. 'I meet with Jether the Just.'

'Then it is war,' Lucifer declared.

Lucifer strode to the outer balcony of his ice palace portico and raised his scarred imperial features to the raging, dark ice blizzards, staring up at the thirty-nine crimson moons rising high above the White Dwarf Pinnacles.

'I am ready for my legal visitation to the First Heaven. Prepare my chariot.'

Safe House
London

One of Assad's men entered the front door, followed closely by a short, stocky man.

'This is Sarge,' said the first man. 'He's one of us.'

'I'll be looking after you while the professor is gone,' said the second in his strong Cockney accent.

Jason frowned. 'Lawrence, you're going where?'

Lawrence stood and smoothed his Savile Row trousers.

'If you'll excuse me, I have an appointment with a group of very old . . . ahem . . .' He coughed politely into his handkerchief. 'Let us just say that I'm afraid that I have some pressing personal business to attend to.'

Maxim helped Lawrence on with his houndstooth coat and handed him his cane.

'Maxim will ensure that all your food and sleeping requirements are met. Sarge will ensure your protection.'

He handed Jason an old pale-pink diary with a gold lock, then a tiny gold key on a necklace.

Jason frowned.

'Julia's diary,' Lawrence said. 'The year you first met.'

Jason took a deep breath.

'How long will you be gone for, Professor?' Alex asked.

Lawrence and Maxim exchanged a long glance.

'The answer to that, young Alex,' said Lawrence, pulling on his kid gloves, 'is *as long as it takes.*'

CHAPTER FIVE

Tower of Winds

The First Heaven

Jether the Just, known in the world of the race of men as the indefatigable Lawrence St Cartier, stood in the lush gardens of the Tower of Winds, scanning the horizons intently.

All vestiges of Lawrence St Cartier had vanished. Jether stood regal, nine feet tall, his golden crown, embedded with jacinth, resting on long pure white hair that blew in the zephyrs. Imperial warrior, he was ruler of the twenty-four ancient monarchs of heaven – the Ancient Ones, stewards of Yehovah's sacred mysteries. On his shoulder perched his enormous white owl, Jogli, with searching, gentle brown eyes.

He paced up and down relentlessly, staring across to the Mount of the North, where thousands of battalions of Michael's angelic armies were gathering in formation.

Suddenly, he shivered.

He turned to Michael.

'He is here.'

I watched that day, as my elder brother stepped down from his monstrous chariot under the crimson moons rising on the horizon.

He stood in his usual arrogant stance.

His bearing still kingly, escorted by his Machiavellian royal guard.

An evil smile lingered on his lips as he walked nonchalantly through the gates of the First Heaven.

And I watched, almost mesmerized, as his scarred features metamorphosed into the noble, exquisite features of aeons past.

He closed his eyes, as though mainlining the atmosphere.

Then ran his fingers over his perfect features.

It would be almost the last time that my brother Lucifer would ever enter these gates with the legal authorization of the Royal House of Yehovah.

And well he knew it.

Tower of Winds

Lucifer turned his gaze upward.
He nonchalantly waved his gauntlet at Michael.

Michael gave no response.

'Your solemnity distresses me, brother!' he shouted.

Michael watched Lucifer. Silent.

'No matter, brother' Lucifer said dismissively. 'When I take the throne, I shall make you my jester . . . my light entertainment.'

Eden
The First Heaven

Lucifer strode rapidly toward the eastern side of Eden, Yehovah's garden. He knew precisely where he was heading.

He strode past the cherubim guarding the Tree of Life, past the Tree of Knowledge of Good and Evil, then walked through the Eastern Gates.

He followed the familiar path that wound toward the gardens of fragrance that grew far below the plains.

He walked under the narrow pearl harbour covered with pomegranate vines laden with lush silver fruits, his breathing shallow, treading frantically over beds of gladioli, past the rows of frangipani trees, across the familiar lawns of golden bulrushes and buttercups with fine crystal stamens, toward the intense shafts of blinding crimson light radiating from far beyond.

Across the vale, he came to the inconspicuous grotto at the very edge of the Cliffs of Eden, surrounded by eight ancient olive trees. Christos' garden.

It was there. Just as Lucifer had known it would be. He pushed open the simple wooden gate.

The garden was empty.

Christos was nowhere to be found.

Lucifer gazed in frustration out across the vast, seemingly bottomless chasm below, towards the magnificent Rubied Door, ablaze with light, that soared hundreds of feet high in the jacinth of the tower walls – the entrance to Yehovah's throne room. As the door swung ponderously open, the blue lightnings and thundering grew in intensity. A tempestuous wind began to blow.

In the centre of the Rubied Door, barely visible, an immense white form swathed in blazing light stood watching him.

Lucifer lifted eyes filled with terrible yearning and looked at the figure.

The majestic form watched Lucifer silently.

Lucifer clutched Christos' bench, strangely weakened.

The response from the blazing light was complete silence.

Suddenly, a pulsating wave from the form fell onto Lucifer's face. The fierce light hovered over his body until his entire form was wrapped in the wondrous pulsating luminescence.

He drank it in hungrily, desperately, bathing in the streams of compassion, of the unimaginable mercies of undying love that consumed him.

'I did it for you!' he shouted. 'I did it all for *you*! To show you that the race of men will desert you. They will fail you. They will betray you.'

Sobs racked his body.

'Just as I betrayed you,' he sobbed, falling to his knees, staring transfixed at the form, now partially visible through the incandescent light.

Michael and Jether watched in awe as Yehovah, the omniscient himself, moved towards Lucifer.

No one will ever know what passed between Yehovah and my elder brother that day.

Only that when my brother Michael found him in the East of Eden, he was pinned to the ground as by an invisible force, trembling violently, unable to rise to his feet.

Lucifer stared down in torment at the blood dripping from his hand, staining his white robe crimson.

Rapidly regaining his strength, he savagely pushed Michael from him.

'I don't need your help, *brother*,' he snarled.

Michael stared at Lucifer, his eyes expressionless.

'The next time you enter these gates, brother, will be your last.'

Lucifer raised his face in hatred to where the form had been standing.

'By the setting of these thirty-nine crimson moons, the

throne shall be mine,' he hissed. 'I will defeat you the day of the fortieth crimson moon, brother!' he spat. 'I will defeat the Nazarene!' he screamed to where the blinding light still stood.

The First Heaven was completely silent. Then, through the horizon of consuming, blazing glory, echoed the sound of Yehovah.

Weeping.

CHAPTER SIX

Julia St Cartier's Apartment

Kings Road, Chelsea, London
Twenty-Six Years Earlier, August 2000

Julia St Cartier sat barefoot, in her pale-pink silk pyjamas, cross-legged on the white satin bedspread that covered the treasured king-size bed that she had purchased on an antique-hunting trip to Paris. Her long blonde hair was pulled back into a ponytail, her face *sans* any make-up. She blew her nose for what must have been the tenth time in five minutes, then flung the tissue dramatically on top of a pile of tear-stained tissues. Her eyes were swollen from crying.

Rachel Lane-Fox lay with her long shapely legs draped across the end of the bed. 'Jules, you've *got* to get hold of yourself. So you and Jason had a fight.' She shrugged.

'It was more than a *fight*, Rach,' said Julia. 'It was a total misunderstanding. He wants time and space.' She looked up at Rachel through her tears. 'A whole lot of space, Rach.'

'He's cut you off?'

Julia blew her nose, nodding. 'You know how stubborn

he is. He won't even hear me out. And six thousand miles between us only makes it worse.'

'So phone him.'

'He's not accepting my calls. And he's blocked my texts and emails.'

'Wow.' Rachel eased herself up off the bed and walked to the window of Julia's Georgian Chelsea flat. She turned around. 'You really got to him, didn't you?'

Rachel reached and grabbed another tissue out of the almost empty tissue box and held it out to Julia. 'No man's worth this, Jules.'

'Except your Jonathan,' Julia sniffed.

'Jonathan and I never fight. I mean, even he admits Jason is stubborn as a mule.'

'Well,' said Julia. 'I wish he'd never introduced us via Uncle Lawrence.'

Rachel gingerly picked up the used pile of pink tissues and dumped them into the wastepaper basket next to the wardrobe.

'Come on. There's a whole queue of men gagging to date you. You've been invited to Milan by Fabio in two weeks, to the most prestigious party in the fashion industry. Rich Avi's jet is waiting and fuelled to fly you to the Grammys. George Smyth, who's a multi-millionaire, is literally begging you to meet his family.'

Julia picked up her Blackberry and scrolled down her messages.

'Have you ever been with a man and you felt so safe . . . so safe that it felt like the entire world could burn around you and you'd be okay. Because he's there. Safe, secure. You know me, I've had to be strong the whole of my life, never able to lean on anyone.'

'Yes,' said Rachel, with quiet sympathy. 'That's exactly how I feel about Jonathan.'

Julia closed her eyes.

Rachel stood up to her full supermodel height, five foot ten, with her hands on her slender hips and her glossy low-lighted dark hair swinging.

'Jules, I've told you this before. You've got to get *tougher*, darling.'

'I *am* tough,' Julia blurted.

Rachel grimaced at her. 'No, *I'm* tough. *You've* always been a pushover. You've got to be tough in love. You're too soft. You always have been, even at school.'

Julia glared back at Rachel and threw a tissue at her. 'I'm tough in business,' she exclaimed. 'I didn't get shortlisted as New Journalist of the Year in the British Journalist Awards for nothing.'

Rachel looked at Julia in amazement.

'You got *shortlisted?*'

Julia nodded, picked up a newspaper and placed it in front of Rachel. She pointed to an article at the top of the page.

'There. Julia St Cartier – shortlisted. Newcomer of the Year, freelance journalist for the *Sunday Times*.'

'Oh! This is totally amazing, Jules!'

'The *Press Gazette* announced it today. The awards dinner's in December, ironically at the De Vere Connaught Hotel. It would have to be De Vere, wouldn't it? Anyway, I've got two extra tickets. Will you and Jonathan join me?'

'Jules!' Rachel hugged Julia tightly. 'We wouldn't miss it for the world. It's Mayfair, isn't it?'

Rachel walked across the bedroom and opened the doors of Julia's crammed wardrobe, rifled through her clothes and brought out a beautiful figure-hugging black dress.

'Get your mind off Jason, girl! I've got some *real* news for you.' She twirled around. 'Julia . . . I'm pregnant!'

'You're *what?*'

'Twelve weeks. If it's a girl we'll call her Alexa. If it's a boy, Alex.

'Now get up. Brush your hair, put on your little black dress. We're going out to celebrate!'

The excitement in the iconic grand hall of the De Vere Connaught Hotel was almost tangible. Rachel and Jonathan Lane-Fox kissed each other passionately.

Rachel lay back in her chair, looking around the table of twelve.

'Where's Julia?' Jonathan asked. 'I haven't seen her since the drinks reception. They've already announced seven awards.'

'In the ladies. She's really nervous.'

'Well,' Jonathan smiled broadly, 'being shortlisted for New Journalist of the Year – it's real kudos.' He stared up at the ornate arched ceilings and the enormous crystal chandeliers. 'Impressive. *Very* Julia.'

He grinned. 'Speak of the–'

Julia walked towards them, her long blonde hair glossy and swinging free. She was dressed in a fitted silver sheath, tottering in her silver Miu Miu five-inch heels. She sat down next to Rachel.

'Nervous?'

Julia nodded, peering in her compact as she reapplied her candy-pink Mac lipstick.

Rachel gestured towards a suave, extremely handsome man seated next to Jonathan. 'Tristan Conway,' she whispered, 'he's got a beautiful home in Richmond, loads of money. He's handsome and newly divorced.'

'I don't care about money,' Julia muttered, snapping shut her compact.

'Yes, you do!' interjected Jonathan and Rachel at the same time.

Rachel held up a glass of sparkling water. 'Glad you're over Jason, Jules.'

Julia downed her full glass of champagne.

'She's obviously not.' Jonathan Lane-Fox removed his glasses.

'Jonathan, please talk some sense into her,' said Rachel. 'You've known Jason for years.'

Jonathan studied Julia intently. 'Have you heard from him?'

'No,' muttered Julia, lighting up a black Sobranie cigarette.

'Not a single *word*?' exclaimed Rachel.

'Listen, girl.' Rachel placed her hand on Julia's arm. 'You're the most exciting new journalist on Fleet Street. You've got six international job offers: *Washington Post*, *New York Times*, *The Times* in London, the list goes on. You've got the whole *world* at your feet. Tristan's invited you to his house party in the country next weekend. Forget Jason. Forget New York. You need a man who looks after your heart, not one who breaks it.'

Jonathan tapped his horn-rimmed glasses on the table. 'I think Jason will come round.'

Rachel glared at him.

Jonathan lifted his hands in surrender. 'Yes, he's the most stubborn man I've ever known. But I've never before heard the tone in his voice when he talked about Julia.'

'That was before Meg Ryan and the vodka bloodbath happened.'

Jonathan leaned forward. 'The *what*?'

Rachel sighed. Julia glared at her darkly. 'Never mind.'

'Jules,' Jonathan sighed, 'it sounds like you scared Jason out of his mind.' He cocked his head to one side, unable to hide his smile. 'He needs her, Rachel. Julia's everything he lacks in his life: emotion, a little unpredictability, huge heart, kindness, laughter.' Jonathan sipped at his coffee. 'It's just a matter of patience.'

'It must have slipped your mind,' said Rachel drily. 'Julia doesn't have patience.'

Jonathan grinned. 'She'll have to with Jason De Vere.'

He patted Rachel's tummy. 'Four months pregnant.'

Julia smiled weakly. 'It's amazing. I'm so happy for you both.'

Jonathan put his head to hers. 'Patience, Julia. Patience,' he whispered. 'Immerse yourself in your work. It's cathartic.'

He winked at her.

'And give up the fags.'

The lights dimmed once more and conversation came to an abrupt halt.

All eyes were on the high-profile British celebrity who walked onto the stage.

'It is our great pleasure to announce the British Journalism Award for New Journalist of the Year.' He removed a card from the white envelope, scanned it and looked straight at their table.

'The winner is . . . Julia St Cartier.'

London
2000

Julia sat at her study desk in her pale-blue dressing gown, a face mask on, her hair swept into a towel, as she stared blankly at the screen of her large white Apple Mac.

Rachel popped her head round the door. 'Jules? Writer's block?'

Julia looked up from the keyboard and threw up her hands. 'I've been working on this piece for an entire fortnight. I've never had this kind of block before.'

'You need a break, Jules. All you do is work. All work and no play makes Julia St Cartier . . .'

'Stir-crazy,' they cried in unison, laughing.

'Jules. You got a moment?' The tone of Rachel's voice had changed.

'Of course.'

'Okay, listen up. I've got something serious to ask you.'

'What's up, Rach?'

'*Very* serious, okay?'

'Okay,' agreed Julia tentatively.

'Listen . . . uh . . .' Rachel paced up and down the study.

'It must be really serious if you're pacing.' Julia removed her glasses, saved her document and turned to Rachel.

'It *is* serious, Jules,' Rachel sighed. 'Okay, here goes. If anything ever happened to me or Jonathan . . . will you promise to take care of my baby?'

'What do you mean if something happens? Nothing's going to happen.' Julia frowned. 'But yes, of course. You know I would.'

'Promise.'

'Absolutely. I promise. Rachel Lane-Fox, I've known you since I was thirteen. This isn't like you at all. What's going on with you? You've got my full attention.'

'Jules, Jules. Look, I don't know how to say this.' Rachel took a deep breath. 'I'm involved in stuff.'

'In *stuff*? What do you mean you're involved in stuff?'

'I'm investigating something, Julia. Something really serious. I'm in over my head.'

Julia took Rachel's hand in her own and clasped it tightly. 'Rach, I've got connections. Informants. I've done some research of my own. I know who you work for. I'm an investigative journalist. You had to know that I'd find out.'

Rachel nodded. 'I guessed you would sooner or later.'

'You're Mossad, aren't you?'

Rachel nodded.

'Being an international supermodel on the ramps is a great cover.'

Rachel smiled, a glint of steel in her eye.

'And Jonathan. Does he know?'

Rachel shook her head. 'No, my Jonathan's an investment banker, an intellectual. He doesn't know. It keeps him safe.' She paused. 'Jules, listen. This investigation I'm involved in . . . it's a black op, off the books. I'm investigating some extremely high-powered people who've done some extremely dark things.'

Rachel hesitated again. 'It's dangerous. The most dangerous thing I've ever done. I'm resigning after this.' She placed her hand on her tummy. 'I'm going to be a real mom.'

'And you can't tell me any details?'

Rachel shook her head.

'Jules, if anything ever happens to me or Jonathan, you've got to promise me you'll look after my baby.' She looked deeply into Julia's eyes. 'I *have* to know he's in safe hands.'

'He?'

'Yes. We had the scan yesterday. It's a boy,' Rachel said. 'We're going to call him Alex. Alex Lane-Fox. Jules, I'd trust you with my life. I need to know I can trust my son to you. Promise me, Jules.'

'Rachel, if anything ever happened to you I would take Alex as my own.'

Rachel leaned over and squeezed Julia's hands.

'But it won't. You're going to be fine.'

'Yes, of *course* I am.'

Julia stood up and embraced Rachel tightly.

'By the way, Jonathan wants you to come to Italy with us. Baby shopping,' said Rachel, and smiled. 'You know you've never been able to resist Rome. Especially the Residenza Napoleone III.'

Julia's mouth dropped open, cracking the face mask. 'Oh my gosh, Residenza Napoleone – it's a total paradise. Antiques, chandeliers, old masters. It's above my pay grade at the moment, Rach.' Her face dropped.

'My treat,' said Rachel. 'I'm paying. The ramp's been good to me lately. The owner's become a good friend. And Jonathan said he's arranging a little surprise for you. To cheer you up.'

'A surprise?'

'Yup. He's keeping me in the dark about it. We leave three weeks on Thursday. There for the whole weekend. Flight leaves from Heathrow at 4 p.m. We'll pick you up at midday.'

Rome
2000

Rachel clung excitedly onto Jonathan Lane-Fox's hand and peered into the window of the most luxurious baby shop in Rome.

'There!'

Jonathan and Julia followed her gaze to an extremely expensive looking pram.

'It's perfect!'

Jonathan shook his head in half-hearted protest. 'We've got to get it back to London, Rach.'

'We'll ship it!' declared Rachel.

Jonathan sighed. 'Listen, darling, the shipping will cost more than the pram.'

'I have to have it. You know how much money I make on the ramp.'

Closing his eyes, Jonathan sighed again. He winked at Julia. 'Never fight with a pregnant Jewish supermodel.'

He fingered the Star of David around her neck tenderly. 'If you *really* want it . . .'

Julia took out a box of black Sobranie cigarettes, tapped one out, and held it to her lips.

'I thought you'd given up,' he said.

'I have,' Julia muttered, lighting up. 'Just not today.'

'I wouldn't do that if I were you,' Jonathan said in a warning tone.

Julia followed his gaze. The Sobranie dropped straight through her fingers onto the pavement.

She stood, white as a sheet, frozen to the pavement.

'It's . . . it's . . .' she whispered. 'Outside, drinking coffee in the square . . . It's *him*!'

She frowned in bewilderment. 'It *can't* be!'

Rachel frowned. 'It's who?'

'Jason.'

'*Jason*? Aw, c'mon, Julia. You're dating *Tristan*. You haven't mentioned Jason for months. Anyway, he's in New York.'

'No, he's not,' interjected Jonathan. 'He's right there, across the street.'

'Oh, my gosh.' Julia smoothed down her hair. 'I look awful. I didn't straighten my hair. 'She pushed her fingers through the blonde curls framing her face.

'*What* am I wearing? I thought we were going *baby* shopping.'

'We *are* baby shopping.'

Rachel looked at Jonathan suspiciously.

'Jonathan, you didn't?'

Jonathan gave a secretive smile, then started to walk towards the alfresco dining area.

'No, Jonathan,' Julia hissed. 'How could you?'

'Could only take so much of you moping around, Julia.' Jonathan grinned, ignoring Julia's frantic hissing.

The two women watched as Jonathan strolled across the street and sat down opposite Jason at the small table.

Julia scrabbled frantically in her bag for her Chanel make-up mirror.

'Breath spray . . . Breath spray!' she muttered, frantically spraying it into her mouth.

'Whoa!' Rachel snatched it from her. 'You're overdoing it.'

Julia spritzed her glossy blonde hair with perfume, re-applied her pale-pink lipstick swiftly and stared at her reflection in her compact.

She glanced up towards where Jonathan and Jason were conversing.

Jason was studying her every movement, a knowing smile on his face.

She scowled at him, then yanked her hair from her ponytail. 'I'm going to run.'

'If you run now,' Rachel said drily, 'you're just going to confirm that you're the crazy Meg Ryan who downed the vodka and landed in A&E. Stand still. Relax. And play it cool.'

'I can't.'

'Well, you'd better.' She watched Jason De Vere get up from the table. 'Because he's coming straight towards us.'

'I'm going into the shop.'

Rachel grasped her arm tightly. 'No, you're not.'

Julia bit her lip hard, trying to stop the stinging tears. She watched Jason De Vere get up from the table.

Oh no. Jason was heading with Jonathan straight for her and Rachel Lane-Fox.

Oh, please don't let Rachel give him a piece of her mind.

Jonathan and Jason drew nearer until they stopped directly in front of the two women.

Six foot tall, with short, well-cut dark hair, Jason held out his hand to Rachel, displaying his usual cool demeanour. Calm as the proverbial cucumber.

'Congratulations, Rachel,' he said with his laid-back smile. 'Jonathan tells me you're expecting a boy.'

She smiled broadly. 'Yes, we're so thrilled.'

Jason slowly turned to face Julia with studied nonchalance. Mustering every ounce of courage, she steeled herself and raised her brown eyes to his.

'Julia St Cartier.'

She would recognize that New York accent anywhere.

'Jason Ambrose De Vere.'

He sniffed the air.

'Still on the cigarettes.' It was a statement rather than a question.

Julia waved the air around her. 'No. I mean hardly.' Her eyes flashed dangerously. 'What are you *doing* here?'

'Business . . . with Jonathan. We've been friends for years.' He stared at her calmly. In complete control.

A seething rage rose in Julia. 'So you've come to berate me on my personal habits that you so abhorred.'

'No, I told you, I came to see Jonathan.'

Julia's heart sank into her high-heeled platform boots.

She scrabbled in her bag for her oversize Chanel glasses and jammed them on to cover the stinging tears.

Jason shuffled sheepishly.

Rachel grabbed Jonathan's arm. 'If you'll both excuse us, there's something I need to show Jonathan.' They both rushed inside the shop, leaving Julia and Jason standing on the pavement.

Julia looked into the shop window, her mind completely frozen.

'You blocked me. Completely cut me out of your life.' She raised her face to him, her eyes flashing with renewed peril. 'From your texts. Your cellphone. As though I was some contagious disease.'

Jason's expression softened. 'You scared me.'

'Obviously,' she said with emphasis.

'Julia . . .' He shuffled his feet. 'Look, you know me. I'm unemotional. Pragmatic. And then . . . this cute little blond-haired journalist bursts into my life. Sunshine and hurricane. And I – I just couldn't handle it. You're quite an agenda.'

'Thank you,' Julia snapped. 'As are *you*.' She picked up her shopping bags, glaring at him icily. 'Plus being a total jerk and the stubbornest man on the entire earth.'

She started to walk away, desperately trying to hold back her tears.

Jason reached after her and grasped her arm. 'There was only one problem,' he said, his voice dropping low.

'And what was that?' Julia snapped, her tone like ice, willing back the tears with iron resolve.

'The problem,' Jason said, 'was that I couldn't ever quite get you out of my mind.'

She raised her eyes to his. The chemistry between them was rocketing again.

'Please let me buy you dinner, Julia.'

CHAPTER SEVEN

Santa Monica

6 September 2001

Rachel pulled up outside the loft style beach apartment in her British racing-green, Range Rover.

Jason and Julia were waiting for her on the pavement in front of their newly leased Santa Monica home.

Rachel swung her long slim legs out of the car in their black leggings, removed her cap and shook free her long glossy low-lighted locks.

'Okay, you two lovebirds. I feel terrible. It's still your *honeymoon.*'

'It's okay, it's okay, Rachel,' Jason grinned. 'We've had ten days of unadulterated passion.'

He caught Julia's eye, grinned and swiftly changed the subject. 'My godson seems very quiet.'

'Asleep,' said Rachel.

'Okay. Let's get unpacked.'

Rachel opened the trunk. Jason stared in exaggerated horror.

'What did you bring? His entire nursery?'

'That's babies, Jason. They come with a lot of stuff,' Julia laughed. 'You might as well get in some practice.'

Jason picked up a folded travel cot, reams of pale-blue bedding and four giant packs of disposable nappies, then headed up the stone steps and through the glass doors into the foyer.

'Couldn't you have hired a removals company?' he shouted over his shoulder before disappearing.

'Oh, Jules, I'm so sorry,' said Rachel. 'Do you think Jason's going to cope?'

'He'll cope. We're both working from home this month.'

Rachel grimaced. 'He's never struck me as the baby type.'

Julia laughed as Jason ran back down the stone steps towards them. 'Hey, Jas. Rachel's not sure you like babies.'

'Where is he?'

'In his car seat. Sleeping.'

'I *like* Alex,' Jason looked first to Julia then to Rachel. 'I do. He's my godson.'

This time he loaded up ten tins of baby formula, bottles, a bottle warmer, and a musical box.

Julia picked up an oversize stuffed panda from the boot. She leaned over, kissed Jason full on the lips, and plonked the panda in Jason's arms.

'If you want me to actually *see* to walk up the steps I suggest you remove the panda,' he grunted. 'I'm stacking it all next to the elevator.'

Jason stopped at the apartment entrance, without turning. 'He doesn't cry does he, Rach?' he shouted. He disappeared into the building.

'Uh-oh, we've got trouble,' said Rachel. 'If Alex doesn't settle, he's going to keep Jason up *all* night.' She winked at Julia. 'And *don't* let him give Alex whisky to sleep!'

'It's only for six days, Rach. Just till you get back. When do you leave?'

'Fly to Boston to see Dad in intensive care for four

days, then on to my photo shoot. Jonathan would have taken care of Alex, but his boss sent him to Hong Kong. They're setting up a satellite office there. Jonathan's in charge. You know investment banking.'

Julia winked. 'You want the low-down, Rach? I think Jason is totally besotted about being a godfather. He's been waiting for Alex to get here since breakfast.'

Jason strode down the steps. 'Okay, where's my charge?'

Rachel, Julia, and Jason looked down at the baby sound asleep in the baby car seat in the passenger seat.

'He's a good-looking baby,' said Jason.

Julia slapped his back. 'Don't sound so surprised. He's gorgeous!'

Rachel bent over and kissed Alex.

'I love you, Alex,' she whispered. 'I'll be back before you know it.'

She handed the car seat to Jason, kissed him on the cheek, and then hugged Julia tightly.

'Give our love to your mum and dad,' said Julia. 'Break a leg, Rachel.'

Alex started to cry as the car roared away, then the crying turned to screaming.

Jason looked at Julia.

'I *told* you: A week of screaming babies.' He sighed, then bent over the car seat, undid the safety belts and picked up the screaming Alex.

He held him up high in his arms.

'Okay, godson. You can sleep in my study – but only if you stop crying.'

Julia held out Alex's dummy, grinning. 'Need some help?'

Jason gazed back coolly. 'Nope, Alex and I have a godson–godfather connection. Watch.'

Julia looked on in amazement as Alex's eyes locked onto Jason's.

He quietened almost instantly. Jason walked into the elevator, Alex in his arms, as good as gold.

'Who would've believed?' She bit her smiling lip, deep in thought. 'Jason De Vere, you are amazing.'

11 September 2001

Julia dished up scrambled eggs and bacon onto Jason's plate. He was burping Alex.

Julia held out her arms.

'He's happy,' Jason protested.

'Yes, but *you've* got to eat.'

'I can eat.' Jason forked the scrambled eggs into his mouth with his right hand, holding Alex over his left shoulder.

'What is this? You and Alex are inseparable!'

'It's a guy thing.' Jason winked at Julia.

'What day does Rachel pick him up?'

'Hmmm . . . she should be just about on her way to LA. She was getting the early flight out from Boston. She's there till the twelfth.

'I'm going to really miss the little–'

They were interrupted by her Blackberry pinging frantically.

Jason frowned. 'Who's that?'

Julia scowled at her phone, which rang again. 'No idea. But I'm on holiday.'

Her Blackberry pinged once more.

She checked it, then frowned at Jason. 'It's *The Times*. They know I'm on honeymoon. Strange.'

Her Blackberry pinged again. Julia stared up at Jason, deathly pale.

'The World Trade Center. Oh my god! Jason, put the television on – now!'

Jason clicked the remote.

They both stared in horror and disbelief at the TV screen in the kitchen and the view of downtown Manhattan buildings . . . and the World Trade Center.

Rooted to the spot, they watched as American Airlines Flight 11 destroyed the North Tower of the World Trade Center, after crashing into it at 8.46 precisley.

The flight that Rachel Lane-Fox had boarded one hour earlier.

One Hour Later

Julia's eyes were red-rimmed from sobbing.

'Here, babe,' Jason passed her another handful of tissues.

'Oh, Jason. Why – why did Rachel have to take the early flight?' She started sobbing again. 'She'd have still been alive. Oh god, Jason.'

It was her plane that rammed into the North Tower. The thought ran through in her head as if on repeat.

Julia's cell rang.

She looked up at Jason in dread. 'It's – it's Jonathan . . .'

'You want me to talk to him?' Jason asked.

Julia shook her head. 'No. I'll do it.' She picked up the phone. 'Oh, Jonathan. . . .'

Julia walked back into the kitchen. She stood, trembling, her phone still in her hand. Jason looked at her questioningly.

'Jas, it's Jonathan. He's – he's not doing well. Rachel was his whole world. I spoke to a doctor who was with him. Rachel texted Jonathan from the plane. He knows she died in the crash. They're sedating Jonathan now. He's collapsed in shock. He asked if we could keep Alex a few more days until he gets home.

'We were cut off in mid-conversation,' she added.

Jason walked to the TV.

'Jules,' he muttered.

He turned from the TV.

'Oh god. The South Tower's just collapsed.'

Julia ran over to the TV. Together they watched in stunned silence at the black smoke spewing out over Lower Manhattan. Both towers were in flames. The only sounds were the screeching sirens of fire engines and ambulances, and the roar of F-15 fighter jets overhead.

Jason looked down at the soundly sleeping Alex.

'Poor little guy. It's just as well he can't understand what's going on.'

'Jason,' Julia took Jason's hands in her own. 'When Rachel first got pregnant, she – she asked me to promise something.'

Julia took a deep breath. 'Rachel asked me to look after Alex if any– if anything ever happened to her. She made me promise.'

Jason kissed her on the forehead.

'He's my godson, Jules. We'll do whatever we can. Alex Lane-Fox is safe with us.'

Seventy-two Hours Later

Rebekah Weiss sat quietly in Jason and Julia's living room. Her face was drawn, gaunt. Her coffee stood untouched.

Julia sat exhausted, silent. She had had three hours' sleep in as many days, covering the attack on behalf of *The Times* as the London paper's American correspondent.

'They're calling it the frozen zone, Rebekah,' she said quietly. 'Only emergency service personnel and officials are allowed in the zone. They're already erecting 12,000 feet of chain-link fence. It's like martial law, soldiers with machine-guns are guarding the perimeter.'

'Alex is sleeping?'

'Yes.' Julia smiled weakly. 'His afternoon nap.'

Julia took Rebekah's hands in her own, her own eyes rimmed with red from crying.

'I'm so sorry, Rebekah. There are no words. Rachel was my best friend in the entire world.'

Rebekah clasped Julia to her chest, her tears falling on Julia's unwashed hair.

'She loved you too, my darling Julia. She loved you like the sister she never had.' Rebekah's American accent was still tinged with a heavy Hebrew inflection. 'We'll get through it. We Israelis always do.'

Julia raised her head to Rebekah. 'And – and Jonathan? Oh, god. Rachel was his entire world.'

Rebekah nodded through her tears. 'Yes. Julia . . .' She raised Julia's face to hers and said as gently as she could, 'He tried to commit suicide.'

'Oh, god, no!'

'I talked to the doctor. He says Jonathan's had a mental and emotional breakdown. He's in a sanatorium in Hong Kong. He's being transferred to a trauma unit in London tomorrow. The neurologist said he's comatose. Locked into his own world. He's not able to deal with the grief. I fly to London straight from here to be with him. David will follow as soon as he's strong enough.'

Julia shook her head in confusion.

'But Jonathan – Jonathan Lane-Fox is always so . . . so grounded.'

Rebekah nodded.

'Yes, he is. A wonderful, compassionate, grounded man. We love him like our own. He's deliberately locked himself away from the real world, Julia. He's living in a world where Rachel still exists. In his subconscious.'

'He's stuck. You've seen it before . . . in the Israeli Defence Force?'

Rebekah nodded.

'I've seen it before. But only in men in combat. It occurs when the trauma is so intense that the stress causes the subconscious mind to lock down completely on that one event, which replays in the mind's eye over and over and over again.'

Rebekah hesitated. 'He . . . he doesn't want to see Alex, Julia. Alex reminds him too much of Rachel.'

She rose to her feet and paced the room.

Julia smiled through her tears. 'You pace just like Rachel.'

The older woman reached her arms out to Julia and they held each other tightly.

Rebekah's hands cradled Julia's face. 'Oh, how my Rachel loved you.'

She attempted a smile. 'Julia, David and I have decided to move back to Israel. We'll take Alex back with us. David will have to resign from NASA. I'll work half days at the Hadassah hospital in Jerusalem.'

Jason stood watching them from the far window. 'Rebekah, Professor Weiss. David is indispensable to NASA. You would have to leave the US. And Rebekah, you're a top-flight surgeon.'

Registering her look of implacable determination, he went on, 'Please hear me out. Julia and I intend to continue working from home for the next few months. She's covering the attacks at the moment; I'm holding the fort with Alex. We've got him in a great routine. He's happy, peaceful. Let us look after him until Jonathan is better, give him time to recover. And it will mean the little guy is in surroundings he knows.'

'We . . . we couldn't do that to you, Jason.' Rebekah shook her head. 'It's not right. Alex is our responsibility. We couldn't burden you with that.'

Julia interjected, 'Rebekah, before she died, Rachel made me promise that if anything happened to her or Jonathan that I would look after Alex.'

Rebekah looked questioningly through her tears at Julia. 'My Rachel made you promise?'

Julia nodded, unable to talk.

She looked over to Jason pleadingly.

'You know,' Jason said quietly, 'Jonathan and Rachel made me his godfather. I take it extremely seriously. Rebekah. He's not a burden. He's a joy. Our joy. Give us the privilege of looking after him. Give us a few weeks. Let's see where Jonathan is. We can regroup and you can both continue with your careers. We love the little guy. Let us keep that promise to Rachel, Rebekah.'

Later

Julia tiptoed into the study which they had converted into a makeshift nursery. Jason was staring down at Alex, who was fast asleep, blissfully unaware of the fact that his mother had died in an inferno in the World Trade Center and that his father was being heavily sedated in a London sanatorium at that exact moment, following a second suicide attempt.

Julia and Jason stood together holding each other's hands tightly, watching Alex intently.

'He looks so peaceful,' Julia whispered, studying Alex's exquisite features. 'His hair is coming in dark, just like his mother's.'

She looked up at Jason. 'He's going to be *so* handsome. He's almost an exact replica of Rachel. I want to look after him, Jason. Make sure that he's all right. Forever.'

Jason kissed Julia tenderly on her forehead.

'We'll never let anything hurt him again, Jules. He's safe. He's with us. He's our family for now.'

Julia wound the key on the small musical box. A tender Brahms' lullaby started to play in the background.

'I wonder what your future holds in store for you, Alex Lane-Fox,' Jason murmured.

CHAPTER EIGHT

London

2026

'Alex, get some kip. You must be exhausted. The professor said Lily won't wake for at least eight hours.'

Alex shook his head at Jason. 'Stuff . . . research,' he mumbled, and looked up.

Jason De Vere must have lost six pounds in the past forty-eight hours. Though freshly shaven, his strong face was gaunt from grief, his blue eyes dull. He ran his fingers through his close-cropped silvering hair.

'You doing okay, Uncle Jas?'

Jason downed the last of the whisky. 'Thanks for your concern, Alex.'

He grasped Alex's shoulder in affection. 'It's a process,' he said. 'Grief, I mean. Something you can't avoid.' He gave a wry smile. 'See you in the morning.'

Alex watched Jason disappear down the corridor to the camp-bed Maxim had set up for him. Then he surveyed the room.

Storm was in a deep sleep under a duvet on the sofa.

Weaver was snoring loudly and intermittently on a mattress on the floor, clutching three grubby eiderdowns to his large bulk.

David Weiss had the main bedroom.

And Maxim was riveted to a rerun of *Doctor Who* on the TV, Jason's revolver in one hand.

'I hope you know how to use that thing, Maxim.' Alex grinned.

Maxim looked up in umbrage. 'I would *remind* you that *I*, Alex Lane-Fox, was in the Royal Grenadiers. I fought in the Falklands and . . .'

A look of faded glory crossed his face. 'And on the Plains of White Poplars.'

Alex stared at him, perplexed.

'Before your time, young *whippersnapper*.'

Maxim gave Alex an icy stare, snorted loudly, and turned up the volume on *Doctor Who*.

Alex settled himself into the worn leather armchair, reached into his satchel, and removed the memory stick his grandfather David Weiss had given him.

What had his godfather Alex Jennings discovered?

What was so incendiary that he had been killed for it?

And how was it all connected to 11 September 2001?

Alex took a deep breath, then inserted his dead godfather's thumb drive into his computer for the fourth time.

He took a sip of lukewarm coffee, his eyes fixed on the computer screen. The evidence that his godfather, former officer of naval intelligence, had uncovered was mind-blowing, overwhelming. He had checked and rechecked it. He studied his notes.

There had been without doubt a group of shadowy puppet masters who had played key roles in the covert activities of Project Hammer and the Black Eagle Trust. All evidence pointed to the fact that the deaths of innocents in the World Trade Center, the Pentagon, and the four planes had been meticulously planned by the very same nameless, faceless perpetrators, to conceal every financial trail that led to the existence of trillions of dollars of Nazi and Japanese gold, and the covert activities the gold had funded for over fifty years.

Jason walked towards him. He held out his hand.

Alex passed him the hip flask.

'Can't sleep?'

'Nope.'

Jason spat the gin out hastily.

'Ugh, meths.'

'It's gin.'

'*Cheap* gin.'

'Maxim? *Maxim*!'

Maxim pulled himself reluctantly away from watching *Dr Who*, rolled his eyes, and pulled a small bottle of Islay from the drawer.

'You know I don't approve, Master Jason.'

Jason got to his feet.

'But, of course, there are extenuating circumstances.'

Jason grabbed the bottle from Maxim, held it to his lips and took a slug.

Alex looked up.

Jason grimaced. 'Julia,' he murmured. 'You miss Polly?'

Alex took a long swig of gin. 'More than I can say, Uncle Jas,' he said softly.

Jason abruptly changed the subject and settled himself in the chair opposite Alex. He frowned. Maxim had by now turned the volume on the television up to noise-disturbance levels.

'Maxim, turn that damn TV *down*!' Jason shouted. 'I can't hear myself think.'

'But it's the Weeping Angels, Master Jason, sir; a powerful species of quantum-locked humanoids,' Maxim pleaded.

'You mean murderous psychopaths,' Alex said, grinning. 'It's a rerun of *Doctor Who*, Uncle Jas.'

'I don't care if it's the Super Bowl. Turn the damn thing *down*, Maxim.'

Maxim grudgingly pushed the remote.

Alex grabbed Weaver's X-pad.

His fingers glided over the keys. He placed it in front of Maxim. 'There, Maxim . . . Weeping Angels.'

He plugged in Weaver's headphones. 'Full volume. No one else can hear.'

Maxim placed the headphones in his ears. Jason shook his head as an inane smile crossed Maxim's face.

Alex grinned. 'Well *he's* in his element.'

'Your grandfather has been telling me that you're investigating 9/11 again,' said Jason. 'Run it by me.'

Alex frowned, waiting for Jason's normal sarcasm.

'You'll listen? With an open mind, Uncle Jas?'

Jason gave his old half-smile.

'You have my ear. You always have my ear, Alex.'

'You may even learn something.' David Weiss stood at the door. 'Can't sleep either.' He smiled into his pipe.

'Okay, Alex. Fire away.'

'Okay, you know I had two godfathers – you, Uncle Jas, and Alex Jennings. I was named after him.'

'Yes.' Jason looked questioningly at David. 'He was an officer in Naval Intelligence, wasn't he?'

David nodded. 'Correct. He was my oldest friend. We attended Harvard together.'

Alex handed Jason a bulging file. 'Okay, first off, my mother was a fully-fledged Mossad agent.'

Jason raised his eyebrows. 'Rachel? You're *kidding* me!'

'It's fact, Jason.' David Weiss removed his glasses and rubbed his eyes. 'Julia knew.'

'Julia *knew*? She couldn't have. She would have told me.'

'Rachel was trained by Mossad from the age of seventeen. Her cover was initially photography, but with her striking looks – from her mother's side, might I add – she swiftly rose to the rank of supermodel. It was a brilliant cover, for a while. Before her death, she was investigating a multi-billion-dollar covert operation, Third-World investment to bring about the collapse of the Soviet Union. Project Hammer.'

'I don't understand,' Jason said. 'Bring about its collapse *how*?'

'Destabilization of the rouble, funding the August 1991 coup against Mikhail Gorbachev, takeover of the key energy and defence industries in the Soviet Union.

'Let me backtrack,' David said. 'Towards the end of the Second World War, the treasury of the Japanese Empire, originally stolen from China, was discovered in the Philippines by a member of staff under General Charles Willoughby, who was General MacArthur's intelligence chief. General MacArthur was alerted immediately and then the staff member flew to Washington, where he briefed President Truman himself. Behind closed doors, in top-secret discussions, the stratagem was hatched – to keep the greatest treasure chest of the twentieth century a secret.'

Alex nodded. 'It was added to the Black Eagle Trust, the gold already confiscated from the Nazis, deposited under utmost secrecy in over 170 banks globally and used to bankroll literally hundreds of black ops.'

Jason stared at them in disbelief.

'That's what Rachel was working on,' David said. 'She was hot on their trail.'

'Even if . . .' Jason hesitated. '*Even if* there were any truth to these claims, how is clandestine gold linked to 9/11?' He shrugged. 'I don't get it.'

'It's mind-blowing, Uncle Jas. Everything I considered in my research as relative conspiracy theory because of a seeming lack of concrete evidence: the research of David Guyatt, UK ex-banker, Peggy and Sterling Seagrave, and other investigative journalists – everything they discovered is meticulously documented in this file.' He held up Rachel's Mossad File. 'As far back as 1998 up to 2000. Plus the documented findings of Alex Jennings.'

He looked up at David and Jason. 'Everything! The evidence that my mother discovered over two decades ago. I've dug deep, checked, and rechecked the facts. Listen to some of the research.'

'Here it comes.' Jason sighed. 'Webster Tarpley, Tom Flocci, Peter Dale Scott . . .'

Alex held up his hands in frustration. 'Investigative journalists with brilliant minds, Uncle Jas. Have you actually ever studied their research?'

Jason held up his hands. 'I plead the Fifth.'

Alex continued.

'Fact. The $243 billion in bonds used to destabilize the Soviet Union was due for settlement and clearing on 12 September 2001. That means it had to be paid back in full.'

Jason frowned. 'A quarter of a trillion dollars, Alex? That's pocket change in the affairs of governments and the world stage.'

'Patience, Uncle Jas! But that's *not* the issue. The issue is that on clearing, they were required by US law to meet the demand for identification of ownership. *Full* disclosure. Once that then came into the public arena in the clearing process, their very existence would expose the illegal covert fund of

104

trillions and trillions dating back to the Second World War and Bretton Woods; to every election engineered for the past decades; every government destabilized or overthrown. Hundreds of CIA black ops and secret operations commissioned by the Pentagon without the official stamp of the White House. The perpetrators behind the trust couldn't allow the trail to see the light of day. All of it would have been exposed. The greatest criminal act of the military-industrial complex exposed to the entire world.'

'How do you think your grandfather Julius De Vere accumulated forty per cent of the world's bullion?' David looked at Jason. 'He was involved actively in the trust.'

'Thousands of prominent leaders, including presidents, chiefs of staff, Pentagon generals, CIA operatives would have spent lifetimes in Leavenworth Penitentiary,' said Alex. 'They had to cover their tracks. They had to somehow get around the insistence on identification of ownership. They *had* to stay invisible. Their overwhelming challenge – the demand for full disclosure *re*: the clearing process of the quarter-trillion-dollar note.' He paused for breath. 'They had to erase any association to its very existence.'

Alex downed the rest of his now-cold coffee.

'Common knowledge . . . documented on nearly every 9/11 truthers site: there were three major brokers in the World Trade Center. What isn't common knowledge is the fact that the largest US securities dealer was actively involved in managing the securities in question.'

'The $243 billion in bonds?' Jason asked.

Alex lit a cigarette and nodded.

'Precisely. Fact. Okay here we go. Kindergarten stuff for researchers into 9/11 – on thousands of sites on the net . . . all facts verified by credible 9/11 truthers and every journalist worth their salt.'

He took a deep breath.

On the morning of 11 September, Flight 11 hit the North Tower at 8.46, right below the floors where the largest securities broker was located.

He glanced up.

Okay, next – massive explosions went off on the twenty-third floor, just under the FBI offices in the North Tower, on the twenty-fifth floor, and in the basement of the North Tower.

'The 9/11 Commission verified the facts: the twenty-second through twenty-fifth floors collapsed into an inferno. Fires were reported on the twenty-second floor at 8.47. At 9.03, Flight 175 hit the South Tower. All three brokers' offices were totally incinerated by the fires.

'At 9.37, Flight 77 hit the newly remodelled section of the Pentagon: the Office of Naval Intelligence. Now hold on to your seats – this is not common knowledge . . . Agents of the Office of Naval Intelligence had been investigating several of the financial transactions linked to securities being managed by the exact same firms in the World Trade Center that were targeted. Forty-one per cent of the fatalities in the Twin Towers came from security brokers. Thirty-nine of forty Office of Naval Intelligence employees died in the Pentagon. In the vaults beneath the World Trade Center Towers, any certificates for bonds were destroyed.'

'And you're saying these agencies were all involved in . . . What was it?'

'The Black Eagle Trust. Yes – involved in keeping it secret, covering it up, or investigating it. But that's not all. Remember Building 7?'

'Vaguely . . .' Jason frowned. 'Wasn't it the building that conspiracy theorists say supposedly was a controlled demolition?'

Alex deliberately ignored the comment.

'Anyone whose done their homework on 9/11 knows that Building 7 housed agencies specifically investigating financial

106

crimes . . . What isn't common knowledge is that their investigations included the clandestine slush fund: These are indisputable facts - Building 7 housed the Export-Import Bank of the US, floor six; US Secret Service, floors nine and ten; Securities and Exchange Commission, floors eleven, twelve, and thirteen; Internal Revenue Service, floors twenty-four and twenty-five; CIA, floor twenty-five. Department of Defence, floor twenty-five . . . The list goes on."

'Alex Jennings here states that fires and explosions spontaneously began inside Building 7 before the collapse of either tower. Evacuees fleeing the building documented witnessing fires that had already started, even dead bodies. The building was eventually destroyed in what many unofficial observers now believe was a controlled demolition.

'Documented fact – US Secret Service Special Agent David Curran, stated on the record, "All the evidence that we stored at Seven World Trade was obliterated. A lot of cases had to be closed as a result of losing that building."

'Building 6 was destroyed by explosions from within, before being buried in the aftermath of the collapsing towers. Guess who was in Building 6.'

Jason shook his head in disbelief. 'Try me.'

'The US Customs Service and the El Dorado Task Force. The El Dorado Task Force was an interagency money-laundering investigation group formed in 1992 from fifty-five agencies responsible for coordinating all major money-laundering investigations in the US. Immediately after 11 September, every one of these . . . groups – literally every one – was redirected . . . off the money-laundering investigations which included ongoing investigations solely into investigating terrorist financing.'

Alex stubbed out his unsmoked cigarette, his eyes blazing with intensity.

'Taking the heat off all the cases they'd previously been working on . . . including the Black Eagle Trust.' David Weiss murmured.

'Exactly! But this is the big one! On the same day, the Securities and Exchange Commission declared a national emergency and, for the first time in US history, invoked its emergency powers under Securities Exchange Act Section Twelve(k).

'In layman's terms, the extremely stringent regulatory restrictions for clearing and settling security trades for the next fortnight were lifted. That's what enabled the estimated quarter trillion in covert government securities to be cleared upon maturity.

'Now look at this, Uncle Jas: without – without – the standard regulatory controls around identification of ownership.

'The securities could be now be electronically *cleared* without anyone asking questions, which happened when the Federal Reserve declared an emergency and invoked its emergency powers.'

'All links to the Black Eagle Trust were expunged. The covert gold war chest and the trail leading back to Nazi and Japanese gold was concealed from any outside scrutiny Thanks to the events of 9/11, a literal veil of secrecy now cloaked the entire clandestine operation. The criminals were home and free. No disclosure.'

Alex brushed his ever-straying long dark bangs out of his eyes and slammed his Xpad shut.

He looked up at Jason, Lawrence, and David Weiss.

Jason looked directly into Alex's gaze. Sombre.

'Alex Lane Fox, if there's any truth to this, it exposes the real criminals of 9/11.'

'The crime of the century.'

They all looked at each other. Silently asking the same question.

Adrian De Vere had commandeered the ten kingdoms under Axis Ten's banking systems including the IMF, the World Bank, and the Federal Reserve.

Where was the gold now?

CHAPTER NINE

Stone Croft

Isle of Harris
Outer Hebrides

If you are reading this letter now, my son, it means exactly what you have by now surmised. Yes, the Harpazo has occurred and I am now with the one I have spent my life for on this earth – my beloved Maker.

Keep well the instructions that I taught you. Keep them hidden in the depths of your heart. You are well aware of the enormity of the sacred assignment ahead, that only you can fulfil.

It will not be long before we meet again. This time, however, in a place where pain and suffering have no existence. Only peace. Purity. And His presence.

Be strong, my son. Be vigilant. Be very courageous.

But above all things, keep your heart attuned to the omniscient, omnipotent lover of your soul.

For it is to him alone we attribute the Kingdom, the power and the glory.

Until we meet again

Your mentor and friend eternally,
Father Columba

The priest slowly refolded the letter. He rubbed his intense grey eyes, then picked up a sheaf of photographs. He laid them out deftly like a casino dealer, then studied them intensely.

Julius De Vere.

James and Lilian De Vere.

Nick De Vere.

Next, he placed Lily and Julia De Vere.

Alex Lane-Fox.

And finally, Lawrence St Cartier.

He hesitated, then picked up the photograph of Jason De Vere – close-cropped silvering hair, severe features – and studied it intently. Then picked up a sheaf of documents from the table.

'De Vere Holdings,' he muttered.

He opened a neat file.

'Treasury, bullion trading, mining, and investment banking,' he muttered, turning the page.

'De Vere Asset Management New York, East Asia . . . De Vere Reserve.'

He took a sip of whisky and studied the documents.

'The subsidiaries of the De Vere family controlled De Vere Continuation Holdings AG.' The priest frowned.

He continued to read aloud.

'De Vere family's assets amount to $40 *trillion*. They own forty per cent of the worldwide bullion market and operate an aggressive monopoly on the diamond industry. Have undisclosed stakes in Russian oil. Operate at the centre of the illegal global drug and arms trade. Run the International Security Fund, set up in the 1990s under the auspices of Julius De Vere.'

He rose from his chair and walked to the far side of the room, toward a large gun cabinet.

His eyes darted over the guns. SAS weapons: three C8 carbines, four modern assault rifles, stun grenades, tear-gas canisters.

He unlocked the cabinet and removed two C8s and a SIG Sauer .40-calibre pistol, walked back to the chair, laid the carbine on the table, flicked off the pistol's safety catch, and held it in his right hand as he continued to study the documents.

Finally, he picked up the photograph of Jason and placed it directly in front of him.

Then took out his rosary.

And prayed.

CHAPTER TEN

Safe House

London

'Lily's awake. She won't eat. She won't speak.' Maxim's voice quavered.

Jason stood up.

'She's asking for Alex, Master Jason.'

Alex plugged his X-pad into charge, then swiftly walked down the corridor to the tiny back basement room and slowly opened the door.

Lily lay on the bed, her deathly pale face framed by her long black hair. She was clutching Julia's cameo so tightly in her hand that her fingers were turning blue.

Alex pulled a wooden chair next to her bed.

Very gently he undid her fingers from the cameo and placed its chain around her neck.

'Inside,' Lily whispered. She opened the silver cameo. On the right was a photo of Lily; on the left, Julia. 'Alex, it's Mum – she's dying.'

Alex sighed deeply. 'I don't know, Lily. I just don't know.'

Tears ran down her cheeks. 'I don't want to live, Alex.'

'Lily, you have to live. You've got so much to live for.'

Lily sat up groggily in bed. She burst into wrenching sobs.

'I'll get your dad.' Alex stood.

Lily reached for his hand. 'No, Alex, don't leave me.'

Alex smiled down into Lily's green eyes. 'I won't leave you, Lily.'

'You *promise*.'

'Remember when we were young. Very young. When I used to come and stay with your mum and dad? You were four and I must have been around eight.'

Lily nodded.

'Your magic book you used to make me read to you. Maxim found it.' Alex brought out an old, torn paperback of *The Lion, the Witch and the Wardrobe*.

'Narnia,' Lily whispered. 'Mum gave it to me. Aslan, Mr Tumnus, the witch . . .'

She made a wry face.

'Polly believed Aslan was alive.'

'Yes,' Alex said softly. 'She believed.'

'Do *you* believe, Alex?'

Alex felt the strange burning in his chest again. 'I don't know, Lils,' he whispered. 'There are times . . .'

Lily snatched the book from him. 'In our world, he is called by another name.' Her head fell back groggily onto the pillow. 'Read some to me.'

Alex opened the book and read softly. *'Once, there were four children whose names were Peter, Susan, Edmund and Lucy. This story is about something that happened to them when they were sent away from London during the war because of the air raids.'*

Immediately, the words of C. S. Lewis began to work their deeper magic, like a breath of spring that could thaw the worst winter. Alex's voice conjured the image of the big old house in the countryside, with its rambling corridors and empty rooms, and its peculiarly wise old professor.

Before the children had even begun their game of hide-and-seek, or Lucy had ever ventured into the wardrobe, Alex silently closed the book.

Lily De Vere had fallen into a deep but restless sleep. He kissed her gently on the forehead, then started to tuck the book next to her pillow.

A photograph fell to the floor.

Alex reached down and picked it up. He frowned. It was a photograph of himself at eighteen and Lily at fourteen, but Lily had drawn a red heart around their faces. He hastily replaced it in the pages and tucked the book under Lily's pillow.

Alex walked as fast as he could to the bathroom. Locked the door. And, for the first time since it had all come down, he sobbed heartrendingly for Polly.

Later

Lawrence St Cartier padded down the corridor in his sheepskin slippers and popped his head around Lily's door.

Jason had fallen into a restless slumber in the chair beside her.

She was in a deep sleep.

'Courage, dear hearts,' Lawrence whispered. 'Courage. *Aslan is on the move.*'

Stone Croft
Outer Hebrides

A crackling sound came from the woods just outside the croft.

The priest was still sitting on the sofa, his eyes closed. He jumped to his feet, instantly awake, C8 carbine in one hand, SIG Sauer pistol in the other. He moved quietly into the tiny kitchen and stood waiting behind the kitchen door.

Ten seconds later, the front door blew open.

Six men in black militia uniforms, wearing night-vision goggles, burst into the croft.

The priest moved stealthily backward and fired both weapons until the ammunition was gone. The six men hit the stone floor like rocks.

The priest stuffed the documents and photographs into his rucksack, grabbed a second revolver and the tear gas canisters, pulled on his anorak.

He frisked the soldiers' bodies, scanning their dog tags, shoved one of their radio transmitters into the rucksack, pushed open the door of the croft.

And ran.

Safe House
London

Lily padded quietly over to where Jason sat, the pink diary still unopened in his hands.

He looked up at her. Her eyes were red from sobbing.

She snuggled in next to him and laid her head on his shoulder.

Tears brimmed over onto her high De Vere cheekbones, plastering strands of her long, gleaming hair to them. Her deep-green eyes flashed. They were her only trait from the St Cartier side, from Julia's beloved late mother, Lola.

Everything else was pure Jason De Vere, right down to the cleft in her chin. There was no fighting it. At twenty-one, Lily was already almost a female version of Jason De Vere in both looks and temperament. And Julia and Jason adored her.

'What's that, Dad?' she whispered.

'Your mother's diary,' Jason said quietly. 'The year we first met.'

Lily stared up at him, perplexed. She blew her nose. 'Where did you find it?'

'Lawrence. Julia was his adopted niece, remember.'

Lily took the diary from Jason's hands. 'Key?'

Jason shook his head. 'I don't think I'm ready for disclosure. I made your mother's life hell the year we first met.'

'You were a jerk,' Lily sobbed, then kissed him on the forehead.

'Yes, I suppose you could say that. Maybe worse.'

He took the tiny gold key from his pocket. 'Prepare for the worst.' He grimaced.

'Even *you* couldn't have been that bad.' Lily smiled through her tears.

'You know how stubborn your mother was.'

Lily laughed out loud. 'Oh, and this coming from the king of all stubbornness. Known to cut people off and not talk to them for a decade . . . like your own brother.'

'Nick,' Jason said softly.

'You didn't cut Mum off the year you met.'

Jason turned red and scratched his neck sheepishly.

'You *did*.' Lily glared at him.

She put the small key in the lock and turned it.

'I'm afraid I did,' said Jason. 'After we first met. I blocked her. We didn't speak for a couple of months. Your mother had been through a horrendous relationship. Let's just say she wasn't at her best.'

Lily shook her head. 'Curiouser and curiouser. How did you meet?'

'She was a young journalist on Fleet Street. Extremely bright, so she came to my attention.'

Lily laughed softly.

'Everything Mum did was high profile.'

Jason smiled weakly. His eyes welled with unshed tears.

'Yes. That was your mother, all right. She had more guts, and more charm than anyone I've ever known.'

He looked over silently into the fireplace and smiled, his eyes tender with memories.

'Your mother had me from the start.'

He closed his eyes.

The memories flooded back like a tsunami.

It was 4 July, Independence Day. A hundred and seven degrees. It had been one of the hottest summers on record.

Julia had flown to America on business, so she stopped in New York on her way home.

Jason drew up into JFK's short-term parking, got out, slammed the door of his four-wheel-drive SUV, and drew a deep breath.

Nervous as hell.

He and Julia had corresponded every day for four months, from the moment they connected. He in New York, she in Chelsea, London. The up-and-coming New York entrepreneur and the edgy London journalist.

Instant chemistry. She had sent him the equivalent of today's Instagram. He sent her songs. He could make her cry with laughter in an instant with his dry, pragmatic humour.

But today was the first time they would actually meet face to face.

He recognized her from her videos and photos the moment he walked into baggage claim.

The edgy blonde beauty, who was bewitching a transfixed businessman into hauling her three pink and silver cases off the conveyor belt, with that same London rock-chick charm that had magnetized him from her very first text.

Everyone in New York was dressed in shorts and T-shirts.

There she stood. Ripped jeans. Black AllSaints leather jacket. Perfect make-up. High cheekbones. Long, gleaming blond hair, waving cheekily at him from across the conveyor belt.

He hesitated, then walked over to her, running his fingers through his short dark hair.

Half an hour later, they were settled on the sofa in his bachelor pad, watching reruns of Moonlighting; *then to the movies, then to dinner; laughing, debating heatedly, and talking into the early hours as though they had known each other for a lifetime.*

The first kiss confirmed everything he already knew.

She was sunshine and hurricane. The yin *to his stoic* yang.

Her perfume, her craziness, her mind-blowing intelligence.

She had got under his skin like a drug, and no matter what lay ahead, he knew he would never be able to get her out of his system his whole life long.

She woke the next morning, her make-up worn off, her normally meticulously straightened hair hanging in unruly curls from the humidity, and he still thought she was beautiful.

In fact, she was unforgettable.

'Dad . . . *Dad?*' Lily's voice brought Jason back to earth with a jolt. 'The next eight pages of the diary are completely blank.'

Jason sighed. 'For eight days, we were never apart. Day and night.'

'Wow, you must have really liked each other.'

Another sigh. 'Yes, we did. Chemistry from the moment we set eyes on each other. She was truly unique.'

119

Lily started to cry quietly.

Jason gently closed the diary. 'One day at a time, my beautiful, brave Lily. We'll get through it together.'

He rocked her in his arms like a baby and sang the lullaby Julia used to sing to her.

Finally, Lily's eyes closed and she fell into a deep sleep.

'One day at a time,' Jason whispered, a tear leaving a silver trail down his cheek. 'One day at a time.'

Armenian Quarter
Jerusalem

Rebekah entered the quiet, peaceful, makeshift sanatorium. She stopped. With her sharp eyes scanning the monitors, her hand reached up to the drip attached to Julia's arm, a smile began to break out on her old face.

Julia's eyes opened. She looked at Rebekah and smiled. A tear slid down her cheek onto the pillow. 'Rebekah, where am I? I thought I heard Jason's voice. What happened?'

She reached out to Rebekah with her eyes filled with wonder.

'Oh, Rebekah, something's changed. I can breathe. I'm going to be alright. I just know I'm going to be alright.

London

Dylan Weaver handed the phone to Jason. 'It's Rebekah Weiss, boss. You've got ninety seconds before they can track the number.'

Jason snatched the phone, his face ashen. 'Re– Rebekah? What's happened to Julia?'

Alex and Lily watched in silence, dread written over Lily's countenance.

'She's . . . she's *what*?' Jason looked over to Weaver, his hands trembling. 'The line's breaking up. I – I can't hear what Rebekah's saying.'

'Take it near the window, boss.'

Jason strode over to the window, ashen.

Alex and Lily watched as the colour drained from his face. 'Oh no,' she whispered, clutching Alex's hand tightly.

'Julia,' Jason whispered. 'When . . . *how*?'

Weaver motioned to him to end the call.

'I'll get back as soon as I can. I *love* you, Julia.' Jason clicked the phone off.

He turned to Lily and took a deep breath, holding out his arms to her.

'It's – it's your mother, Lily.'

Lily ran into his embrace.

Jason buried his face in her long dark hair. 'She's going to be alright!'

CHAPTER ELEVEN

London

Storm snuggled deeply into the leather chair. Fed and bathed, she was untangling her freshly washed long, dark hair.

Alex studied her.

She wasn't pretty; in fact, she could be termed plain, but there was something almost haunting about her. Pale alabaster skin, grey-green elfin eyes like pellucid pools. She must be about twenty-three.

She warmed her hands in front of the fire and tucked them back into Dylan Weaver's oversize Arran knit jumper.

'What I don't get . . .' Weaver mumbled in between bites from a large bar of Cadbury's chocolate.

Jason removed the bar from Weaver's grasp and placed the last four squares in his mouth. 'Nothing like British chocolate.' He was deeply at peace, the strain of the past forty-eight hours erased by the knowledge that Julia was safe and recovering rapidly.

'What I really don't get,' Weaver said, 'is why you came here, and how the hell you found us.'

'I told you,' Storm answered, the spark back in her eyes. She pointed again directly at Jason. 'Him.'

Jason put his hands up in surrender. 'I have no idea what she means!'

Storm scrabbled in her rucksack, opened the file marked *Aveline*, and removed some yellowed legal-looking papers.

She took out a photograph and one document and quietly handed these to Jason.

Alex and Weaver watched Jason intently. He went pale, took out his glasses, studied the papers, then looked at Storm intently.

'It's a lie. He's dead. I saw the death certificate with my own eyes. This is a *complete* fabrication.' Jason rose and headed for the back door. 'I need some air.'

'Be careful, Uncle Jason.' Alex frowned. 'What did you give him?'

'He'll tell you when he's ready,' Storm murmured.

Jason looked down at his watch for the fifth time in as many minutes.

'We should have evacuated over ten minutes ago.'

There was the sound of locks unbolting. General Assad entered, followed closely by Sarge.

'London is not safe,' said the general. 'The leaders of the Resistance in London, Birmingham, and Edinburgh have all been arrested. You have to leave. We have our own plane fuelled and ready to escort you.'

'But they'll track us!' exclaimed Alex.

'No.' General Assad's voice was firm. 'We'll be flying under their radar, using one of our military planes. The flight path is already approved. Where are the others?'

'Packing, General,' answered Jason.

Sarge and General Assad stood in the hallway. 'Hurry. We evacuate now,' said Assad softly.

'You're going *nowhere*.' Sarge lifted his C8 carbine and pointed it at General Assad. Assad reached for his revolver. Sarge shot him point-blank in the head.

He dropped to the floor like a stone. Dead.

Lily started to scream.

Alex held her to him. 'Be quiet, Lily,' he whispered. Jason reached for his revolver.

Sarge grabbed Lily and held the gun to her head. 'Put your weapon down, Mr De Vere.'

Slowly, Jason laid the revolver on the floor.

'I only want *him*.' Sarge waved the gun toward Jason. 'He's got the bounty on his head. We're only here for the money.' He released Lily.

A posse of Special Forces militia, dressed in black, knocked the door flat, surrounding Jason.

'Daddy!' Lily screamed. *'Da-a-a-ad!'*

Jason looked back at Lily and Alex.

'Look after her, Alex.'

'Yes, sir,' Alex answered, trembling in shock.

Sarge rammed the carbine into Jason's forehead. Blood gushed from the gash in his temple.

'Dad!' Lily screamed.

Alex placed his hand over her mouth and dragged her behind the sofa, as a mercenary injected a substance into Jason's neck, roughly placed a black bag over his head and handcuffed him.

Jason collapsed.

The black militia soldiers hauled him out of the flat, leaving Lily sobbing in Alex's arms.

CHAPTER TWELVE

Las Vegas

Lawrence St Cartier walked through the hotel casinos and held out his ticket for the Cirque du Soleil.

'The Right Honourable Grand Vizier Von Slagel is expecting you, sir.'

He was ushered respectfully through the crowds to seats in the very front of the theatre. He would recognize that flamboyant hat anywhere.

Charsoc, otherwise known as Kester Von Slagel, was sitting, rifling through a bag of merchandise, his carpetbag at his feet, his multitude of vermillion rings glittering in the low light.

Lawrence sighed, then cleared his throat loudly. Charsoc looked up.

There was a hiss from behind. *'Take off your bloody hat.'*

Charsoc turned and gave the British tourist a killing stare.

'Ah, Jether, long time no see, as they say in the less educated parts of this stinking planet.'

He looked Jether up and down languidly.

'You are quite the worse for wear, it would seem.'

Jether remained impassive.

'Do you think you could clear your popcorn and other frippery off my seat?'

'Tut-tut, tetchy, tetchy.'

Charsoc gingerly removed a large bag of popcorn, five chocolate bars, and a pile of glittering merchandise off the seat beside him.

Jether sat down heavily.

'Las Vegas,' he muttered. 'Only you would see fit to have our first meeting of the aeon in Las Vegas.'

'Cirque du Soleil,' Charsoc replied, his mouth full of popcorn. 'The arts, Las Vegas, entertainment capital of the world. You know how very partial I am to the arts.'

He gingerly offered a half-eaten Hershey bar in Jether's direction.

Jether shuddered in distaste. Charsoc shrugged.

Jether studied Charsoc's attire.

'Grand vizier? Part of the show?'

'Very amusing, I am sure.' He stretched. 'But yes, you are correct. I feel most at home here.' Charsoc stretched his legs out in front of him, his golden-tasselled slippers in full view.

'Your agenda?'

'Agenda, agenda. Is it imperative we have an agenda? Can we not just be two old compatriots meeting to catch up socially?' Charsoc took out his mobile blood-pressure cuff and proceeded to roll up his shocking-pink sleeve.

Jether rolled his eyes. 'Your blood pressure can wait. I am pressed for time. We are fully aware of all your master's dastardly plans concerning Adrian De Vere's resurrection.'

Charsoc grimaced. 'Gabriel's snivelling little spies have been doing overtime, I see. Our pay is so much better. Maybe there are yet others who will defect.'

Jether heaved a sigh of boredom.

'Those days are long gone, Charsoc. Your master's malevolent agenda is laid bare for all to see. Now, to business.'

'What is it you *want* from me, Jether?' Charsoc snapped.

126

He studied his reflection approvingly in a pale-pink Ted Baker mirror from his cell phone.

'Pale *pink*?' Jether remarked.

Charsoc snapped the cell phone shut in irritation. 'I have developed rather an obsessive penchant for pink since I arrived in this world. It soothes my soul.'

'Your soul obviously requires a vast amount of soothing.' Jether studied Charsoc's outfit, from the pale-pink kid gloves to the shocking pink underdress and vermillion velvet robe. 'Eccentric.'

'*Eclectic* is the word in the fashion industry. Not that you would have any glimmer of comprehension. Your attire is consistently, remarkably bland, Jether. *Beige.*' Charsoc wrinkled his nose in distaste.

'Be that as it may, Charsoc, we have business to discuss. It is thirty-nine moons. Your master was given an ultimatum: desist in his chimeras within the next forty moons, or he will be banished from the First and Second Heavens for eternity.'

Charsoc grimaced, and fished with his long fingers in his carpetbag. He took out a sealed missive and grudgingly placed it in Jether's grasp. 'My master's answer.'

'Your master's demise draws nearer, Charsoc. And yours with it, may I add. I don't imagine there is much pale pink in the Lake of Fire.'

'We will fight you to the very end, Jether,' Charsoc snarled, choking on his popcorn.

Jether patted him rather too hard on his back, then rose to his feet. 'It would be a gross stretch of the English language to say it has been a pleasure.'

'You'll miss the show.'

'You will inform Lucifer that your absence from the greatest angelic battle in the history of the aeons was due to the fact you were watching Cirque du Soleil in Las Vegas?'

Charsoc scowled. 'I shall be there. Make no mistake, Jether. And you will be my prize.'

Jether bowed to Charsoc.

And vanished.

CHAPTER THIRTEEN

Black Site

Undisclosed Location
Israel

Jason pulled on the orange jumpsuit over his knees with difficulty. He winced in agony as he drew it up over his bruised and bloodied ribcage.

His forehead was bruised, the gashes above his eyebrows streamed with blood. He limped across the claustrophobic cell.

There was a slit for a window. Only a hole in the ground, and a bare thin mattress soaked in sewage running from the walls onto the filthy cement floor. The perimeter of the cell was covered in barbed wire.

'Where am I?' he rasped.

'Black site. On the moon.' The savage-looking soldier with shaved head, in black militia garb, grinned lecherously at him, then placed a blindfold over his eyes and pulled the knot tight until Jason screamed in agony.

He thrust his rifle butt against Jason's ribcage. Jason collapsed on the stinking wet mattress. The steel doors locked automatically.

Lily sat curled in a foetal position in the corner of the sofa, trembling uncontrollably, staring at General Assad's bloodied body sprawled out in the hallway.

Alex looked around the kitchen, grabbed a worn blue-checked dishcloth, ran back into the hallway, placed it over the general's bloodied head, and then scrabbled frantically through Assad's pockets.

He looked over to Lily in consternation. 'Lils, try and get yourself together, *please*. Got it!'

He held up a cell phone. He scrolled down the numbers.

'Nothing.' He raised his hands in frustration.

'What?' Lily's voice trembled, 'what are you looking for?'

'Coordinates for our plane. We have to get out of here *now*.

'Dylan!' he shouted across at Weaver, who was hiding behind the sofa with Storm.

'Weaver, for God's sake. Get a grip, man! They're miles away by now.'

He threw the cell phone at Weaver. 'Make yourself useful.'

'What,' mumbled Weaver, 'are we looking for?'

'Call the last four numbers.'

'Dead . . . dead . . . dead.'

Alex swigged down the gin from his hip flask, lit a ciga-rette, and picked up his X-pad.

'Maxim!' he shouted. 'You can come out now.'

Maxim's head appeared from under the table. He was shaking.

'I . . . I removed the bullets in the revolver.' Maxim held back a sob. 'To polish them. And now they've taken Master Jason.'

130

Alex raised his face to him. 'Look after him, Lily, won't you?

'Airports. Private airports,' he muttered. 'I need to know all airports in a twenty-minute radius. Weaver, get to it.'

Weaver switched his computer on.

All the electricity went off.

Storm screamed.

'It's okay,' Weaver said from the darkness. 'I've got a portable generator. Has anyone got a torch?'

Maxim walked over to Weaver, shining a torch in his own face.

'Maxim, you look like a ghoul. Could you kindly pass it to me?'

'*Sh-h-h-h,*' whispered Alex. 'Someone's outside.'

The lock turned.

'Why isn't the alarm working?' hissed Weaver.

'Because we disarmed it.' A soldier wearing night-vision goggles, his head covered with a balaclava, stood in the entrance. 'Resistance,' he added quietly. 'Come with us.'

Weaver nearly choked on the day-old sandwich he was now stuffing into his mouth.

'How do we know you're not going to kill us?'

'You don't.'

Weaver spat the sandwich out, pale.

'You either come with us or stay and get caught. They're ring-fencing the square as we speak.'

'You.' He pointed at Alex and repeated. 'You. Are you Alex Lane-Fox?'

'Yes, sir.'

'Get everyone evacuated into the van outside. Immediately.'

The soldier's voice had an authoritative tone.

'Lily. Go,' Alex instructed.

'They're going to kill us,' said Weaver, a wild look in his eyes.

Alex turned to his grandfather and said in Yiddish, '*Zayde?*'

David Weiss spoke to the soldier in Hebrew. The soldier whispered something in Hebrew back to him.

'No, they're not,' David said. 'They're Sayeret Matkal, Israel's special forces unit. It's okay, Alex.'

'Weaver, Storm, Maxim – out!' Alex motioned them through the door.

'Let's go,' the soldier commanded, 'or we miss our pick-up.'

Maxim was hastily gathering a sheaf of architectural papers in his arms.

'Ahem,' he said, looking flustered. 'Blueprints for my Tardis – have a rather pressing appointment.'

He stood up.

'And I am late.'

And he vanished before their eyes.

CHAPTER FOURTEEN

Lucifer's Bedchamber

Ice Palace
Perdition

Charsoc the Dark stood outside the soaring black diamond doors of Lucifer's bedchamber.

He hesitated, his ears attuned to the sounds of an exquisite, haunting melody coming from within.

He nodded to Lucifer's royal guards. They pushed open the heavy doors, and Charsoc entered, his voluminous canary-yellow night robes swishing across the marbled floors.

The grand casement doors of Lucifer's bedchamber were flung wide. Hundreds of frankincense tapers burned in iron chandeliers overhead.

Charsoc moved nearer.

Lucifer stood in the shimmering light of the thirty-nine crimson moons, playing his viol, his eyes closed in ecstasy. The exquisite, haunting melody echoed across the murky lava wastelands to the White Dwarf Pinnacles of Perdition.

Lucifer's face was raised to the heavens. His raven hair, loosed from its diamond braids, fell gleaming over his bare shoulders. He swept the carved horn bow with long, passionate strokes over the strings of his viol, his long, slim fingers moving dexterously across the fingerboard.

He drew a deep breath, then turned to Charsoc.

'I ordered *no* disturbances, Charsoc the Dark.'

'Your Excellency, I have woken from strange and sinister dreamings.'

Lucifer flung the viol down on a magenta couch, strode to his throne on the east side of the chamber, and sat.

'Jagon,' he called to the gleaming white ice wolf lying by a raging fire in the monstrous iron hearth.

Jagon rose and slunk across the chamber to his master's side.

Lucifer picked up sweetmeats from a golden bowl and gently fed them, one by one, to Jagon, who lay at his master's feet.

'I have no interest in your strange and sinister dreamings, Charsoc the Dark.' He gestured to the balcony. 'The fortieth crimson moon rises on Perdition's horizon. My victory is assured.'

Charsoc drew nearer.

'Your Excellency,' he said, 'I am a dark seer. The Stones of Fire, I know that they magnetize your soul.'

Lucifer's eyes narrowed. 'You speak out of turn.'

'I speak out of supreme loyalty to only one.'

Lucifer flung a sweetmeat into his mouth.

'Speak then, if you must.'

'Your Majesty,' Charsoc drew near to Lucifer, 'I consulted this dawn with the Warlocks of the West and Nakan the Necromancer.'

He hesitated.

'We are all of one accord.'

'One accord?' Lucifer stared at Charsoc disdainfully. 'Naysayers, every one.'

'I speak of the Stones of Fire, Your Excellency.'

134

Lucifer's eyes narrowed.

'I know the intention of your soul,' Charsoc continued. 'They draw your very being. You would enter and take Yehovah's throne through the river of the Stones of Fire. It bodes ill for you, milord. They contain Yehovah's consuming fire.'

'Yehovah has grown *weak*,' Lucifer railed. 'He has not exercised his hand against me in millennia. He believed it was finished with the Nazarene. But I will show him who is king. I will imprison the race of men and take his throne.'

He stroked Jagon's sleek white coat.

'It is a trap, Your Excellency.'

Lucifer rose from his throne and walked to the balcony, staring for a long time at the rising fortieth crimson moon.

'Yes. The Stones of Fire. They call to my very soul,' he murmured.

Then he swung around to Charsoc, his face contorted with malice.

'I walked those stones for aeons when I was his light-bringer, his seraph. Prince Regent, Son of the Morning. I shall walk them again to overtake his throne. No one, NO ONE,' he roared, 'is to be informed of my plans.'

He picked up his viol and smashed it on the marble floor.

His time ran down. He sensed it.

'Armageddon draws nearer, milord. May I humbly remind you, Your Majesty, if we lose, you will be held in the Crypts of Conflagration, then incarcerated for a thousand years in the bottomless pit, before your demise in the Lake of Fire.'

Lucifer carefully sliced a blue fruit with a gleaming dagger. He placed a slice on his tongue, caressing the blade lovingly, then walked over to the trembling Charsoc, grasped him by the hair, and held the razor-sharp blade to his neck.

'Charsoc the Dark,' he hissed, 'if you ever, *ever* bring up the subject again, I will sever your ugly, pasty head from your body.'

He pressed the blade against Charsoc's neck until blood started to seep from his grey skin.

'I will take my brother Michael prisoner as collateral,' he hissed. 'And Jether will be forced to escort me to the Labyrinths.'

He flung the gasping Charsoc savagely onto the marbled floor of his chamber.

'Get out,' he hissed.

Charsoc lay rooted to the floor, trembling.

'*Get out!*' Lucifer screamed. '*OUT!*'

Charsoc gathered his voluminous yellow nightgown in both hands, rose to his feet, blood seeping from his neck, and stumbled out through the glistening black doors.

CHAPTER FIFTEEN

Tower of Winds

First Heaven

Jether the Just hesitated before the small silver filigree door of the Garden of Tempests. As he held his onyx ring over the keyhole, the door slid open. A huge, vibrantly colourful garden stood revealed, and at its centre the Tower of Winds.

He walked towards the very centre of the tower gardens, where six of the ancient angelic monarchs of the Royal House of Yehovah sat on golden thrones around a large table, the azure breeze teasing at their white hair and trailing beards. Their heads were bowed in supplication. They were the devoted executors of Yehovah's unutterable marvels and governors of the three great portals. They were the custodians of the sacred vaults of the flaming cherubim and seraphim – vaults that housed countless billions of DNA blueprints, genomic codes, and the boundary lines of Yehovah's innumerable galaxies, seas, and multiple universes.

Obadiah and Dimnah were Jether and Xacheriel's youngling attendants, tasked with assisting the Ancient Ones in their custodianship of Yehovah's countless new galaxies.

Blissfully oblivious to Jether's arrival, they lay on their backs in the fountain, wearing what looked like inflatable neon-green armbands. The two younglings – of an ancient angelic race possessing the characteristics of eternal youth, a remarkable inquisitiveness, and bright orange hair – were sucking on sweetmeats and slurping loudly at the thick chocolaty mixture that was now gushing from the fountain.

'*Humpf.*' Jether cleared his throat. Obadiah glanced up at his master and started to sink beneath the chocolate-covered water in sheer panic. Dimnah pulled a lever on one armband. Green smoke erupted, and the unfortunate youngling was catapulted straight into the unsuspecting Lamaliel, who had just come through the gate.

'Ticklish. Oh, my, ticklish,' the gentle Lamaliel giggled, pinned to the floor by the chocolate-covered Dimnah.

Xacheriel, known among the race of men as Maxim, entered in his galoshes, panting loudly, clutching a yellow sou'wester to his unruly curls and his blueprints to his chest. In the First Heaven, he was Curator of the Sciences and Universes for the Ancient of Days, and one of the twenty-four ancient kings under Jether's governance.

Jether raised his bushy eyebrows.

'Ahem! I was detained on serious business.'

More giggles from Lamaliel.

Jether and Xacheriel turned their gaze to the younglings, who were tickling Lamaliel with eagle feathers.

'*Desist, Dimnah*!' Xacheriel roared.

Dimnah froze as though paralysed, while still pinning Lamaliel down.

'Dimnah,' Xacheriel plodded heavily toward him. 'Get *off* Lamaliel.'

'Yes, milord,' Dimnah replied, and pulled a lever on the second armband.

The entire table of ancient monarchs watched as Dimnah

accelerated a hundred feet into the skies in a frenzy of green smoke, made three supersonic spins, then plummeted back, head first, towards the middle of the table.

There was an almighty crash. Then silence.

'You're a *disgrace,* Dimnah.'

Xacheriel yanked the reeling, sprawling youngling off the chocolate-splattered table.

'A disgrace! Give me those contraptions.'

Sheepishly, Dimnah removed the armbands and placed them reluctantly in Xacheriel's hands.

'A thousand pardons, milord Xacheriel. A thousand pardons.'

'My *personal* boosters,' Xacheriel muttered. 'From my private cloisters. A disgrace!' He glowered at the petrified Dimnah.

Jether shook his head at Obadiah, who sat frozen in the fountain. 'Clean yourselves up,' Jether sighed, 'then return on your best behaviour. We converse about weightier things than your youngling heads can accommodate.'

Both Dimnah and Obadiah closed their eyes and ran at full speed toward the gate, slamming into Michael and Gabriel as they entered.

Michael picked them both up by their feet and flung them over the gate, laughing.

'Dunderheads!' Xacheriel muttered, sticking his finger in the chocolate on the armband. 'Mm-m-m.' He stopped himself as he caught Jether's eye.

Jether bowed to Michael, then to Gabriel, and they seated themselves on his left and right.

'Lamaliel, my dear friend . . .'

'A great adventure.' Lamaliel giggled. 'A respite from my supplications.'

'Yes, that may be, but we are convened here for the most serious of meetings, gentle Lamaliel.'

'Of course, of course,' whispered Lamaliel, smoothing his robes. 'Forgive me, my honoured friend.'

Jether frowned as Xacheriel removed a model of a Dalek and the Tardis from *Doctor Who* and placed them directly in front of him with a satisfied smile.

'Ahem.' Jether raised a bristling eyebrow.

'Inspiration,' Xacheriel declared.

Jether sighed loudly and pointed to Xacheriel's sou'wester. 'Matters of *State*.'

Xacheriel yanked the rain hat off his head with an ungracious huff and replaced it with his crown, askew as usual on his uncontrollable grey curls.

Jether stood with one hand resting on the pages of an enormous volume covered in gold filigree-work. When the assembly had fallen still, he said, 'Revered compatriots. The council is summoned today to meet the gravest of needs.

'Since Lucifer was overcome at Golgotha, almost two millennia have rolled past. Armageddon approaches – the great battle. My revered compatriot, Issachar.'

Issachar the Wise folded his hands, his normally gentle features grave.

'My honoured compatriots, the fortieth crimson moon rises as we meet. This day is a day that will be written in the annals of the First Heaven, as well as the annals of the race of men.'

'From Lucifer.' Jether held up a missive with the black, smouldering seal of Perdition. 'His answer to Yehovah's ultimatum, in accordance with the legal requirements of the Supreme Councils of the First Heaven. He was given forty crimson moons to retract his diabolical plans regarding the Nephilim gene and the creation of his hybrids and chimeras. Failing that, it is the final war.'

Slowly he broke the seal and unfolded the ancient parchment. He studied the exquisite copperplate italic lettering and sighed.

'His final answer to Yehovah's ultimatum. He declares war. A formal declaration of war, in legal conformity with Eternal Law.'

Jether turned to Xacheriel.

Xacheriel extricated his overlarge feet in their yellow galoshes from under the table. He cleared his throat loudly. Then, putting his monocle to his eye, he thumbed through his scientific papers.

'Honoured compatriots; my revered Jether. So he disregards Yehovah's ultimatum and continues with his ill-founded schemes to mutate the genetic code of the race of men. I have the evidence here, received from Gabriel's revelators, that the Twins of Malfecium have been extremely busy in their sweltering laboratories. The Pale Horse, alias *the chip*, which they created has now been perfected. Once it is inserted into one of the race of men, the DNA codes interact instantly with the recipient's genome. A masked genetic marker is activated by a second chip in the forehead. It is programmed to rewrite the race of men's genetic code, and will simultaneously transform them into transgenic organisms. With DNA inserted from a non-human species. Nephilim DNA, the source codes of the Fallen. The race of men's own source codes will be mutated forever.

'Four billion humans implanted with the DNA of the Fallen,' Xacheriel declared. 'Four billion mind-controlled, demonic super-soldiers.'

'Under my insane brother's control.' Michael slammed his gauntleted fist on the table in frustration. 'And he wants the throne, too.'

'Yes,' continued Xacheriel. 'He would mutate the race of men's gene pool as he did in the days of Noah and the Great Flood, but now using the scientific strides of the race of men over these past two decades.'

Jether slowly refolded the missive. 'He writes that he would storm Yehovah's throne at the setting of the fortieth crimson moon. Gabriel and his revelator eagles will alert us to their advance. Michael's armies will be in position.'

Gabriel stood. 'As written in the tenets of Eternal Law, the fortieth crimson moon is our brother's last legal access through the gates of the First Heaven. We have no option but to conform. Yehovah himself will open the Pearl Gates to Lucifer for the final time.'

Jether nodded. 'I sense Lucifer's true intention,' he said softly, and walked to the edge of the Tower of Winds, his robes and long white hair blowing in the tempests. 'The Stones of Fire,' he said softly. 'I am a seer, and his old mentor. At times I can read his very thoughts.'

'The Stones of Fire,' Gabriel gasped.

'Yes, Gabriel.'

'Honoured Jether,' Michael said, 'surely even my brother would not be so foolhardy.'

'In worlds long gone when I alone was Lucifer's mentor,' Jether sighed, 'his greatest ecstasy – like your own and Gabriel's – was to walk through the sacred river of the Stones of Fire, directly into Yehovah's heart.'

'Direct access to the throne,' Gabriel uttered. 'But even he could not be so shortsighted.'

'They draw him,' Jether murmured. 'The Stones of Fire magnetize his soul today, as intensely as they did in aeons past. His dreamings are filled with the idea of possessing their power, overthrowing Yehovah's throne, and taking it as his own. He has been yearning to walk amid the Stones of Fire again for aeons. It has now become his driving obsession. This is his last chance to experience their immense power.'

Michael's eyes narrowed. 'So his secret intention becomes clear. He will seek to deflect my armies at the gates, but his true aim is through some devious scheme to enter through the Labyrinths and to descend the golden stairway to the Stones of Fire . . . and gain direct access to Yehovah's throne.'

'But *how*?' Gabriel uttered. 'The warring seraphim and cherubim protect the way. He'll never pass the first gate.'

Jether looked back at Michael and Gabriel.

'There is no doubt he incubates some malevolent strategy. Gabriel, you and your revelators will guard the Rubied Door from inside the throne room. Michael, prepare your armies. This convocation is adjourned.'

One by one, the angelic kings and Michael bowed to Jether until only Gabriel remained. He stood silent, his eyes drawn to the very far corner of Eden, where a beautiful young girl with daisies woven through her hair was walking arm in arm with an older man, in deep discussion.

Jether walked over to Gabriel, his owl Jogli on his shoulder.

'You are enjoying them as I do,' said Jether softly.

Gabriel nodded.

'Polly and C. S. Lewis,' he murmured. 'They walk together each evening as dusk falls, talking about Narnia and discussing his writings.'

Gabriel looked at Jether in wonder. 'I have wept many dusks watching them.'

Jether smiled, his eyes distant.

They stood looking out over Yehovah's garden. A great and terrible glory began to descend across Eden.

'He comes,' whispered Gabriel in awe. 'He comes as the great lion.'

Gabriel and Jether watched, deeply moved, as a majestic white lion padded regally through the garden of Yehovah, past the Tree of Good and Evil, and stopped under the blue fruits of the Tree of Knowledge.

The lion raised his head, shook his mane, and roared.

From behind the trees, hundreds of children ran headlong towards the lion, flinging their arms around his neck, burying their faces in his thick mane. Little girls covered him with daisy chains and kisses. Toddlers swung on his tail. The lion lay on his back, purring loudly.

'Oh, how he loves the children of the race of men,' Gabriel whispered.

Then, quite suddenly, an upright figure stood in the place of the the lion, shining with luminous brilliance. Yehovah picked up all the children, every one, placed them tenderly in his blazing rainbow cloak of light, and vanished through the great Rubied Door.

Jether shook his head in wonder.

'It is storytime,' he murmured. 'He goes to give them gifts, each one.'

Jether turned from the garden and placed his arm in Gabriel's, and together they walked in silence toward the fountains.

Finally, Gabriel spoke.

'Revered Jether, Lucifer would wreak vengeance on the race of men here. He is jealous of their place in heaven. I have set King Aretas the Great as their protector. Lucifer's troops will not be allowed to break into that area of the First Heaven.'

Jether nodded. 'Yes. There will be a time when the redeemed of the race of men who dwell with us will join us in the battle, but not until the last battle – Armageddon. Gather your troops, Gabriel. The war of the First Heaven is upon us.'

Ice Wastelands
Perdition

Lucifer stood on the precipice of the war chamber, brandishing his sword, his robes blowing violently in the dark blizzards, six enormous black seraph wings extending from his spine. All across the plains, as far as the eye could see, the Fallen armies were gathering, answering the call to the Last Great War in the Heavens.

The monstrous bells of limbo pealed.

He raised his sceptre.

'*We will WAR!*' he roared.

A monstrous cry erupted from the armies of the damned.

'*We will WAR! We will WAR! We will WAR!*'

CHAPTER SIXTEEN

The First Heaven

Jether sat erect on his white-winged charger, encircled by the twenty-three angelic monarchs, on the soaring white crystalline Cliffs of Eden. Imperial and forbidding, in their right hands the ancient kings held their lances high, flashing with the lightnings of Yehovah.

A battalion of younglings held blazing crimson standards aloft, carrying the emblem of the Royal House of Yehovah.

Directly ahead of them, led by Gabriel attired in full battle regalia, marched his vast company of swift and agile archers, the revelators, in suits of gleaming silver armour. Overhead the revelator scouts filled the length and breadth of the skies – the First Heaven's huge white-feathered warrior eagles. Around each eagle's neck was a circlet of gold embedded with rubies: the warriors' homing beacons.

Filling the plain to Gabriel's right Michael's imperial knights, mounted on their gold-caparisoned war stallions. Their gleaming broadswords were raised high as they followed the mighty commander of heaven's armies.

Michael rode in his war chariot, pulled by enormous white-winged war stallions. He wore his ceremonial golden armour and held high the Sword of State in his right hand.

The fearsome company of the White-Winged Lions of Yehovah ranged at his right.

The great and terrible armies of the Lord.

Jether surveyed the Pearl Gates from his vantage point on the eastern Cliffs of Eden.

The macabre drumbeat of the Shaman Kings resounded through the First Heaven.

The angelic monarchs saw the horizons darken as the black cloud of the Fallen, astride their dark-winged leviathans and griffons, or riding their iron war chariots, drew closer with each passing second.

Jether raised his face to the soaring Rubied Door in the distance.

'They are here,' he whispered. 'The battle commences.'

Pearl Gate
First Heaven

Lucifer stood in his monstrous iron war chariot, its silver wheels sprung with jagged war blades. His raven hair, plaited with flaming rubies and diamonds, fell past broad shoulders to his garments of state. His white velvet cloak, hemmed with diamonds and ermine, was draped across his shoulders, covering platinum armour. On his head rested a crown of pure gold embedded with chrysolite and black rubies. He held the royal golden sceptre of Perdition in his right hand, his sword in his left.

The King of Hell.

The ghoulish battalion of the sinister hooded Shaman Kings stepped forward: hell's macabre drummers.

The ground started to shudder violently as if in the throes of a terrible earthquake. Slowly the soaring gates of the First Heaven opened.

'Armies of hell, I salute you!' Lucifer cried.

The slow, menacing throb of Shaman drums pulsed beneath his voice.

'Slaughter our enemy. Today the throne becomes mine!'

A terrible, bloodcurdling roar went up from the armies of hell.

Moloch stood twelve feet tall in his war chariot, licking his sword lecherously.

'Michael, my pretty,' he roared, 'we have unfinished business!'

He turned to his armies.

'Storm the First Heaven!'

Michael stood in his chariot, his valiant angelic battalions waiting for his signal.

'Now!' he cried.

The immense company of the lions of Yehovah, their white manes gleaming, their enormous white wings extended, flew toward Lucifer's armies. Their thunderous roaring resounded across the horizons of the First Heaven.

Lucifer's twelve Satanic Princes, the rulers of the dark world, thundered through the open gates in chariots drawn by winged leviathans. Following them came thousands of Lucifer's menacing satanic royal guard, the Black Horde.

Lucifer stood upright in his war chariot, in the very centre of the gates, his eyes scanning the savagely fighting angelic armies for one figure and one alone – his brother Michael.

He caught sight of him in savage combat with the prince of Grecia and watched as Michael, with one skilled move of the sword, brought the satanic prince to his knees.

'Shackle him!' cried Michael to his guards.

Lucifer rode toward them, brandishing his broadsword high.

'Brother!' he cried. 'Let us fight one to one on the beaches, as in aeons past.'

Gabriel rode up behind Michael on his white-winged stallion. 'He calls you to war,' he warned his brother. 'I sense some evil strategy.'

Their enemy's voice came insistently. 'Michael and Lucifer, two brothers, fight one to one as in aeons past.'

'Do not *heed* him, Michael.' Gabriel's voice was intense. 'He has some evil strategy afoot.'

Michael looked past Gabriel, his gaze fixed on Lucifer.

'You wish to *fight*, Lucifer?' Michael cried, brandishing the Sword of State. 'One on one? Then we will fight!'

Gabriel raised his visor and grasped Michael's arm.

'Michael! No!'

'My brother calls me to war. I will war, Gabriel!'

Gabriel watched in frustration as Michael's war chariot and winged steeds rose into the skies and flew after Lucifer's chariot in the direction of the Crystal Sea.

Both war chariots landed on the vast expanse of the white pearl beaches beside the Crystal Sea, where the two brothers had long ago spent their days racing and jousting in their chariots, careering in camaraderie across the white sands of the First Heaven. In worlds long since departed.

'Brothers!' cried Lucifer as his war chariot ploughed into the sand. 'It has been many aeons since we tested our swordsmanship, Michael.'

Michael raised his Sword of State, his gaze locked onto Lucifer's.

With one hand gripping the reins of his eight black war stallions, Lucifer raised his broadsword to the crimson moons overhead.

'Today I occupy the throne that was always my inheritance,' he cried.

'Not on *my* watch,' Michael shouted.

Michael's and Lucifer's chariots thundered across the beach, the jagged silver war blades of their chariot wheels grinding against each other as they raced neck and neck on the sands.

The two brothers fought violently, as in millenniums past, steel against steel, blow upon savage blow.

'This day, brother, you will be cast out from the First Heaven for eternity.'

Lucifer threw back his head in Machiavellian laughter.

The parrying and thrusting became more intense, the clashing of steel more violent.

'You have grown *soft* these past millennia, brother!' Lucifer shouted derisively to Michael.

'You have never forgiven me for the *greatest* humiliation of your life,' Michael cried. He flung off his silver war helmet, his noble face fierce, his blond hair now loosed to his shoulders. 'Golgotha . . . brother!'

'Golgotha!' Lucifer's eyes grew dark with sheer hatred. 'The Nazarene.' He stood, ferocious in his war chariot, his waist-length ebony hair flying in the zephyrs rising from the Crystal Sea.

'I shall defeat the Nazarene and his pathetic armies at Armageddon. But first, Michael . . .' He laughed dementedly as he removed his own helmet. 'But first I seize our Father's throne!' The rivets flew from the princes' chariot wheels, the stallions straining to breaking point.

'Let us fight – brother against brother,' Lucifer snarled. 'As in aeons past.'

Lucifer tore off his breastplate and mantle, revealing his sinewy muscles. Six black Seraph wings rose from his spine.

'You hide behind your armour, brother,' he taunted.

Michael tore off his breastplate, bronzed and muscular, his immense white wings arced from his spine.

Lucifer looked at Michael sideways, crouched down, then jumped across into Michael's chariot, brandishing his broadsword.

150

'I was always seconds ahead of you, brother,' he hissed.

In a split second, he lunged savagely at Michael with his sword and wrestled him to the floor of his careering chariot. The two brothers fought hand to hand, Lucifer raining violent blows onto Michael's chest with his broadsword.

Michael grasped Lucifer's long, matted raven hair in his hands, twisting it around his fingers savagely till Lucifer screamed in agony. He grabbed Lucifer's head with both arms with his immense strength, blocking the air from entering his brother's windpipe.

Lucifer gasped violently for breath as the pressure intensified, struggling frenziedly to escape from Michael's iron grip. His head began to swim. Sweat poured from his forehead as he drifted in and out of consciousness.

With a final desperate surge of strength, he wrenched his dagger from his boot and plunged it savagely in the direction of Michael's bare chest.

Michael collapsed to his knees in sheer agony.

In a split second, Lucifer clasped Michael's head in a vice-like grip and threw him violently to the floor of the racing chariot, holding his broadsword to his throat.

Moloch and Dagon appeared to his right and his left.

'Shackle my brother,' Lucifer gasped. 'We have our collateral.'

West Wing
Palace of Archangels

The Warlocks of the West circled the skies above the Palace of Archangels astride their six-winged leviathans, while the Satanic Princes patrolled the perimeter in their griffon-drawn war chariots. Thousands of the Black Horde, Lucifer's elite milita, surrounded the Palace of Archangels, their yellow eyes blazing with demonic red fire.

Lucifer rode triumphantly through the Western Gates,

past the vast desolate orangery that had once been vibrant with the heliotropes and lupins that he had so loved, past the drained Pools of the Seven Wisdoms, drawing to a halt directly in front of the two towering golden doors of the West Wing of the Palace of Archangels. His chambers before his banishment aeons previously.

The doors opened.

Charsoc stood in the flowing, bright vermillion- and fuchsia-striped robes of Chief Magus. His jet-black hair fell past his waist. His rubied shoes were long and narrow, and curved upwards at the toe. Charsoc held his crooked magus rod high and bowed deeply to Lucifer.

'We have commandeered the palace, Your Majesty. Michael's, Gabriel's, and your own quarters in the West Wing are now under the control of your royal guard and have been made headquarters of the Fallen.'

Moloch and Dagon shoved the limping Michael through the doors of the West Wing.

'Shackle my brother, then bring him to me,' Lucifer commanded.

Lucifer dismounted from his chariot. Slowly he walked through the two golden doors of his chambers, under the vaulted ceilings of his pre-banishment inner sanctum, his eyes riveted on frescoes exquisitely painted in hues of azure and indigo, heliotrope, damson, and amethyst that merged into magenta and vermilion. He hesitated, strangely moved, drinking in the spectacular panoramas and majestic trompe l'oeils that covered the ornate carved ceilings of his long-gone world.

He wrapped his ermine-trimmed cloak tightly around him, then strode down the corridors of the West Wing. On his approach Huldah, Shaman King, unshackled the soaring doors to Lucifer's ancient chambers.

Lucifer walked inside and went straight to the crystal doors on the far side of the chamber. He flung them open, then walked out onto the balcony, staring out towards the towering golden, ruby-encrusted door, ablaze with light, that was embedded into the jacinth walls of the tower of Yehovah's palace. An immense flaming rainbow was suspended directly over the mountain. Hues from the entire spectrum ebbed and flowed in intensity, from violets and indigos through pinks and vermilions. They marked Yehovah's eternal remembrance of the race of men.

'The race of men.' Lucifer slammed the doors shut, then walked to the very centre of the chamber where a huge golden aeolian harp stood. He reached out his hand, his fingers gently strumming its strings.

Then he strode across the gleaming sapphire floors, flung his cloak and helmet onto one of seven enormous golden thrones, and walked between the jewelled columns towards the most ornate throne, dark beneath hundreds of unlit frankincense tapers. He sat.

'Bring my brother to me,' he commanded.

Dagon and Moloch dragged the struggling Michael in front of Lucifer, who was now reclining on his throne and fingering a golden goblet.

Michael's fierce, intelligent green eyes were glazed with pain. His normally gleaming flaxen braids were loosed, his hair falling to his shoulders and matted with blood, his cheeks bruised.

Michael stared at his brother with disdain. 'You are a *monster.*'

Lucifer toyed with a sweetmeat in his fingers. 'I may well be a monster, Michael,' he said carelessly, 'but may I remind you, *you* are a monster's prisoner.'

He grinned at Michael. 'My prize. Chief Prince Michael!'

Charsoc entered.

'Charsoc the Dark, go immediately to your former compatriot Jether the Just. Tell him I hold captive their commander, Chief Prince Michael of the Royal House of Yehovah. He is my prisoner. Relay to the Angelic Council my demands. Then bring Jether and my brother Gabriel to me, unarmed. They will escort me personally to the Labyrinths – to the very entrance of the stairway to the Stones of Fire.'

He smiled carelessly. 'Chief Prince Michael's armies will stand down immediately or I will sever their commander's head and display it on their Pearl Gates for all to see.'

Charsoc hesitated. 'Milord, they will require proof you have the Chief Prince.'

Lucifer picked up his dagger.

'I am, according to my younger brother, a *monster*.' He laughed insanely. Then, with one swift move of the dagger, he sliced Michael's left thumb cleanly off his hand.

Michael stood, blinking tears of agony as the blood drained from his face. Silent.

'You have a monster's proof,' Lucifer said. 'Well, what are you waiting for?' he screamed.

Later

Jether entered Lucifer's chambers, followed by Gabriel.

Lucifer sat languidly on his throne, goblet in hand, now attired in his pre-banishment ceremonial jacket of embroidered white silks and his gauntlets of soft white leather. The imposing diamond crown of Prince Regent rested on his braided ebony locks. His fingers were adorned with rings of rubies and sapphires set in gold.

'Welcome, my old mentor, Jether the Just.' Lucifer glanced down at the silver and gold medals of Prince Regent pinned to his breast. 'How thoughtful of you to have kept my wardrobe intact.' He smiled lazily at Jether. 'I'm playing House.'

Gabriel stared at Michael, then at Lucifer, trembling with rage and shock.

'And welcome my youngest brother . . . Gabriel.'

Jether placed his hand firmly on Gabriel's shoulder. 'We are not *all* barbarians.' He looked at Lucifer grimly.

'May I?' He gestured to Michael, who stood shackled in the corner, silent, mastering the agonizing pain.

Lucifer nodded, toying with his goblet. 'If you simply *must*.'

Jether walked over to Michael and placed both hands over his. Instantly, Michael's thumb grew back and the pain was gone.

Jether turned to Lucifer, his eyes piercing through him like steel. 'What is it you want from Yehovah, Lucifer, son of iniquity?' His voice was dangerously soft. 'Apart from his throne.'

Lucifer sipped delicately from his goblet.

'You, Jether the Just, as head of Yehovah's ancient monarchs, are to call Michael's armies and the revelators to stand down immediately. I demand clear passage to the Labyrinths. You and Gabriel will escort me personally. My brother Michael will be my collateral. Once I enter the river of the Stones of Fire, he is yours.'

CHAPTER SEVENTEEN

Labyrinths

First Heaven

The forty blazing crimson moons hung high in the horizons of the First Heaven. Gabriel and Jether escorted Lucifer and his small entourage through the skies towards the Holy Mountain. Their wings carried them with the speed of comets across the celestial firmament.

The Holy Mountain was so vast that its seven spires were visible long before they reached the end of their journey. Slowly the seven needle-like points grew into immense edifices – towers beside which Earth's greatest Gothic cathedral would be just a glimpe in miniature.

Seraph wings beat against the onrushing air and slowed to a standstill. The angels, Unfallen and Fallen, alighted outside the looming golden seventh spire.

Inside the adamantine rock of the mountain, a single staircase descended in seven headlong flights, passing through seven hidden chambers. By uncountable steps, it spiralled downwards into the inner sanctum of the Labyrinths and to the river of the Stones of Fire.

Jether raised his hand. The crypt-like door, the sacred entrance to the Labyrinths, swung open. Behind it was darkness.

Jether entered, followed by Lucifer and Charsoc. Behind them stalked Gabriel. The warlock kings holding the shackled Michael brought up the rear.

At the top of the next flight of stairs, Jether halted. The stairs were not carved from the opaque rock of the mountain, but built into it with transparent diamond and ruby.

Down the first flight of the jewelled stairway they went, until they reached a level floor – a landing lit by a flaming torch high against the wall. Its eternal flame was fuelled by the burning coal of the first of the seven spirits of Wisdom.

Lucifer grimaced, then followed Jether into the cavern. Charsoc shuddered on the threshold before following at a distance.

Beyond this first chamber, the downward climb resumed. After what seemed a long time, a new glimmer from beneath them grew into the glare of another torch, the burning coal from the second spirit of wisdom.

The stairhead now overhung what looked a virtually sheer drop.

Lagging behind Jether's surefooted lead, the Fallen continued their descent, painstakingly picking out step after diamond step. They passed the third torchlit landing and crossed the third chamber. Then more stairs, more darkness, as the ill-assorted party continued downward in complete silence.

When the steps brought them to the fourth gate, which was closed, Jether halted beside the torch. 'You well know the way, Lucifer,' he said.

Michael fell to his knees in the shadows, his hands and ankles chained, his mouth bound. Dagon held a dagger to his throat.

Without a backward glance, Lucifer pushed at the door. Light spilled out of the chamber. He walked away across the threshold and out of sight. With clammy fingers, Charsoc clutched his robes and followed. Cruelly, Dagon forced Michael to his feet and impelled him into the chamber, the other warlocks following up the rear.

The Crystalline Hall

After the steps of the Fallen had faded to silence, Jether led Gabriel into the fourth chamber, a vast hall irradiated with light from the amethyst crystalline floor, blazing with an inner luminescence.

'I schooled Lucifer here, in worlds long departed, just as I did you, Gabriel, and Michael.'

'Why do we pause?' asked Gabriel.

'The approach to the Stones of Fire is Lucifer's path, and its consequences are his to bear. These things are not ours to share.'

'The holiness and the fear of Yehovah will be exponentially intensified because of Lucifer's inherent darkness,' Gabriel said.

'You speak truly, Gabriel,' Jether nodded. 'Lucifer's first downfall was because of pride. His downfall this fortieth crimson moon will be no different. He will grow weaker and weaker the nearer he draws to the throne room.'

Jether nodded to Gabriel, then beckoned him to a pillar of crystal that rose upward like a tree to meet the roof in the centre of the cavern.

They gazed into the multitudes of holograms visible within the crystal. Jether raised his hand and instantly a hologram of Lucifer appeared, descending the glistening crystal glass spiral stairway somewhere far beneath them towards the mountain core.

The image of Lucifer reached the foot of the spiral and came to a halt, staring entranced at a line of imposing forms.

There, at the gate to the fifth chamber, the Watchers gazed impassively back at him. Tall and silent guardians, they held flaming broadswords before their faces. No word had ever issued from their mouths, for their mouths had been sealed with the very coal that they were guarding.

Even as Jether and Gabriel watched through the crystal hologram in the chamber far above, the silent Watchers bowed in recognition of Lucifer's ancient rank.

A voice from somewhere deep within the chamber echoed, 'Fallen prince, thou who wast once full of holiness and valour. Let the son of iniquity pass.'

As one, the Watchers raised their flaming swords. Then, as Lucifer and his party passed beyond into the fifth chamber, their line of figures returned to their worship of Yehovah.

The Glass Stairway of Infinity

Lucifer continued to walk steadily downward through the darkness, the sixth flight of stairs. Charsoc followed, holding his own voluminous train in both his jewelled hands, trembling behind his master.

Lucifer passed the Watchers at the fifth chamber, descending the glistening crystal glass spiral stairway.

As they entered the sixth cavern, Lucifer's limbs started to tremble uncontrollably. Marshalling all his iron discipline, still he descended, to the sixth eternal flame, past the very fear of Yehovah. One intention drove him – access to the Stones of Fire, the final stairway of living molten rubies.

He hesitated. Ahead of him stood the Watchers of the seventh flame, before sapphire doors that soared three hundred feet high. The dread warriors' faces were as flint. As one, they lifted their weapons, barring his way through to the doors to the seventh chamber. It was the entrance to the Stones of Fire.

'Let him pass,' the thunderous tones echoed. The huge sapphire doors slowly opened. There was complete silence.

Lucifer stared, magnetized by the river of blazing, glimmering jewelled Stones of Fire flowing a full thousand feet below the rubied stairway. Sapphires, diamonds, rubies, emeralds, each at least six feet in diameter, glimmered there with the consuming fires of Yehovah.

As far as his eyes could see ahead, the blazing river of jewels ran.

Lucifer, more than anyone, knew where the river led: straight into the heart of the hallowed mystery of the Holy Trinity. The most sacred place in the universe – the abode of Christos and the Holy Spirit. The place that only three others had been permitted to enter: himself, Michael, and Gabriel.

The place that had haunted his dreamings day and night for aeons since his defection. The thing he had yearned for, ever since his banishment – to walk once more in the sacred abode of Yehovah, in the river of the sacred Stones of Fire. In Yehovah's heart.

Slowly, so slowly, Lucifer placed one foot on the first rubied step of the spiral stairway.

Instantly it erupted into a living, burning mass of gleaming rubied fires.

His entire body trembling uncontrollably in a strange mix of ecstasy and terror, Lucifer walked down the first flight of the rubied staircase until his way became barred by a huge iron grid.

Facing him was a strange and twisted crown.

He could hardly withdraw his eyes from its strange yet terrible beauty. As he studied the crown more intently, he realized that it was made of huge, ugly, jagged thorns.

Transfixed, he reached out his hand. As he touched it, it ripped the flesh of his palm.

He screamed in agony.

Trembling, he moved deeper into the intense darkness of the seventh cavern. As he did so, the Watchers drew back and disappeared.

Slowly, his eyes became accustomed to the dark. He could discern the dim outline of a large hill far in the distance.

He was about to descend further down the rubied spiral stairway when suddenly his attention was drawn upward. He stared into the darkness. The hill had disappeared, replaced by the outline of an enormous wooden cross that towered ahead of him. All at once, a great terror gripped him.

'Golgotha,' Lucifer hissed, now utterly powerless to move.

He looked down at his white robe and ermine cloak in horror. It was stained with blood.

He stared at the cross in terror, the pungent acrid odour of blood invading his nostrils.

Reminding him of that day.

The day when he, King of Hell, had been vanquished.

The day of the Nazarene.

He could vaguely make out a form hanging from a cross. Directly above his head, a pair of feet were impaled on an enormous crude iron nail.

Fresh blood dripped from the feet onto his raven hair.

Lucifer flung his cloak to the floor, desperately tearing his bloodstained mantle from his neck.

Paralyzed with terror, he slowly raised his head to the form hanging on the wooden cross.

A chilling scream rang out from the impaled figure: *'Eli, Eli, lama sabachthani!'*

It resounded throughout the Holy Mountain as if the echo would never stop. *'Eli, Eli, lama sabachthani!'*

Lucifer clapped his hands over his ears in a desperate attempt to block out the awful, chilling scream of desolation.

He flung himself onto the blazing rubied stairway as vision after vision of Christos' sufferings passed before him.

He watched, immobile, as the crown of thorns was pushed savagely into Christos' head until the blood saturated his already matted hair.

He watched as Christos was scourged.

Once, twice . . . then again and again.

'Stop!' Lucifer cried in a long wail as he flung himself to the cavern floor.

The sound of the flogging stopped.

Slowly, Lucifer lifted his head off the ground.

A lamb stood before him. It had seven horns and seven eyes.

The lamb took the scroll from the right hand of he who sat on the throne.

The voices of the Angelic Host thundered, 'Worthy is the lamb, who was sacrificed, to receive all the power and glory.'

Lucifer clasped his hands to his ears.

'To him who is seated on the throne, and to the lamb, be ascribed the blessing, and the honour, and the majesty, and might, and dominion forever, through eternities of eternities!'

He rose to his full height, still magnetized by the blazing path of molten, golden fire.

Then he stared, rooted to the ground in terror.

Christos. Lucifer watched as the images flashed in front of him.

Images of him clasping Christos' hand; of a heavy, sweet-smelling golden liniment that ran down from Christos' palms, anointing Lucifer's forehead.

Images of that day before his insurrection.

Images of himself kissing Christos lovingly, first on the right cheek and then on the left. Christos stared back at Lucifer, a strange and terrible sorrow in his gaze.

The words . . . the torment.

'Son of the Morning, many moons hence when many worlds have long risen and fallen, there will be another garden' – Christos' voice was barely audible – 'another kiss.

'Another garden . . . another kiss.'

Lucifer clasped his hands over his ears, trying desperately to drown out the sound of Christos' voice that seemed to be coming toward him from every direction.

'Another garden . . . another kiss.'

'Why did you betray us?' Now it was Gabriel's voice mingled with Christos'.

'Why did you betray us?' The voices merged with what seemed to be hundreds of other voices, out in the darkness.

'Oh how thou art fallen.'

'Thou art fallen. Thou art fallen. Why did you betray us? Another garden . . . another kiss. Betray us. Betray us . . . *Why did you betray us?*'

Lucifer flung himself to the ground, his hands over his ears.

'Stop . . . stop!' he wailed dementedly. 'I beg you, stop tormenting me!'

Finally – after what seemed an eternity – silence fell.

Christos and the cross had vanished. There was only the intense darkness that seemed to be closing in on him.

And the intense, unrelenting thudding of Lucifer's heart.

Gabriel walked towards him, out of the darkness, his hand on the Sword of Justice. He stared at his bloodied, half-naked brother in horror.

'Lucifer, brother, desist,' he said softly. 'You of *all* well know where the river of the Stones of Fire leads. You are tormented. You are losing your mind, brother. Desist.'

Lucifer pushed his fingers through his raven hair, matted with blood, then stared up at his brother, his face contorted with malice.

'Naive, malleable Gabriel,' Lucifer spat. 'Before this hour is over, I shall be your king. I shall sit on his throne.'

'Your insanity is now evident to all. Look well at your bloodied hands, Lucifer. This is only the beginning.'

'Gabriel.' Yehovah's voice resounded. 'Let him pass.'

Lucifer smiled in triumph.

Gabriel grudgingly removed his hand from his sword. 'My deluded brother,' he said, 'you walk the river of the Stones of Fire at your peril.'

'You have grown *weak*, Gabriel,' Lucifer hissed. 'You could have shared his throne with me.'

'No, Lucifer!' cried Charsoc, staggering towards Lucifer from the entrance to the seventh gate. 'Your brother speaks the truth, Your Majesty. The darkness inside you is too strong. You will be destroyed on the path of consuming fire. Only the holy, only the pure can walk the Stones of Fire,' Charsoc screamed in agony, prostrate at the entrance.

'Our powers grow weaker!' Charsoc cried. 'His light is become our tormentor.'

Lucifer! Yehovah's voice was coming from inside his head. *How art thou fallen from heaven, O Lucifer, Son of the Morning! How art thou cut down to the ground, which didst weaken the nations!*

Lucifer clasped his head in his hands.

'Don't you hear it?' he cried. 'Gabriel, don't you hear it?'

Jether came up quietly behind Gabriel. 'Yehovah speaks to Lucifer,' he said. 'He alone can hear.'

The noble tones reverberated in Lucifer's head.

For thou hast said in thine heart, I will ascend into heaven, I will exalt my throne above the stars of God: I will sit also upon the Mount of the Congregation, in the sides of the north: I will ascend above the heights of the clouds; I will be like the Most High.

Lucifer held his head, disorientated.

'Let my brother Michael go, Lucifer,' Gabriel cried. 'You have achieved your objective.'

'Unchain my brother Michael!' Lucifer cried distractedly. He stared, still magnetized, at the path of molten gold ahead of him, the river of the Stones of Fire.

Charsoc raised his head, burning in agony.

'Lucifer!' he whimpered. 'Our powers fade.'

Lucifer stepped into the midst of the burning sapphire stones. Euphoric, his soul in ecstasy, he bathed in remembrance.

Jether watched as Lucifer walked in complete obsession with his flaming and bloodied garments clinging to his burning limbs.

The blazing fires continued to rise, licking at his thighs. Still he walked the river of living molten Stones of Fire, his face contorted in agony.

'Yehovah!' he cried.

Charsoc lay screaming, burning at the gate.

'Lucifer, stop! Turn back!'

'No!' hissed Lucifer, the flames encircling him. 'I enter through Yehovah's heart!'

With immense difficulty and iron discipline, he rose to his full height and placed his feet solidly on the blazing path, screaming in torment as he trod the sapphires and diamonds.

'It is *bewitchment*!' Charsoc screamed. 'Yehovah's enchantments.'

'It is his presence,' Jether whispered. 'He is a consuming fire.'

'Your obsession will destroy us all!' Charsoc screamed in agony.

Jether watched, silent.

Lucifer, Son of the Morning, you who once sang with a thousand flutes and tabrets in my presence. Yehovah's noble tones resounded in Lucifer's head. Tears of rage and yearning coursed down Lucifer's face as still he walked.

'Yes, I am obsessed with you, my father. *Obsessed*!' he screamed.

Tearing at his crimson-stained mantle as one deranged, yet still walking, he turned a corner.

Seven fiery seraphim stood.

'Let him pass,' came the divine voice.

Lucifer's monstrous black seraph wings were now burning in the flames. His agonized screaming echoed through the caverns.

Thou wert the anointed cherub that covereth; and I had set thee so: thou wast upon the holy mountain of God; thou hast walked up and down in the midst of the Stones of Fire. Thou wast perfect in thy ways from the day that thou wast created, till iniquity was found in thee.

Lucifer fell to his knees, into the blazing jewelled River of Fire, scrabbling his agonized way to the last gate, bruised and bloodied, his long ebony hair and wings on fire.

I cast thee, O covering cherub, out from the midst of the Stones of Fire.

'No!' Lucifer wailed in utter torment. 'No, Father! Do not cast me out, away from you!'

He fell facedown, his hands clutched over his ears, screaming dementedly. Burning in the midst of the blazing river of sapphires, he lay a full league from Yehovah's heart.

In his hand, he still clutched an immense ruby.

'*Yehovah*!' he screamed.

Jason rolled from side to side in agony on the soaking mattress, his wounds burning. There was only the sound of crows and the acrid smell of old urine and faeces.

Then a clattering under the door.

He crawled over to the door. In a filthy metal bowl lay one-and-a-half spoons of uncooked rice.

Jason held the bowl up to his parched lips and scooped the rice ravenously into his mouth with his fingers.

He looked down at his ring finger and frowned. His wedding ring was intact.

'Julia,' he rasped. 'Always . . . *Julia*.'

Rubied Throne Room

Lucifer's agonized screaming filled the throne room and resounded to the First Heaven's horizons. '*Yehova-a-a-ah!*'

Finally, Christos spoke softly. 'Go to your brother, Gabriel.'

Gabriel walked the river of fire to where his elder brother lay whimpering, burning on the blazing sapphires.

He stared down in horror at Lucifer's ebony hair and wings, all aflame. He closed his eyes and bowed his head. Then he bent over Lucifer and, with all his strength, lifted his tormented brother in his arms.

Slowly, step by step, he carried Lucifer through the River of Fire and out, past Yehovah's heart.

Into the throne room.

Gabriel laid him on the golden floor directly in front of the blazing iridescent throne. Lucifer writhed from side to side in agony, his entire body ablaze from the inside, his wings and hair still burning outwardly. His agonized screams resounded through the rubied throne room, through the Labyrinths, through the seven spires and out across the horizons of the First Heaven.

The Fallen stood paralyzed in their tracks, trembling at their king's tormented screaming.

'Now!' shouted Michael to his generals. 'Tell them that we have their king, shackled and in chains.'

Lucifer lay immobilized only six feet away from the rubied throne of Yehovah, shaking uncontrollably, his face and limbs disfigured, his long ebony locks burnt beyond recognition.

'Lucifer, Son of the Morning, you have been found wanting. The sentence of the royal courts of Yehovah is pronounced upon you.'

Jether moved forward. He nodded to Michael.

Michael grasped Lucifer fiercely in an iron grip and hauled him up onto his knees. Lucifer stared at him in a mixture of absolute terror, unbridled rage, and venom.

Jether removed a burning sword from one of the eternal flames and held it directly over Lucifer's head. 'You and your Fallen – Satanic princes, demonic powers, warlocks, necromancers – are hereby banished for eternity from the First and Second Heavens. Your ice palaces on Mars and throughout the Second Heaven are, from this moment on, the property of the Royal House of Yehovah.

Jether turned. 'Chief Prince Michael.'

Michael bowed.

'Your armies are ordered to take possession of every castle, every palace, every citadel of the Fallen in the Second Heaven. You, Lucifer, will be cast down to Earth by your own brother, Michael, never to enter these gates again – banished for all eternity until you are cast into your eternal doom in the Lake of Fire.'

Jether stood back, and Christos appeared out of the midst of Yehovah's presence.

He stood, King of Kings, fierce, noble, beautiful even in his ferocity.

He walked towards where Lucifer knelt, then kissed him tenderly, first on his left cheek, then on his right.

His voice was very soft.

'Another garden. . . . Another kiss.'

He turned to Michael.

'Remove him from our presence.'

CHAPTER EIGHTEEN

Black Site

'My, my. If it isn't the long lost Jason De Vere. My *dear* boy! What *have* they done to you?'

Jason woke up disorientated. He stared at the shadowed form standing in the gloom. It was Xavier Chessler.

'I should really call a doctor.' Chessler frowned. 'Those wounds look as though they may be infected.'

'Chessler, you bastard!' Jason growled.

'Now, now, no need for vulgarity, dear boy. You'll have the starring role in the greatest TV event in the history of mankind: your execution, live in front of six billion viewers.'

'You evil son of a *bitch*.'

'I did warn you at our little tête-à-tête at the Ritz in London not to cross us, my dear. But oh no – you evaded us in Babylon, then resurfaced just in time to assassinate your own brother. Which, of course, was *precisely* what we'd planned.'

He kicked the small metal bowl with his extravagantly expensive Testoni shoes.

'You, my dear godson, have always been . . . how should I phrase it? . . . a tad predictable. We *banked* on your losing that tenuous De Vere temper, my dear. You played your part to perfection.'

He glanced at his watch. 'You'll have a last supper, of course. And a priest will deliver the last rites.'

'I don't *want* a goddamn priest.'

'Your time on this planet is running out. I'd make good use of them, if I were you. They'll come for you the morning of your execution, at 6 a.m., if I'm correct. You're in good company, by the way – the Jewish High Priest is to be executed before you. You will be obliged to watch, of course.'

Chessler walked to the door, then turned.

'It didn't have to be this way, Jason. If you had played with us nicely, you would have lived to tell the tale.'

He smiled, his eyes hard as nails. 'But no. Jason De Vere, stubborn to the last, like your poor deceased father before you, god bless his pathetic soul. *Such* a waste.'

The cell door locked behind him.

Military Plane

'Where are we headed?' Alex asked the soldier seated beside him, who still wore a balaclava.

'You'll see soon enough.'

Alex looked over at Lily. She was curled up in a foetal position at the back of the military transport plane as it flew through some bone-rattling turbulence.

At least thirty soldiers sat in the open cargo bay.

'We're joining with the Resistance,' the soldier said.

'The Resistance? In the US?'

The soldier shook his head. 'We go to the headquarters of the underground. We're headed for the Middle East.'

Alex walked to the cockpit, then turned to the soldier in the balaclava, frowning. 'You're not expecting us to go back to Israel? Are you *insane*?'

'There are no parachutes, Alex Lane-Fox,' the soldier said drily. 'So I suggest you sit back down and enjoy the flight.'

Old City
Jerusalem

Rebekah sat at a small aluminium table on a back terrace in the Old City, across from a craggy-faced man with an unruly mop of silver hair.

He poured strong coffee from a cafetière into Rebekah's cup.

'You have worn well, old friend,' the old man said in a thick Hebrew accent.

Rebekah sipped the coffee and studied him intently. 'As have you, old friend.' She shook her head. 'Still the old war dog.'

The old man laughed, reached in his pocket, and placed a small package on the table.

'This is everything you require. The most sophisticated technology in the world of espionage.'

'Of course.' Rebekah studied the weathered face before her. 'Do you miss it, Avi?' she asked softly. 'Active service, I mean. Since Mossad was deactivated?'

'Ah!' Avi Cohen drank a third of his coffee down in a gulp. 'You of *all* should know, the Resistance Mossad is a thousand times more powerful and dangerous in hiding.'

He finished his coffee. 'I am *always* active.'

'I didn't think anything less,' she replied.

Avi leaned back in his chair. 'We had some fun, though,

didn't we? Munich, the Cherbourg Project, Black September. Thank you for saving my life,' he murmured. 'And the life of my son. I am forever in your debt.'

He pushed the package over to Rebekah.

'This is what you need. *Be-tachbūlōt ta'aseh lekhā milchā māh*. Proverbs 24: 6. For by wise counsel thou shalt make thy war.'

'Our old motto,' she said. 'I always preferred it to the new.'

He nodded at the parcel. 'You have in your hands the most sophisticated remote neural-monitoring technology in existence. Only we have access to it. Inside this package is a transmitter the size of a grain of rice. You surgically implant the nano-scaled camera into the cornea of your subject. When it is activated, you will see exactly what they see. The second component activates a microphone attached to the camera. It can be activated up to 10,000 kilometres away from the subject. You will hear all conversations, see exactly what the subject is viewing.

'General Mahmoud is receiving the activation codes in Jordan as we sit here. I took the liberty of sending him an extra transmitter. It is undetectable by even the most sophisticated tracking devices.'

His eagle eyes bored into her soul.

'What are you involved in, Rebekah? I sense great danger.'

She held his gaze and did not speak.

Avi studied her intently. 'It is a long time since you were active in Kidon, Rebekah,' he said, referring to the secretive Mossad special ops unit. 'You are eighty-three years old.'

'But a strong eighty-three. My reflexes are fast.'

'Ah, the indefatigable Agent Rebekah Weiss.' Avi unclipped the holstered pistol at his waist. 'This always brought me luck,' he said, handing it to her.

'Your Magnum Desert Eagle. Oh, Avi, you've carried it everywhere for decades. I can't accept it.'

'I insist.' His voice had a steel edge. 'Use it, Rebekah. It's old, but indestructible. Like me,' he smiled. 'You'll need it.'

Rebekah took the revolver, studying it closely.

'I haven't used one of these in over two decades.'

Avi nodded. 'Your reflexes are still fast, Rebekah. It is ingrained in your psyche.'

'I am ready to meet my maker, Avi. I sense my time draws to a close. But I will take a few down with me.'

'Then, it is *shalom*, Agent Rebekah Weiss, old friend.'

Rebekah stood up from the table.

'Yes,' she said softly. 'It is *shalom*, Director Avi Cohen, old friend.'

She started to walk back inside, then hesitated and looked back.

'Avi, look after my David for me. And my grandson. Promise.'

The old man nodded.

Rebekah walked away without a look back.

'I promise,' Avi murmured.

CHAPTER NINETEEN

Aqaba, Southern Jordan

The plane began its descent. Dylan Weaver stared down in horror.

'Look at the landing strip – it can't even be four thousand feet long! And it's not even tarmac. Oh god, the pilots will never make it.'

He grabbed the soldier next to him, deathly pale. 'We're going to *die*!'

Alex glared at him. 'Shut up, Weaver.'

The Resistance soldier shook Weaver off. 'Yes. Get a . . . What is it you say in English? Get a grip, computer man – but not on *me*, if you don't mind.' He spoke with a strong Hebrew inflection. 'Relax. It's *designed* for this. We land on runways like this all the time. Mogadishu, Helmand . . .'

'I'm going to throw up.'

The soldier threw the trembling Weaver a sick bag.

'Weaver, calm *down*,' Alex said. 'You're in a C-Seventeen Globemaster Four. This baby can land on strips as short as 3,500 feet. In all weathers, on unpaved runways.'

Sweat dripped from Weaver's forehead as he held the sick bag over his nose and mouth and started breathing heavily into it.

There was a thud as the plane touched down and rapidly decelerated.

Alex frowned. 'There's no airport.' He looked out at the vast expanse of desert.

'Stealth,' the soldier replied. 'Time to go.'

The small party walked down the jet's rear cargo ramp, shielding their eyes from the sand sweeping through on a strong southerly breeze from Egypt.

'We have a welcoming party,' David Weiss said.

Five black Range Rovers arrived as if out of nowhere, followed by three armoured troop carriers.

Four Jordanian generals dressed in desert camouflage alighted from the vehicles and approached the plane.

Alex watched in amazement as the oldest and most authoritative-looking general saluted the Resistance soldier. The soldier pulled the balaclava off his head and shook his long black hair free. He was a handsome Israeli, around twenty-three.

'Generals Mahmoud, Mustafa, Khalistan, and Soliman at your service,' growled General Mahmoud. 'Any friend of the Ghost is a friend of ours. Welcome to the kingdom of Jordan. I greet you on behalf of His Majesty, King Jibril. It is our privilege to escort you to your destination in Petra.'

Alex exchanged a glance with General Mahmoud.

'*King* Jibril?'

'His Majesty was Crown Prince. Now he is king. He is expecting you, Alex Lane-Fox, and you, Madam Lily.'

'They've taken my Dad, General. You've *got* to rescue my dad,' Lily pleaded, her eyes wide with dread.

The general leaned over and kissed Lily softly on both cheeks. '*Salaam*, little one. We are in strategy meetings even now as we speak. In case of arrest, everyone is inoculated against the Mark. We have forty thousand crack troops; an underground base twenty miles wide and half a mile deep;

176

tanks; Special Forces; even nuclear-armed cruise missiles. You name it, we have it. Come.'

He gestured to the convoy of Range Rovers.

'We have a two-hour drive ahead of us. Enjoy the scenery.' He gestured at the empty sand around them. 'We should arrive at Petra in two hours.'

Monastery
Petra, Jordan

The Range Rovers sped across the sands of the sprawling Western Desert, leaving long dust plumes in their wake.

Lily stared out towards the mountains, transfixed by the spectacular views over the Great Rift Valley.

'*Match me such a marvel save in Eastern clime,*' Alex murmured. '*A rose-red city half as old as time.* Nick's favorite quote.'

'I miss Uncle Nick so much,' Lily said softly. 'Petra was his favorite place in the world.'

Alex fell silent. A tsunami of memories; of that insane unspeakable day in Damman, Saudi Arabia. Images of Nick flooded his brain. The day Alex had tried to blot from his memory – until this moment.

The Saudi Incident.

He put his head in his hands, remembering.

He and Nick had flown to Damman in Saudi Arabia to rescue Princess Jotapa of Jordan – the love of Nick's life – and her adored younger brother, Crown Prince Jibril, from their imprisonment by the brutal Mansoor.

Jotapa's father, King of Jordan, had died suddenly from a heart attack. Jibril as Crown Prince was next in line to the throne of Jordan, but his cunning and cruel half-brother, Faisal, had taken the Jordanian throne by force. The evil Faisal had immediately given Jotapa's hand in marriage to the depraved Mansoor, who had held Jotapa and Jibril literal prisoners in Damman for months. By the time Nick and Alex had arrived, Faisal and his brutal private army were dead, shot by Jordanian troops loyal to the old king. Mansoor had met the same fate.

Nick and Jotapa had flown into each other's arms, inseparable.

Jibril had been shell-shocked from his savage treatment at the hands of his jailer, Mansoor. No one knew the real story of what he had suffered at the hands of his jealous, psychotic incarcerator.

It was only a few hours after their arrival in Damman that things started to go crazy, surreal. Nick had started acting strangely. Alex had lost his temper – he remembered it now as though it was yesterday.

Don't think I don't know what you are talking about, because I do. Polly had gone on endlessly at the airport. Polly, Nick, Jotapa. They were all talking about the 'Rapture', some happy-clappy urban myth that Jesus Christ was just going to walk through the door and transport them to another dimension. They were all completely deluded. Meanwhile, what were they going to do, stay in Damman until He came to get them?

He pressed the speed dial to Polly's mobile phone, it connected but it was emitting some strange jamming sound. The call to the landline at the London flat rang and rang. It was so frustrating.

At least Jibril remained sane preparing to catch the flight to Petra.

Alex had been trying to reason with Nick when it had started – the strange bizarre turn of events; the Saudi Incident that – try as he might – Alex could not erase from his memory. It wasn't so much an incident as a person.

First the room had filled up with what could only be described as the fragrance of jasmine.

Then the fragrance had been followed in quick succession by an intense blinding light.

And then it had happened. Or rather, *he* had happened.

The stranger had appeared in the doorway, barely distinguishable through the translucent light.

Alex had watched as Nick, completely magnetized by the stranger, had stepped directly into the light.

Then the stranger had started to speak. *Nicholas.*

It is time? Nick had whispered.

It is time. The stranger had bent down and gently wiped the tears from Jotapa's face.

Arise, Jotapa, princess of the House of Aretas.

Alex remembered Jotapa rising to her feet and clinging to the stranger as though her life depended on it. Then the stranger had spoken again – this time to Jibril, who stood trembling, dumbstruck.

Jibril, Crown Prince of Jordan, you shall yet be as King Aretas, protector of your people. The stranger smiled. *And of mine.*

Alex had backed away until he stood in the far corner of the room, unsuccessfully trying to protect his eyes from the blinding light, and getting as far as he could from the stranger.

And that's when everything had spiralled completely out of control. What had happened next was . . .

'Alex? Alex!' Lily's voice became more insistent. 'Where *are* you?'

Alex stared up at her in a daze as the Range Rovers lurched to a halt outside the towering western gate of the Monastery of Petra.

'Just Nick,' Alex muttered. 'This place reminds me of Nick.'

They drove past the deserted former five-star Mövenpick Resort, located directly at the entrance to the historic city.

'And Polly. We came here five years ago,' Alex muttered. 'So this is where we go on foot or horseback, I presume.'

'You presume incorrectly, Master Alex,' General Mahmoud said softly.

The Range Rover came to a halt, and the driver killed the engine.

As if out of nowhere, at least twelve members of the Jordanian Royal Guard surrounded the van. General Mahmoud passed a biometric card through the window.

'The Shaya al Shayada, the Jordanian Royal Guard, the elite unit for protection and defence of our king. They have been expecting you.'

He nodded to a soldier at the entrance to the Siq, the narrow gorge that gave access to the ancient city of Petra. Instantly, the Range Rover dropped ten feet, twenty, a hundred feet downward, then another fifty feet until it stopped directly in line with a gaping entry-point in the rock.

More papers. More biometric identification. Soldiers holding machine-guns lined the entrance. The Range Rover was waved through.

The visitors stared about them, incredulous, as they drove through the entry-point, deep into the rock, and through miles of a vast underground city. Eventually, they reached what appeared to be almost a replica of the old Mövenpick hotel, complete with its beautiful gardens.

A red carpet was laid out before them.

'Where's the professor?' David Weiss asked General Mahmoud.

'He had to attend to some pressing business. He should return in seventy-two hours.'

Jibril, now the reigning monarch of Jordan, walked in, straight towards Lily. Six feet tall, with thick black hair that fell to the nape of his neck, he moved with a regal bearing.

He kissed Lily's hand, and his eyes met hers.

'Finally, I meet the beautiful Lily De Vere.'

Again he kissed her hand.

'I heard so much about you from Alex and your uncle Nicholas.' He hesitated. 'I am so sorry about your father, Lily,' he said. 'I give you my word, we are doing everything in our power to rescue him. In the name of my forebear King Aretas the Great.' He bowed.

Lily's eyes sparkled with barely restrained tears.

'Thank you, Your Majesty,' she said softly.

Jibril turned to Alex. They embraced fiercely, as brothers. 'Alex, my friend.'

Dylan Weaver, now recovered, stared wide-eyed. He nudged Alex hard in the ribs. 'You know the *King of Jordan*?'

'Yes.' Jibril smiled at Alex. 'I am King of Jordan now. Alex Lane-Fox and I were bonded together for life in Damman.'

He looked deeply into Alex's eyes. '6.07.'

'6.07 a.m.,' Alex echoed.

'The Saudi Incident.' Jibril fell silent.

Alex frowned. This was not the same angry young man he had last seen in Arabia. The young man standing in front of him was confident, regal, at peace – a far cry from the bearded youth with long, matted black hair who had stood, pistol raised at him in Damman, violent hatred in his eyes.

Images flashed before Alex.

'*Don't shoot. Hold your fire*' General Kareem had

ordered his forces. He turned, laid his gun carefully on the floor, stepping with outstretched arms toward the Crown Prince.

Jibril, shouldering a loaded assault rifle, finger poised on the trigger, his face bloodied and bruised, 'I'll blow your head off, don't come any closer.'

General Kareem had dropped to one knee 'Your brother King Faisal is dead. I am General Ahmed Kareem of the Jordanian forces – Safwat's brother.' And with that the old battle-worn general, visibly moved, had announced. 'We have come to take you and the princess home . . .'

Returning to the present, Alex stared at the young noble King of Jordan in wonder and said, 'You've changed.'

Exuding an air of calm authority, Jibril nodded. 'Yes. I have changed.' He studied Alex, then smiled broadly. 'As have you. You were the youngest investigative journalist in the world. Went into war zones at seventeen – Congo, Somalia, Iraq, Syria. Caught by the Turks straight after returning from Damman. British Consul got you out, but then you were caught by De Vere's Butcher, Kurt Guber. You've suffered from PTSD ever since.'

He grinned. 'I keep track of you, Alex Lane-Fox. How do you think your name was erased from Interpol's blacklist? Ah, Alex, danger calls out to you. You're in good company here.'

He held out his hand to David Weiss.

'An honour to meet you, Professor. You oversaw NASA's covert UFO programme for thirty years until your retirement. You have in your possession the only untampered-with evidence in existence of the counterintelligence programme at NASA. Also a fully-fledged member of the Collins Elite.

'And Dylan Weaver, worked the past fourteen years for the Directorate of Science and Technology, CIA; one of the masterminds of its golden age of technical innovation.'

He winked at Lily, who was staring at the young king in disbelief.

'My intelligence brief me well, Miss De Vere.'

He turned to a short, chubby woman with silvering hair and twinkling kind dark eyes.

'Let me introduce you to Nana, the Palace's housekeeper. Nana has looked after me since I wore a nappy! Nana, take Lily and Professor Weiss to bathe and eat and have a change of clothes. You, too,' he smiled at Maxim and Weaver and Storm.

'Come, walk with me, Alex.'

King Jibril's Quarters
Petra

Jibril and Alex walked through the Palace Halls. 'Alex. I experienced post-traumatic syndrome too, after my treatment at the hands of my brutal half-brother Faisal. I understand exactly what you're going through.'

'I remember the day we found you,' said Alex. 'You must have been through hell. But you're okay now?'

Jibril smiled. 'More than okay.'

'Alex,' Jibril began, then fell quiet. 'Alex, there's something I have to ask you. About . . .'

'About the Saudi Incident.'

'Yes.'

'Did you receive the intelligence?' Alex asked softly.

'I did. Sworn statements from seventeen witnesses. They all correlate precisely. General Khalid – a lieutenant general; three captains; the special forces team; the Crown Prince. And yourself. Nick and Jotapa disappeared at precisely 6.07 a.m. on 14 December.'

Jibril paused, and continued, 'It wasn't a one-off incident, Alex. I've been supervising my own ongoing investigation

183

globally. So far, we have evidence from 168 nations. All from credible witnesses testifying under oath to the disappearance of millions of men, women and children . . . '

'At exactly 6.07 a.m. Saudi time,' Alex finished the king's sentence softly. 'Exactly how – how many disappearances, Jibril?'

Jibril stopped in mid-step. He turned to Alex. 'Over one billion.'

Alex looked at him in shock. 'One *billion*?'

'1,140 million to be more precise. The documentation is staggering. The majority were in China.'

The king added: 'The strange thing was, there was an entire region that was virtually unaffected.'

'The Middle East,' Alex whispered. 'Israel and the Muslim nations.'

Jibril nodded. 'You know my forebear, the Great King Aretas, was a believer, as was his daughter. Stories still circulate that . . . that Christ appeared to him on his deathbed.'

'Jibril . . . ' Alex hesitated. 'You saw exactly what I saw.'

'I did.' Jibril grasped Alex's arm.

'Know this, Alex Lane-Fox. You are my brother in arms for life.'

'As you are mine.'

The regal young King of Jordan and the intrepid adventurer embraced each other fiercely.

Brothers.

Underground Base
Petra

Lily and her companions followed Nana as she led them through a winding underground tunnel. General Mahmoud was deep in conversation with David Weiss, walking behind them at a discreet distance.

'I do wish you were here under more pleasant circumstances, Miss Lily. We are all so sorry about your father.

'The guests' quarters,' he added as Nana stopped outside a small cloister door.

'Oh, my,' Lily breathed.

They stared around at a suite worthy of Claridge's.

Nana smiled in satisfaction. 'We only modernized the sleeping areas,' she said. 'The remainder of the monastery remains true to its ancient origins.'

Weaver, now fully recovered from his plane ride, peered into the bathroom.

'Shower, Jacuzzi, marble. Very James Bond.' He grinned. 'Maxim . . . *you're* the Doctor.'

General Mahmoud frowned. 'The Doctor?'

'*Doctor Who*,' Weaver explained. 'Maxim is obsessed with his Tardis.'

Maxim gave a smug smile. Lily glared at both of them darkly.

'Just saying.' Weaver held his hands up in surrender.

They heard the sound of voices raised in a heated argument.

Maxim frowned. Then a broad smile spread across his face. 'No . . .'

Nana smiled broadly and nodded.

'Yes, indeed. Brother Castigliano is with us.'

General Mahmoud chimed in. 'His spiritual advancement and temper have not improved with time, I'm afraid. He's our chef, and a fine one, I must say. The gentlest of souls, but once he's in the kitchen his Mediterranean blood tends to stir up easily. Finest cook in the Middle East.'

Weaver flung his grubby yellow anorak onto the bed. Maxim tut-tutted, then picked it up gingerly and dusted it off. Nana grabbed it from Maxim. 'I'll have it back like new within the hour.'

185

Maxim raised his bushy eyebrows at Nana. 'A woman after my own heart.'

Nana looked up at Maxim towering over her and blushed.

Maxim opened the massive wardrobe and beamed again. 'Ah, Miss Lily. Four pairs of Hollister jeans – your favourite brand. Lululemon T-shirts.' Maxim shook his head. 'Nana, methinks you and I are kindred spirits,' he declared, as Nana started unpacking Lily's small suitcase and folding her clothes with absolute precision.

Nana blushed coyly for the second time.

Lily walked over to the window and stared out at the lovingly maintained olive grove growing underground.

'Oh, Dad,' she whispered. 'Where have they taken you?

The tables groaned under the weight of food.

'Ah,' said Jibril to the company already assembled. 'My honoured guests are here. Bathed and refreshed.'

David Weiss nodded, silent.

'Madam Lily sends her apologies,' Maxim declared. 'She is resting. Nana has delivered a tray to her room.'

Jibril winked at Alex. 'I hear that you and Nana have really hit it off, Maxim.'

Now it was Maxim's turn to blush. 'A fine woman,' he said. 'A fine woman indeed.'

Weaver stared at the trays of chicken shish taouk, hummus with lamb, falafels, fattoush and tabbouleh salads, mixed grills, rice, halloumi cheeses, lamb, huge jugs of freshly squeezed lemonade with mint fresh from the monastery kitchen gardens, rice pudding with ambrosia orange, rose-water, baklava. He grimaced and gingerly picked at a falafel.

Maxim raised his head to Brother Castigliano and winked.

Brother Castigliano laid down a large silver-covered dish in front of Weaver, then removed the cover with a grand flourish. 'Battered fish, thick-cut chips, and tartar sauce,' he announced.

'High five!' said Weaver.

Brother Castigliano beamed in satisfaction as Weaver started to devour the fish and chips.

Storm sat next to Weaver, picking at her plate. David nodded to her. 'Storm, show the general your credentials . . . your documents.'

Storm passed General Mahmoud her credentials, then the set of black embossed files.

General Nasser studied the gold crest of vipers. 'Babel?'

Storm nodded. 'Secret files. From the hidden archives at CERN, to which only three people had access. My . . . my mentor at CERN, Professor Alessio Bernoulli, knew they existed. He became obsessed with these files in the fortnight before the monsters murdered him.'

The general placed his glasses on his nose. He studied the first file silently.

'My, my,' he said at last, handing the file to David.

He turned his chair to Storm's.

'We have had surveillance on CERN and its puppet masters since 2018. But never an insider.'

He studied the second file.

'The powers that be at CERN, under the leadership of the Jesuits and their masters . . . This is a blueprint of every aspect of Babel and their supercollider.'

He looked up from the file, to Storm. 'You know that Lorcan De Molay and his Fallen, in association with evil men, have been preparing for their habitation for the past seventy-five years. Blueprints of a hundred Gothic castles above ground: Glamis Castle in Scotland; Pendle Hill in Lancashire; St Ives in Cornwall, where Aleister Crowley lived; London's Highgate Cemetery. Castles all down the Rhine: Malbork Castle, Poland; Hunyad Castle, Transylvania. The same in India, Turkey, Russia.'

Storm shook her head.

'No sir. I only knew what I was given access to. None of us had access to the whole picture. We just did our jobs. But the files you hold are the entire jigsaw.'

She hesitated, looking pale. 'Professor Bernoulli became a changed man in the fortnight before his death. Not sleeping. Not eating. As though haunted by some terrible secret. I've been trying to piece it together. If it's what I think it is, their plan is the ultimate evil.'

General Mahmoud inhaled deeply. 'The top level of physicists at CERN had no idea of the penultimate plan. Most are like you, Storm Mackenzie: inherently good, noble men and women, passionately invested only in the pure science. But their puppet masters . . .'

'They cast no shadows,' David murmured.

Storm interjected, 'There is an underground railway from CERN direct to Mont St Michel, overseen by a man called Guber.'

'We know this,' General Mahmoud said softly. 'We already possess those blueprints.'

Alex and Jibril exchanged a quick glance.

'The supposed nuclear spill in Iraq was a false-flag operation,' Storm explained. 'To clear the area of all human habitation. File 8. Locations all across the earth have been earmarked as habitations for the Fallen.'

'You believe in these dark entities?'

Storm began to tremble violently.

'I . . . I saw the . . . the monster. It murdered my supervisor in cold blood.' She laid her face in her hands. 'It severed his carotid artery, with its teeth.'

She began to hyperventilate.

'It had two rows of teeth.'

Alex placed a hand on her arm.

'There . . . there were others,' Storm breathed deeply.

'She saw everything first-hand,' Alex said quietly. 'The only witness.'

'What did they look like, Storm?' David asked, his voice gentle. 'We know it's terribly hard, but try and remember. It's important.'

Storm nodded, trembling.

'They were flesh and blood; giants at least eighteen feet tall. Strange matted orange, no, yell– yellow hair past their shoulders. Lilac irises. They were all chained, at the ankles and wrists. The leader kept asking, *Is it time? Is it time?* But . . . but it was the monster.'

Alex said, 'We know this is so hard for you, Storm, but it's of utmost importance. Can you describe the monster?'

'It – it was huge. Three heads: a lion; a hideous goat's head, a leviathan. Its tail wasn't a tail. It was a serpent's. There were so many writhing serpents.' Storm put her head in her hands, shaking as if she were suddenly freezing.

When she had largely regained control, she unclasped the back of her watch and removed a minute computer chip, handing it to Alex.

'Encryption codes in file 9.'

She got up, pale. 'I apologize. I need to go to my room.'

Still trembling, she ran from the terrace, Maxim following.

King Jibril stared grimly at Alex. 'The shadow families of the Illuminati have been planning the Fallen's residency on earth for thousands of years.'

'But look,' said General Mahmoud, opening a file marked *Babel 10* and thrusting it down on the table.

'Just as we suspected! They have their own supercollider. Twice the capacity of CERN. Linked from Switzerland, under the earth's crust, to the Mediterranean, to the Euphrates.'

Alex cleared his plates to the side and placed the computer chip in his X-pad, then scanned the yellowed papers from file 9.

'Got it!' he exclaimed, then almost immediately cursed, 'Damn! It's rejecting the code.'

Weaver pushed the last handful of his lunch into his mouth and grabbed Alex's X-Pad. 'These guys didn't want anyone to access this. I'm going to override their encryption.'

He inserted a second computer chip.

'In!' he exclaimed. His sausage-like fingers flew over the X-Pad keys.

'Architectural blueprints. Fifty miles of laboratories underground. Buried 2,000 feet below the surface of the earth. It makes Dulce and Area 51 look like kindergarten.

'Hang on. There's more. It's an underground superhighway from CERN to Babel itself.'

'What are they planning?' Alex asked.

David looked up from the documents. 'Thousands of transports are at this moment being prepared to travel at Mach 5 back and forth beneath Switzerland and Italy, under the Mediterranean, straight to the Euphrates. Their intention is to link the two wormholes – the stargates. CERN and Babel.

'The Fallen are planning a mass exodus to Earth.'

CHAPTER TWENTY

Lucifer's Ice Citadel

Mars

Lucifer stood, his fur cape wrapped tightly around his lean imperial form, the freezing arctic winds lashing his scarred face. Heavy iron chains shackled his hands and ankles.

'Is this really necessary, *brother?*' he spat at Michael.

'Ah, how the tables have turned . . . *brother*,' Michael said, pushing him forward. 'Drink it in: the sight of your defeated armies.'

Lucifer dropped his gaze to the wild, barren ice plains surrounding his great, forbidding fortress. As far as the eye could see, legions of the damned were being shackled and chained by Michael's great armies.

Jether and the twenty-four Ancient Monarchs sat on white chargers in a semicircle at the gate. In front of them, the thirteen dread Warlock Kings of the West, their pale-green parchment-like skin and hooked noses visible beneath their crimson hoods, stood shackled in huge chains, an unearthly scream of torment erupting from their lips.

Raphael approached Michael and bowed.

'Your Excellency, the Satanic Princes' royal palaces on Saturn and Jupiter, Uranus and Venus have been ransacked. Closed for eternity.'

Lucifer watched, pale, as his menacing giant six-fingered Satanic Princes arrived one by one in their winged chariots of the damned, prisoners of Michael's elite militia.

Zadkiel entered. He bowed deeply to Michael.

'The Fallen's citadels in Orion and Draco have been stripped, milord. In Centaurus and Ursa Minor. Their palaces in the Second Heaven above Ethiopia, Grecia, and Babylon are now abandoned for perpetuity.'

Lucifer stared with hatred in his eyes as the great and terrible rulers of darkness assembled on the ice wastelands of Mars. Following them were the sinister black Ice Magi, escorted by Michael's great armies – prisoners of the elite guard of the Royal House of Yehovah.

Close behind, rounded up by Michael's chariots, flew the ghostly Witches of Babylon, from Venus, and the dread Warlocks of Ishtar, from Mercury, on the backs of winged werewolves and dragons, their pale faces raised in terror.

From under the oceans and from the desolate lunar depths of the Marianas Trench they came: Hera and the Banshees of Valkyrie, riding on leviathans and giant sea serpents. From the molten centre of the earth came the Wort Seers of Diabolos.

The Necromancer Snow Kings and the one-eyed Ice Cyclops flew through the ice crevices on their six-headed gargoyles. As far as the eye could see, the Fallen were being incarcerated on the great ice plains.

A ghoulish screeching filled the solar wind as the thunderous pealing of the monstrous bells of Limbo echoed from the spire across the bleak Ice Plains of Gehenna.

Michael lifted his sceptre, his white fur cape billowing in the violent ice tempests. 'Secure the gates!' he commanded.

Instantly, a hundred thousand of the Black Horde, Lucifer's elite militia, appeared from their snow caverns, their yellow eyes blazing with demonic fire, their wrists and ankles chained with heavy iron shackles. There was a great shuddering as the gates of the Ice Citadel closed.

Suddenly, the entire ice wastelands began to shudder. A monstrous gold chariot appeared on the far horizon, pulled by twenty winged white stallions ridden by fiery seraphim. The shuddering became more and more violent.

Then, all at once, it stopped. Lucifer started to tremble.

Michael watched as the entire army of the Fallen erupted in anguished cries of torment.

An immense rainbow arced over the Ice Citadel, blazing sapphire, orange, vermillion, and emerald as the golden chariot landed outside the gates. A regal form descended from the chariot, surrounded in an arc by the fiery seraphim.

Slowly the seraphim parted.

Christos stood, fierce, regal. Garbed in the crimson and ermine robes of the Royal House of Yehovah, he wore a golden crown with three rubies on his gleaming shoulder-length dark hair.

Breathtaking. Beautiful of countenance.

The seraph to his right handed him a magnificent sceptre embedded with stones of fire.

Lucifer raised his burned head, magnetized by the king. 'The Nazarene trespasses,' he hissed.

Michael hauled his brother to his feet. 'My deluded brother, watch as the reign of the Fallen comes to its end in the First and Second Heavens.'

Jether alighted from his charger, followed by Obadiah, who held a giant scroll in an engraved casing adorned with gold filigree. Jether bowed deeply before Christos and kissed his signet ring.

'The books of the race of men's iniquities,' Christos said softly.

Jether nodded to Gabriel.

Gabriel rode toward Christos on his white steed, followed by a battalion of revelators and scribes, carrying hundreds of black onyx caskets bearing the inscription *The Books of Iniquities*.

Jether removed a scroll from its golden casing and handed it to Christos. Christos slowly unwrapped the scroll and spoke.

'The edict of the Royal House of Yehovah. From the rise of the forty-first crimson moon, Lucifer, Son of Perdition, and his fallen hosts, necromancers and warlocks, are hereby banished from the First and Second Heavens for all eternity. Banished to the abode of the race of men – Earth.'

'How will the Nazarene keep us *out*?' Lucifer hissed to Michael.

Christos handed the edict back to Jether and walked towards the petrified Shaman Kings, who were still screaming in torment.

'Bring their king.'

Michael hauled Lucifer to his feet and flew over the parapet with him in tow.

He flung Lucifer onto the ice, directly in front of Christos.

'You will never keep me out of the First and Second Heavens, Nazarene,' Lucifer hissed.

Christos nodded to Michael, who dragged Lucifer up onto his knees.

The shackled Fallen watched in terror.

Christos raised his sceptre to the petrified host amassed on the ice wasteland. The fierce blue lightning engulfed the Fallen. As one, they vanished.

A haunting, eerie silence fell across the icy wastelands of Perdition.

Christos walked slowly to where Lucifer knelt trembling uncontrollably.

'Oh, how thou art fallen, Son of Iniquity.'

Then he pointed his sceptre directly at Lucifer.

Instantly, a raging blue lightning erupted from the sceptre, engulfing Lucifer's entire form.

The blazing light hovered for a full minute as Lucifer screamed in torment, then disappeared.

The fiery seraphim surrounded Christos once more, and they ascended in the golden chariot, returning toward the First Heaven.

CERN
Switzerland

Xavier Chessler, Kurt Guber, and a Jesuit priest stood in the remote viewing area. 'The underground transports and the flying craft are ready,' Chessler said. 'Ten seconds . . . eight seconds . . .'

The rotation of the wormhole accelerated above the skies over CERN.

All eyes were riveted on the stargate 645 metres underground.

Suddenly, a sound reminiscent of a tornado filled the air. Chessler and Guber were flung to the ground.

'Oh, my god.' The Jesuit priest held his cross so tightly that his fingers turned white.

Monstrous apparitions began to materialize. Fifteen feet tall with black wings, hip-length black hair and yellow eyes.

Twenty, then a hundred . . . then thousands.

Chessler watched as the leaders were placed in what seemed to be extraterrestrial flying ships, bound for Babylon.

Thousands upon thousands were then escorted to Mach-5

railcars, ready to be propelled straight under Europe and the Mediterranean Sea to the Euphrates.

The Fallen had landed.

Mount Quarnel

Lucifer lay facedown in the burning desert. Suddenly, he stirred and looked around him in horror. He stumbled to his feet, spread his six enormous dark seraph wings, and ascended into the skies until he reached the Kármán Line, the divide between Earth and the Second Heaven.

He plummeted back down to Earth at supersonic speed and landed on his face in the wilderness.

'The Nazarene!' he hissed.

Far in the distance Michael watched him.

'What has he done?' hissed Lucifer, clawing his way through the dirt, towards Michael.

'What . . . has . . . the Nazarene done to me?' he screamed.

Michael walked slowly towards him. He removed his helmet and shook free his long flaxen hair.

'Christos altered the frequencies of your angelic DNA. You have lost your ability to access the First and Second Heavens for all eternity. You now have no capacity in your frequencies to ascend any further than Earth's horizons, until your ultimate demise in the Lake of Fire.'

Lucifer stared in sheer hatred.

Michael vanished before his eyes.

'Hear me, Yehovah!' Lucifer screamed into the skies. 'I will destroy the race of men, your Achilles' heel. I will not rest until I have destroyed every last one of them.'

He raised himself up to his full height, limping. 'You defeated me on this parched tract of dust,' he hissed. He raised his fingers to a face burned almost beyond recognition,

196

then pushed his fingers through the stubble that remained of his long ebony hair.

'*I will destroy them*!'

Lucifer's frenzied scream echoed through the Judean wilderness, across the horizons of Israel.

Laboratories
Petra

'We're dealing with antimatter,' Von Bechstein said brusquely. 'Roll your sleeves up, everyone. We have work to do.'

'Stormie!' Dylan Weaver shouted in exasperation from under the table, where his ample girth had stuck fast. 'Well, *help* me, girl!'

Storm ran over. 'What are you doing?'

With difficulty, Weaver, wheezing and red-faced, extricated himself from under the table.

The seven Jordanian astrophysicists smiled at his struggles.

'There.' He pointed to the highly sophisticated wall of computer screens. 'Help me with the cables.'

Storm plugged each cable in meticulously, assisted by a trembling novice priest.

'What are you doing?' Storm asked.

Weaver held up a black box. He plugged it in, and neon-blue lights flashed. 'This little baby . . .' He rubbed his thick fingers together in triumph.

Storm frowned.

'Look,' Weaver said. 'It reads antimatter.'

Storm sat down, entranced. She fumbled for her large black reading glasses.

'You're saying that it can translate entities made up of antimatter?'

'Precisely.'

'From another dimension?'

Weaver stuffed half a bag of crisps into his mouth. 'Yes.'

'Onto those screens?'

Weaver nodded, crunching loudly. He pointed a greasy finger at the screens. 'Those babies there will reveal *any* extradimensional movement by any entity. In real time.'

Storm gazed at him in wonder. 'That's . . . that's incredible.'

Weaver tapped his nose. 'If any paranormal being intends to take over Adrian De Vere's body, we'll be able to view the moment the exchange happens, right here – miles away.'

He clapped his hands at Storm. 'C'mon, copilot, rev it up. Time waits for no man.'

He tipped the last of the crisps into his mouth. His fingers flew over the keyboard, then froze. He stared above him at the screen broadcasting a live feed from the BBC.

'Oh, god! Look over Jerusalem. Von Bechstein, turn it up.'

This is the BBC. Over to our correspondent in Jerusalem, came the announcer's voice.

The correspondent spoke in urgent, dramatic tones. *This is unprecedented. Thousands of unidentified flying craft have been circling the skies over Jerusalem since dawn today.*

As you can see on your screen, more craft are appearing every second.

'Oh, god, it's *The X Files*,' said Weaver, staring transfixed at the TV screen. 'Thousands of them. It's *got* to be a hologram.'

Alex, Jibril, and David Weiss entered. Their eyes followed Von Bechstein's to the portable computer screens that Weaver and Storm had installed.

David shook his head. 'Not a hologram,' he said softly. 'NASA has been aware of extraterrestrial activity for decades.

Those are real flying craft. In 2017, the Pentagon was already operating a $22 million programme monitoring UFOs. Roswell was no fabrication.'

'Two minutes, thirty-six seconds,' Von Bechstein announced.

Adrian De Vere's body was still visible in the open casket, in the mausoleum of Jerusalem's Third Temple.

'He looks like a Madame Tussaud's wax effigy,' Lily whispered. 'Oh, I can't believe Dad shot him. It's a nightmare. He's stone-cold dead.'

'Not for long,' Jibril muttered.

Third Temple
Temple Mount, Jerusalem

Lucifer landed on the roof of the Temple, his monstrous black wings at full span, his features set in rage. The Warlocks of the West surrounded him.

'It is time, Your Majesty.' Dracul, their king, bowed low.

The atoms of Lucifer's body started to gyrate faster and faster until he vanished completely.

Laboratories
Petra

'Corneal tracking device active,' Weaver declared.

'Copy that,' replied Storm.

Von Bechstein moved nearer to the screens. 'There,' he said softly. 'Watch the antimatter. The gold doors. By the eastern entrance.'

All eyes fixed on the faint but visible silhouette moving rapidly through the open doors, past the long queue of dignitaries still paying homage to Adrian. The pulsating silhouette moved nearer and nearer the mausoleum.

'Five seconds,' Storm announced quietly.

The silhouette flew directly over the casket and entered, disappearing into Adrian De Vere's inert body.

The BBC correspondent's voice continued from the screen. *Dignitaries from all across the world are still queuing night and day to pay their respects to the President of the European Union, Adrian De Vere. We are about to–*

The voice was interrupted by a major outcry around the casket.

Oh, my god! The correspondent's voice spiked. On screen, her face was suddenly pale. *Zoom in on the coffin. Now!*

Old City
Baku, Azerbaijan

The priest sat huddled in his grey windbreaker in the corner of the coffee house, a black knitted cap covering his head. He was the last customer.

He spooned the final dushbara dumpling into his mouth, wiped his lips with the cheap paper napkin, then walked over to the crackling fire.

He pointed to the wide-screen television above the bar. '*Vklyuchite yego?*'

The barman grunted and pushed up the volume on the remote.

The priest shook his head. '*Medeniyyet.*'

The barman clicked his tongue in irritation, flicking through the channels and stopping on Medeniyyet TV.

The priest stared, riveted, at the images of thousands of flying craft still descending over Jerusalem. The images on the screen suddenly juddered.

The presenter stared into the camera lens, speechless. Then the images switched to pandemonium breaking out in the Temple.

The priest clutched his rosary, rose to his feet, and moved closer to the screen.

The images changed again, this time to a close-up of the coffin.

The barman, wide-eyed, pointed to the television.

The priest watched in silence as Adrian De Vere, President of almost the entire Western world, sat bolt upright in the casket.

Pandemonium broke out in the Jerusalem Temple as the Secret Service gathered around the coffin, gesticulating wildly to the television crews to cut away.

The priest watched new images of women fainting in the crowd of dignitaries.

Finally, a strange silence fell across the entire Temple as the cameras zoomed in on a glaringly empty casket.

The barman dropped to his knees. 'He is God!' he whispered, crossing himself. 'A resurrection. He is God.'

He flung himself to the floor.

'He is *God*!'

'Switch it!' The priest gesticulated to a second man, who was now sweeping up. 'What is it saying? Turn it to the BBC!'

The man shrugged and switched channels with the remote.

Over and over again, images were rerunning: the assassinated President sitting bolt upright in the coffin.

The man slapped the priest on the back.

'He is a god, yes?'

The priest laid a fifty-manat note on the table, looked back at the barman still facedown on the floor, and walked outside into the snow.

He pushed a number on his mobile phone: a 'burn' phone for untraceable calls.

Cyrillic letters appeared on the screen: **Конца дней**. *Kontsa Dney.*

He clicked the phone off and threw it away in a rusted bin on the dirt road.

Waving a taxi down, he shouted through the window. 'Heydar Aliyev Airport. I'm late.'

CHAPTER TWENTY-ONE

Citadel of Babel

Babel

The Fallen had landed. The twelve golden palaces now inhabited by the fallen Satanic Princes gleamed in the harsh sunlight of Babylon. The princes of Grecia, Babylonia, Persia, and Magog were guarded by the Black Horde, Lucifer's elite milita.

The palace's crystal spires soared a hundred feet into the air, surrounding the impenetrable fortress that was Lucifer's abode and the headquarters of the Fallen: the monstrous six-hundred-foot gold and crystal tower that overwhelmed the desert horizon.

The new Tower of Babel, Lorcan De Molay's personal pièce de résistance.

De Molay's palatial gold-leafed royal quarters on the uppermost levels were a fantastical expanse of two hundred works by Old Masters, with the finest Savonnerie and Aubusson carpets. Floating glass walkways hovered four hundred feet above pools lined with mature cypress trees. A library spanning six floors, panelled with antique British oak, was filled with priceless ancient scrolls gifted from the secret archives of the Vatican and the damned. Painted frescoes adorned every ceiling. Exotic and lush hanging gardens surrounded the Tower. A rushing waterfall fell thousands of feet to the glistening azure infinity pools far below.

The monstrous crystal spire, where the newly designed Bells of Limbo hung, housed the Warlocks of the West.

Moloch and Dagon raced in their monstrous chariots along the four-hundred-foot walls surrounding the sprawling city of the Fallen – New Babylon.

All humans had been evacuated, and any who had refused the warnings – investment bankers, stockbrokers – were now the shackled slaves of the Fallen.

No human now dared enter Babylon.

The rumours of cannibalism, of thirty-foot giants, monsters and chimeras, of the bartering of women for oil, and of magical powers were rife throughout the Western world.

Even the bravest military pilots gave it a wide berth. The eye in the skies over Babylon was savage – no pilot lived to tell the tale.

Thousands of UFOs, armed with electromagnetic scalar weapons, circled the skies day and night.

The Fallen had taken over the entire Middle-East oil supply. The Satanic Princes of Persia once again ruled what had been the ancient lands of Persia: Turkey, Syria, Iraq, Iran, the Persian Gulf.

The stage was set. The Warlocks of the West gathered at the very summit of the Tower of Alexander, pronouncing their evil incantations, awaiting their master – the Son of Iniquity himself.

There was a tentative knock on Alex's door. 'Come in,' he shouted, splayed out on his bed in his jeans and T-shirt.

Lily entered, dressed in her Hollister jeans and Lululemon T-shirt. 'I think I could really get used to this place. Can I sit?'

'Sure. You're still walking, kiddo.'

Lily swirled around, then stood *en pointe*.

'I certainly am, Mr Lane-Fox, though I don't remember a thing about that night. I fell down a cliff, crippled, then woke up in Egypt. Walking.'

Her eyes shone with exhilaration. 'No more wheelchairs for me.'

Lily frowned. 'Alex, what *happened* to you?' She touched Alex's neck gently.

'My neck? Oh, it's nothing, just a little run-in with . . .' Alex stopped in mid-sentence.

Lily stared at him for a long time, silent. Finally she spoke.

'No, Alex,' she murmured. 'My room's next to yours.' She looked up at him with big troubled eyes. 'You were screaming last night, Alex. In your sleep. I came into your room. Your granddad was here. Your sheets were soaking with sweat. He couldn't wake you. He told me you had post-traumatic stress.'

Alex sighed.

'Who hurt you, Alex?'

'I ran into Guber and his thugs.'

'Kurt Guber? Adrian's Nazi sidekick?'

'Yup. They hung me upside-down for two days. Beat me senseless. Waterboarded me.'

He grasped Lily's hand.

'You can't tell my grandparents I was waterboarded. Our secret. Promise?'

Lily nodded. 'Promise. How did you escape?'

'One of my fixers bribed a guard with a wad of cash. I ran. Didn't even look back. I got away.'

Lily picked up Alex's wallet and studied the picture of Polly.

'You must miss Polly so much, Alex. I'm so sorry.'

'Like I would miss the air I breathe, Lils. You must miss her, too.'

Lily gulped. 'So much, my heart literally hurts.'

They sat in silence.

'Remember,' they both blurted out at the same time, then laughed.

'You first,' said Lily. 'Greatest memory.'

'It was at the airport in New York when I flew out to Saudi. It was the way Polly looked into my eyes, Lils. Like she knew she wasn't coming back. Almost as though she knew she was going to . . . to . . .'

He stopped short, his memory returning to the airport three months earlier.

They had barely made it, running like crazy through the airport. As he was clearing check-in, Polly was in floods of tears. His heart contracted as he remembered. It was the Rapture thing again. They had been over it a million times. Polly was convinced it would happen while he was gone, and that they would never be together again. He remembered like it was yesterday. Polly. How he loved her, he wanted to be with her forever. That was . . . to be the last time they would ever be together.

Polly had turned to Alex.

'Pol . . .' He frowned. Tears were streaming down Polly's cheeks.

Alex sighed. 'It's this Rapture thing again, isn't it? It's got you all wound up. You think it's going to happen while I'm gone, and you won't see me again.'

He held up his hands. 'Pol, we've been over this a million times.'

'Look after Lily,' Polly whispered. 'She loves you.'

Alex took back his passport and walked towards security. He turned back to Polly. 'Didn't get that, gorgeous.'

He grinned and waved to her, standing behind the ropes.

'I love you, Pol. I'm going to spend the rest of my life with you!'

That was the last time he'd seen her alive . . . except for the Saudi Incident.

'Alex . . . *Alex*!' came Lily's voice.

'The last time I saw Polly was in New York when she saw me off at the airport,' he said, and fell silent. Then he mumbled awkwardly, 'Did Polly ever mention the . . . the . . .'

Lily smiled gently, encouragingly.

'The Rapture?' he finished.

'Yes,' she said.

'But you didn't believe her?'

'Alex, I didn't know what to believe. Polly was the most grounded person I ever knew. But she honestly believed that she'd get, I suppose, *taken* . . . out of here in the End of Days.'

'Lily, if I tell you something, you won't think I'm crazy?'

'Try me.'

Alex laughed. 'You're a chip off the old block. That's just what your Dad always says to me. Okay. Brace yourself. Something happened. When I was in Damman.'

'The Saudi Incident?'

Alex nodded.

'I lost my temper with Nick – badly. He refused to leave with us. As though he was waiting for something.'

'Or someone,' Lily added softly.

207

Alex pushed his dark fringe out of his eyes.

'It wasn't only Nick. It was Jotapa too. I knew exactly what Nick was waiting for.'

'The Rapture.' Lily murmured.

'Yes. I thought he was delusional.'

'What happened, Alex?'

Alex again pushed his ever-straying fringe off his face.

'Everything started to go crazy. There were four of us in the room. Myself, Nick, Jotapa, and Jibril. And then – then it happened.'

Lily looked at him, listening intently.

'Suddenly this incredible fragrance filled the whole room.

'And then the stranger came into the room. Well, he didn't exactly come in because the door was closed. He just *appeared.*'

'He appeared?'

'Look, I know how crazy it sounds. That's why I've never talked about it. He was around Nick's age – twenty-nine, thirty. But the weird thing was it was as though he and Nick were long-lost buddies, the way he embraced him. And Jotapa too.'

'And Jibril was there?'

Alex nodded. 'He'll corroborate everything I'm telling you. But that's not the craziest part. Look, Lils, I don't know how to say this.'

'Try me,' Lily said softly.

'Lils, the stranger knew *me*. He knew my name, he spoke to me.'

'What did he say?'

'*Alex Lane-Fox. You've searched for truth all your life. I am the truth*. But that wasn't it. Lily, this is the part that is completely insane.' Alex hesitated. 'Polly . . . Polly came into the room.'

'*Polly?*' Lily's eyes were wide with confusion.

'Yes. I told you it was crazy. That's why I don't talk about it. Polly. Flesh and blood. Long blonde hair. Gentle smile. Dimples. She stood there smiling at me. But she was real, Lily. As real as you standing in front of me now.

'But here's the thing, Lily,' he went on. 'When I returned from Damman I did some intensive research – General Assad managed to obtain records from the internment camp she was in.' Alex walked over to the small table in the corner of the room and picked up his X-pad. His fingers flew over the keyboard. 'Here, take a look. Polly's death certificate.'

'It says she was beheaded, but then . . .' Lily looked up at Alex, a strange faraway look in her eye. 'Then she disappeared. Dematerialized.'

'Yes, and it gives the precise time of death as 11.07 p.m. Eastern Standard Time.'

'My watch stopped precisely when the Saudi Incident happened. The hands, they wouldn't budge.' He rummaged in his rucksack and handed a watch to Lily. 'Look, the electromagnetic field was so strong it stopped, and it's never worked since. General Khalid is a witness.

'Lily,' he added, 'Polly was executed at exactly the time I saw her in Damman. Which was precisely . . .'

'6.07 a.m. in Damman.' Lily finished his sentence softly.

Alex nodded, 'They all disappeared at the same time. Lily. Nick, Jotapa, and Polly were all believers. Jibril and I weren't.'

He drew in a deep breath. 'Remember that book about the Rapture in Walmart in the early 2000s? I picked it up from Polly's shelf one day and skimmed through it; dismissed it as raving fundamentalist delusions.

'Lily,' Alex looked at her, trembling, 'Jibril and I were left behind.'

Michael stood, arms crossed, surveying the barren wind-swept vista of the crumbling crematoriums and gas chambers – all that was left of the grotesque Nazi factory, the Birkenau concentration camp.

He frowned. The soft sounds of a viol lingered in the wind, haunting, almost bewitching.

'Show yourself, Lucifer! I have no patience for your dramatics this dawn.'

He was met with silence.

Michael's eyes narrowed. 'Show yourself,' he cried.

Slowly a long shadow fell.

Lucifer walked towards him on the deserted train tracks, still playing his viol. On his head was a golden crown with three enormous black diamonds.

His features started to transform in the moonlight. Michael studied him.

'You have many thoughts, brother,' Lucifer remarked.

Michael stared at him, his eyes hard. 'I have many thoughts, Lucifer, but none you would be glad to hear.'

Lucifer threw his head back and laughed capriciously.

'You have not missed me, Michael? Our tête-à-têtes? Our brotherly chats?'

'I do not miss what no longer exists.'

'Ha! You are sombre. Serious.' Lucifer flung the viol to the dust. 'Nothing has changed.'

He circled Michael tauntingly.

'Why so serious, baby brother?' His tones were wheedling, cosseting.

'Taking over an entire planet of such mewling pathetic creatures is . . . such fun. It is my *sport*. Come visit me at my new Palace, in Tiberius, right next to the sea *he* used to walk across. The Nazarene. Now, naturally, I walk across it at my choosing. *That* must gall Jether.'

Michael stared back, silent.

Lucifer sighed. 'Your mood vexes me, brother. No matter.'

He gestured dramatically to Birkenau.

'Mark well my greatest handiwork. The ravages of the Final Solution.'

He smiled malevolently. 'I, Lucifer, demanded a sacrifice. Of God's chosen people – the Jews!' he hissed. 'A literal holocaust. The burnt offerings of the ovens in Auschwitz and Birkenau, Treblinka, and Sobibor. Each time the stench of death filled my nostrils, it was to me the stench of *him*.' Lucifer shook with loathing. 'The stench of the Nazarene, born a Hebrew.

'But still my vengeance was not complete. Hitler failed me,' he hissed. 'He sits enchained in the lower parts of the underworld, a laughing stock to all who gaze upon him.'

'You summoned me with Royal Seal,' said Michael. 'You try my patience, Lucifer.'

'*You* are guardian of that parched tract of dust – Archangel over Israel; of the Hebrews. I have a new strategy up my sleeve.'

'You disgust me.'

'The catalyst to his return is when the Hebrews cry out to him as Messiah. My strategy is simple. The Nazarene returns for Armageddon; I spend a thousand years incarcerated in the bottomless pit. I have seen my fellow rebel angels, the Watchers, who reak of sulphur.' Lucifer stared distastefully ahead. 'They are anything but fair to look upon, thanks to their five-thousand-year punishment in dungeons deep below the ground.'

He stared at Michael, his gaze filled with hatred.

'Tell my father, Lucifer will use any and every means to stay out of the prison he has prepared so compassionately for me.

'I am compelled to implement a second holocaust. This time *every* Hebrew will be slaughtered. There will not be even one left who will call out for his return. And I, Lucifer, will reign forever as their Messiah in *his* place.'

'You have finally reached the brink of insanity, brother.'

'That may well be, brother, but my diabolical plan is about to be revealed to the entire world of the race of men. Times have changed since 1945, Michael. The race of men is so easily bought: money, power, hatred . . . sex.' He grinned lecherously.

'Everyone has their price. We have paid the world's leading geneticists over and above what their callow minds requested. They work day and night in Babel creating their dastardly cocktails. We have created a fully working genetic programme that can detect Jewish DNA and lineage to the fourteenth and fifteenth generations. It is an ethno-specific biological weapon, tailored to activate only on Jewish DNA. A genetic bomb.'

Michael stared at him in horror.

'Relay to my heartless father my intention. Tell him Lucifer in his magnanimity gives him an ultimatum: he retracts my eternal punishment, or I will slaughter every single Jew on this entire planet.

'The words of Robert Oppenheimer, creator of the atom bomb are quite apt, I think.' He raised his six black Seraph wings and his face to the skies. 'Now I am become Death,' he cried. 'I, Lucifer – the Destroyer of Worlds!'

CHAPTER TWENTY-TWO

Third Temple

Twelve Jewish priests blew their silver trumpets as Adrian De Vere entered and was escorted to the ornate Chair of State on the podium.

The Jewish High Priest stepped forward, dressed in his holy vestments of blue and gold thread, wearing a breastplate with twelve precious jewels representing the twelve tribes of Israel. He turned to the multitude of kings, queens, presidents, and dignitaries from the Axis Ten kingdoms presently under Adrian De Vere's rule. 'I here present unto you Alexander VIII, your undoubted king. All you who are come this day to pay homage and serve, are you willing to do the same?'

The crowd replied in unison. 'God save King Alexander!'

'Adrian De Vere, will you solemnly promise and swear to govern your peoples of the ten-kingdom axis, and of your possessions, and other territories to any of them belonging or pertaining, according to their particular laws and customs?'

Adrian replied, 'I solemnly promise so to do.'

The High Priest continued. 'Will you, to the best of your powers and abilities, cause law and justice, in mercy, to be executed in all your judgements?'

'I will.'

'Adrian De Vere, will you, to the utmost of your power, maintain and uphold the laws of God?'

'All this I promise to do. The things which I have here promised before the world, I will perform and keep, so help me God.'

A hundred-member choir sang *Zadok the Priest* as two pages removed Adrian De Vere's crimson robe, and Adrian proceeded to the coronation chair directly in front of the Holy of Holies, for the anointing ceremony.

Four knights held a canopy of golden cloth over his head.

The High Priest poured consecrated oil from a lion-shaped ampulla into a filigreed golden goblet, recalling the anointing of King Solomon by Nathan the Prophet and Zadok the Priest.

'In my office as High Priest of Israel, I anoint you, Adrian De Vere, as King Alexander VIII.'

As the High Priest was about to anoint Adrian, two Secret Service men grabbed him firmly, escorting him away from the Holy of Holies. Shocked murmuring rippled through rows of dignitaries in the Temple, their gaze riveted on the High Priest. His own face registered complete shock. The Secret Service sat him forcibly between them on the front row.

Dracul, the King of the Warlocks of the West, and Baron Kester Von Slagel, dressed in full military regalia, stood over Adrian, muttering in a strange angelic tongue, and anointed him with a thick, dark elixir from a golden chalice.

Von Slagel handed a golden crown, inset with three huge black diamonds, to the Dracul, who placed it on Adrian's gleaming black hair.

Von Slagel handed him a golden sceptre.

Slowly Adrian rose and presented himself to the congregation and to the audience of six billion television and internet viewers

He bowed his head, then rose, addressing the camera.

'There has been but one resurrection in the entire history of mankind – here in Jerusalem, two thousand years ago.'

He hesitated for dramatic effect, his eyes sweeping over the packed chamber.

'I have chosen the name of my ancestor, Alexander. I will be known as King Alexander VIII.'

He turned and walked up the steps of the podium, to the throne, and sat.

'My intention is to reinstate a monarchy. A monarchy of our ten-kingdom axis. Ten kingdoms that will exemplify government as we have never experienced it before on the Earth today.'

Petra

Alex, Lily, Dylan Weaver, Storm, David Weiss, and King Jibril sat in Jibril's suite, each riveted to the giant television screen.

Third Temple

Adrian turned to Kester Von Slagel, who handed him a document with a seal. 'It is my great honour, on the day of my coronation, to ratify the Edict of Alexander. From this day forth, we issue a new decree, implementing new times and seasons throughout our Axis Ten zones.

'The terms *anno domini* and BC, which have been used to number years in the Julian or Gregorian calendars for many centuries, are now permanently overruled. Every kingdom in the Axis Ten will now adhere strictly to the new Alexandrian calendar, with the new designations *Anno Alexander*, or AA, and *Before Alexander*, or BA.'

D avid Weiss's eyes remained fixed on Adrian.

'The Book of Daniel the prophet, 7: 25,' he said softly. 'The lawless one's intent will be to change the laws and times.'

Third Temple

A drian continued. 'All members of the ten-kingdom axis will be eligible for the Mark of Alexander.'

The camera slowly panned across the leaders of Canada and the United States, Japan, Australia, New Zealand, South Africa, Israel, the Pacific Island nations, Eastern Europe, Latin America, North Africa and the Middle East, Central Africa, South and South-East Asia, Central Asia, and the Western European Union.

'Those of you who have already received the vaccination against the black plague have already discovered the salutary properties that our scientists have been working on intensively for years. The Mark of the Pale Horse, our trial run, has now been perfected in the Mark of Alexander.

'We have discovered the healing codes not only for cancer, multiple sclerosis, and Alzheimer's, but also for one hundred other grave diseases. Once the chip is inserted into your right arm, the DNA codes interact with your own genetic code and instantly destroy any malfunction and damage in your own personal DNA.

'This, my friends, is the greatest day in the history of mankind as we know it. From this day forward, hospitals and medical centres will be a thing of the past. Sickness and every physical malady known to mankind will be permanently eradicated.

'We have over four billion chips immediately available,

and precincts are being set up in major cities all across the globe in the ten-kingdom axis even as I address you. The precincts will be named *Shangri-La* – your earthly paradise.'

Petra

David Weiss shuddered visibly. 'The Mark initiates inter-cellular change. When activated, it will rewrite the human genome.'

'He's creating an army of super-soldiers,' Alex said. 'The extra gene is the DNA of the fallen angels.'

King Jibril shook his head. 'Not super-soldiers, Alex. Billions of human beings turned into demons. The Mark of Alexander is the Mark of the Fallen.'

David bowed his head. 'It is the Mark of the Beast.'

Third Temple

'Banks, cash, credit cards will all become artefacts of the past,' Adrian intoned from his throne. 'The chip will contain all your personal financial information, your medical records, your identification records. We are moving our entire financial system over to the gold standard.'

Adrian nodded to Charsoc, who flung back the veil in the Holy of Holies to reveal Darsoc and the Grey Magi, Lucifer's cultured, sinister demon sorcerers. Archivists, philosophers, intellectuals, these were his finest informants and his senior intelligence corps. They stood with their white hoods pulled down over their faces, shadowed in the darkness.

'As you can see from the stellar ships that have appeared in the skies over Jerusalem since the early hours of this morning, we have interstellar visitors. I welcome Darsoc of the Nordics.' Adrian raised his sceptre.

The Grey Magi raised their hoods as one, their beauty bewitching. Tall and pale, their waist-length platinum hair fell like glass over billowing white velvet cloaks fastened with silver clasps intertwined with live asps.

'These, ladies and gentlemen, are the enlightened ones – what humanity call "aliens". They will form my supreme council. Christ was no more and no less than one of them. Jesus Christ was an ascended god, as are we.'

Adrian hesitated.

'As am I.

'*We* were your creators, the creators of the human species. Of this, there is no doubt. We, the ascended gods, created *you* – the human race. We created the human species, genetically manipulated early man. We created the world's greatest civilizations. Now at this time in human history, we are here to usher mankind into a new world order of peace, enlightenment, and a united one-world religious system.'

A voice cried out: 'Alexander the Great!'

The steady chant spread throughout the Temple.

Kings, queens, presidents, dignitaries rose to their feet as one, their hands lifted in the air steadily clapping, their voices raised.

'Alexander the Great! Alexander the Great! *Alexander the Great*!'

Adrian smiled, raised his hands. Instantly the crowd fell silent.

He motioned the Israeli President and the Prime Minister onto the podium.

'There is one final edict I must implement today, which brings me the greatest satisfaction of all.'

He held his hand out, and Kester Von Slagel handed him a sealed document.

'The Solomon Concordat: a seven-year guarantee by the

EU and the United Nations to defend Israel as a protectorate, bound by international law. Israel, in exchange for her immediate denuclearization, has been protected both diplomatically and militarily against Russia, the surrounding Arab states, and any enemy third parties, by both the European superstate and the United Nations. Israel has, however, retained a sufficient measure of sovereignty and therefore has remained a state under international law.' Adrian rattled all this off with scarcely a breath.

'Israel has been at peace with every Arab nation on her borders since the Accord and is four years into the implementation of her seven-year denuclearization strategy. A UN peacekeeping force occupies the Temple Mount. Israel's boundaries have reverted to the borders of 1967. Jerusalem is undivided. Muslims, Christians, and Jews have free right of passage to the holy places in Jerusalem, regardless of their religion, gender, or race.'

Adrian turned and shook President Levin's hand warmly, then shook the outstretched hand of Prime Minister Perlman. Cameras all across the Temple flashed.

'Today is the greatest day in Israel's history. Today I announce the dissolution of the Solomon Concordat.'

The Prime Minister and the President of Israel stared at him in undisguised shock.

'The Concordat was in force for seven years,' the Israeli Prime Minister stammered. 'I – I don't understand,' he continued in his thick Hebrew accent. 'We have adhered to *every tenet* of the Concordat for three and a half years precisely.'

Adrian clicked a silver cigar lighter and placed the flame at the bottom of the document. He smiled faintly as the flames turned the Solomon Concordat to ash.

'Jerusalem is mine,' he declared.

He turned to two generals at his side.

'Disband the Israeli Government. Incarcerate them all. All those with Jewish DNA will be moved to internment camps and executed. As I address you, arrests are taking place of everyone with Jewish heritage, by military police in London, Los Angeles, New York.'

He gestured to the horrified High Priest, the Israeli President, and the Israeli Prime Minister.

'Arrest them.'

Adrian rose and moved to the veil covering the Holy of Holies. He rent it in two, then moved toward the Israelis' most sacred possession – the Ark of the Covenant.

'On this momentous day, the Ark of the Covenant is to be replaced. It will no longer reside in the Holy of Holies.'

He stared at it with undisguised hatred, then nodded to the Warlock Kings of the West, who surrounded it as one. Blue electric currents raced towards them from the sacred artefact as they placed it on their shoulders and marched through the nearest exit, their faces contorted in agony.

Adrian motioned to Kurt Guber, who pressed a remote.

Slowly, a statue created of pure gold rose from beneath the floor of the Holy of Holies. The audience stared silently, their eyes riveted to the golden image that was appearing. It was at least thirty feet high.

A perfect rendition of Adrian De Vere.

Then the statue spoke.

'This momentous day,' it cried, 'I, as your King, Aexander the Great, declare myself the only Living God!' The statue raised its arms.

'*I am* greater than Moses, than Daniel, than Solomon and David. Greater than Jesus Christ. I receive your worship!'

Adrian walked over to the now fully visible statue and stood in the Holy of Holies.

'I am the *I Am*. I am God!'

Complete and utter pandemonium broke out as he was

220

escorted off the stage. Hundreds of journalists, dignitaries, and members of the Israeli Cabinet were encircled by military police and rounded up.

The television screen changed to an advertisement for the Mark and Shangri-La.

Jordan

Alex, King Jibril, Storm, and Weaver stared in horror at the screen.

Lily placed her hand gently on David Weiss's shoulder as tears ran down his cheeks.

'And he had power to give life unto the image of the beast, that the image of the beast should both speak, and cause that as many as would not worship the image of the beast should be killed,' he whispered, placing his prayer shawl over his head.

'It is the Abomination of Desolation.' He wept. 'In our Temple. The Great Tribulation has just begun.'

CHAPTER TWENTY-THREE

Armenian Quarter

'Julia, I am going to have to sedate you for a short while to remove the remaining scar tissue.'

Julia frowned.

'I thought it was all taken care of, Rebekah.'

'No, my darling Julia.' Rebekah said softly.

Julia sighed and held her arm out. Rebekah injected her with a strong sedative and removed the nano-camera from the contents of Avi Cohen's parcel.

'Let these old hands be as deft as when I was young, *Adonai.*'

She checked that Julia was sleeping, then swabbed Julia's right eye and deftly inserted the nano-camera into the cornea.

Jordan Underground Base
Petra

General Mahmoud took a puff from his cigar and pointed with a wand to an enormous map on the wall.

'De Vere' – he made a wry grin – 'or Alexander the Great, if you like, has a problem. He is distracted on three levels, which is good for us, because as we speak, the majority of his troops are being deployed out of Israel to the borders of Turkey and Russia.'

He hesitated for effect.

'In fact, he faces *three* major challenges: one, the Pan-Arab Alliance in the south – that's us; two, the Russians.' General Mahmoud pointed to Jerusalem. 'Russia's getting back on its feet after the Third World War. Its latest radar and its scalar weaponry now have the potential to neutralize the Axis Ten's fighter jets.

'De Vere's headquarters, as we know, is right here in Jerusalem. *But* – and a big but it is – he's diverted trillions of dollars into the construction of his new military head-quarters; a monolithic, sprawling complex on the flats of Megiddo, in the Valley of Jezreel. It's a virtual Pentagon, as well as the most advanced missile-deployment site on the planet. He's building miles of underground bunkers, housing the deployment sites, and the most highly developed technology to protect his global positioning systems, satellites – all Axis Ten communications.

'In the past eighteen months, he's been focusing all his energies on purchasing stolen and bartered armaments from Russia, the United States, and the global armaments black market – care of his exotic weapons specialist.'

'Guber!' Alex exclaimed.

The General nodded. 'Kurt Guber and his nuclear intelligentsia are now in the final stages of creating the equivalent of China's Sunburn supersonic missile. The new Axis Ten supersonic missile can be armed with a nuclear warhead equal to over 300,000 tons of TNT – 100,000 tons greater than the Sunburn. Guber's endgame is stockpiling nuclear, biological, and horrific chemical weapons that he'll release at the slightest provocation.

'The greatest threat, however,' General Mahmoud continued, 'is the top-secret arsenal of scalar and nuclear weapons and the malevolent bio-terror viruses, hybrids, and chimera that Guber's incarcerated super-scientists are presently creating in their underground laboratories in Babel, alongside their battalions of artificially intelligent super-soldiers and use of reverse-engineered alien technology.

'De Vere started moving his top militia to the construction site at Megiddo two weeks ago. Axis Ten special forces; Navy Seals from the States; the SAS from the UK, Scandinavia, sub-Saharan Africa. He's preparing to annihilate his biggest headache of them all.'

He pointed to China.

'*Tidings out of the East shall trouble him*,' David Weiss said.

The general frowned.

'The Holy Scriptures. The prophet Daniel. China.'

'The gold,' Alex murmured.

The general stopped and gave him a hard look. 'What do you mean – the *gold*?'

'The Rape of Nanking.'

'He's an investigative journalist,' David said.

'It's a long story,' Alex answered.

'I'm listening.' General Mahmoud looked at Alex intently.

'My mother was a Mossad agent, killed in 9/11 while investigating the gold trail and the Black Eagle Trust.'

'The quarter-trillion treasury note,' the general said softly.

'Yes, sir. Precisely. They had to find a way to get the note cleared without disclosing their identity. Once the $243 billion was identified, it would lead straight back to the trillions used for covert purposes since 1944: to initiate wars, depose governments, and manipulate elections and uprisings here in Egypt, Libya . . .'

General Mahmoud took another puff on his cigar. He stared at Alex impassively.

'Oh, my god!' Alex stared at the general in dawning

wonder. 'China's going to attack the Axis Ten kingdom because *Adrian* has possession of the gold.'

'Bright young man.' The general turned to David.

'Sorry,' Weaver interjected. 'Don't get it.

'The gold that MacArthur discovered in the Philippines didn't belong to the Japanese!' Alex explained. 'The Japanese stole it from the Chinese during the Rape of Nanking. The Chinese want it *back*. This is Adrian De Vere's third challenge.'

He looked back to the general.

'So they discovered that Adrian had it.'

'They did indeed,' said the general. 'And now their over-riding goal is to reclaim it. Our informants confirm that the Chinese plan to march across Asia directly towards Jerusalem. As we know, the Chinese military's greatest strength is their patience. Their advance could be in two years or two months. Our intelligence operatives are keeping them under intensive scrutiny.

'The Chinese Government has also spent incredible sums of money building a military superhighway across Asia, heading directly toward Israel. The superhighway starts here.' The general pointed to a second map. 'It crosses over the Chinese border, into Kashmir, along the Karakoram Highway, west through the Karakoram Pass – a huge danger point. India *could* feel threatened enough to attempt to intervene. If China fights back, India could be annihilated.'

He pointed to Afghanistan, then to the flat terrain.

'The Chinese have a problem though. When they hit Iraq. Babel, Babylon, they'll have to deal with the supernatural aspects of the Fallen, and with De Vere's Eye in the Sky scalar weaponry.'

'What about the Anatolia Dam Project?' Alex said.

General Mahmoud beamed across at Lawrence. 'Where *did* you find this young man?'

He turned to Alex. 'Correct. Turkey has constructed a

225

whole series of dams which it can use to strangle the River Euphrates in its cradle, completely shutting off its waters before they reach Iraq. The Chinese will come directly from the east, heading for Megiddo. We believe that Russia has its sights set on capturing Haifa, Israel's key port. From there, they will eventually advance to Megiddo from the west. Adrian De Vere will eventually be surrounded.'

'*Armageddon*,' David whispered.

'What has any of this to do with Jason De Vere's rescue?' said Alex.

'Adrian's focus is presently removed from Jerusalem onto the construction of his military headquarters at Megiddo,' said the general. 'Jerusalem is guarded by a few top battalions from Axis Ten, NATO, and the UN.'

Alex paced the room. 'Yes, but I know Jerusalem like the back of my hand. His Axis Ten Defence Force there is still ten thousand strong. They're constructing the glass death cell in the Holy of Holies as we speak. There's no way to break through the Temple to get to Jason.'

The general stood to his feet.

'Oh, but there is, Alex Lane-Fox. We have exactly forty-eight hours. Jason De Vere's execution is set for precisely 3 p.m. on Friday.'

He pressed a buzzer.

'Bring Colonel Zawarhi down from the north. And now let us adjourn, gentlemen. We reconvene in three hours.'

Armenian Quarter
Jerusalem

Kurt Guber raised his hand. At his signal, eight members of the Axis Ten SWAT team burst through the entrance of the Petrosians' apartment. Grigor Petrosian grabbed desperately for his old Uzi sub-machine-gun.

226

Too late. The militia mowed him and his family down in a burst of gunfire.

'Take her alive,' commanded Guber.

Four militiamen burst through the back bedroom door to find Rebekah standing in front of Julia, her compact X95 Micro Tavor assault rifle raised. Seconds later, the four men lay stone dead at her feet, each shot through the forehead.

Before she could turn, Guber shot her clean through her right wrist.

The assault rifle clattered onto the floor. Guber slowly removed his helmet.

'What do you want with her?' Rebekah stared at him, in pain but unafraid.

Julia sat trembling on the bed.

'The king needs a queen,' Guber declared in his guttural German accent.

He circled Rebekah, enjoying the horror on her face.

'But you . . .' He gestured to the four dead militia on the floor. 'You, Rebekah Weiss, ex-Mossad . . . *a Jew.*'

He gave a thin smile. '*You* are disposable.'

She lunged with her left hand for Avi's Desert Eagle at her waist.

Guber shot Rebekah at point-blank range through the head. She dropped like a stone to the floor.

'Take *her.*' He waved his revolver at Julia, who was sobbing, her brown eyes wide with sheer terror.

'*Mein* little *Schatz,* you have been summoned . . . by Alexander the Great.'

CHAPTER TWENTY-FOUR

Prison

Israel

'Get up! Get up!' the soldier screamed. 'You have a visitor.' He hauled Jason up roughly, then turned. 'Your Majesty.' He bowed deeply to the figure at the entrance of the prison cell, then exited swiftly.

Standing in the doorway was Adrian De Vere.

Jason stared in shock. He fell back heavily on the mattress. The door closed behind them.

Adrian circled the cell slowly, deliberately.

Jason stuttered. 'But – but – you're –'

'Dead?' Adrian gave Jason an evil smile.

'Dead,' Jason whispered, rubbing his eyes. 'I must . . . I must be hallucinating.'

Adrian grasped Jason's arm in an iron grip.

'You're dead!' Jason protested. 'I killed you in cold blood.' Jason stared at Adrian in horror. 'I *saw* you die!'

'Yes. *Dead* – that's a flexible term. Murdered in cold blood by my own brother.' Adrian lit a cigar.

'But you don't smoke.'

'Things change when you've been dead for three days. By the way, Jason, you may address me as *Your Majesty*. I've just been crowned Alexander VIII.'

He drew a long puff of his cigar.

'Alexander the Great, Ruler of the World.'

He sniffed the acrid urine odour in distaste.

'I see they are treating you well.' A Machiavellian smile played on his lips. 'But that's nothing compared to the surprises I have in store for you.'

He circled the cell again very slowly.

'The live execution of Jason De Vere, cold-blooded murderer of the most adored president and king in the history of the Western world. Six billion viewers, every one of them howling for revenge. They're baying like wild dogs for their revenge, Jason. And they will surely have it. My workers are already constructing the glass box that will be your death cell. Sarin gas. I have it on watertight evidence that the process of death by sarin is among the most agonizing in the world.'

He drew on the cigar.

'After direct inhalation of a lethal dose, it takes a human as little as sixty seconds to die, but I can assure you, we will keep you alive to experience the full effects for as long as possible. Your nose will start to run. You'll experience tightness in your chest and constriction of your pupils. In two minutes, you will begin to lose control of your smooth muscles and all bodily functions. You will vomit, I've been informed by our experts; a revolting mix of yellow and green bile. Then you will defecate. In full view of the whole world.

'In three minutes, you'll begin to twitch and jerk uncontrollably. Nearing ten minutes, muscle spasms will have made it impossible to breathe. If you're lucky, Jason, you'll become comatose and eventually suffocate in a series of spasms. A Jesuit priest will give you the last rites tonight.'

He crushed the cigar under his shoe.

'Shackle my brother.'

The cell door opened, and two militiamen entered and shackled Jason's hands and feet.

'This isn't necessary,' protested Jason.

'Very necessary, I'm afraid, big brother. Bring her in.'

Adrian turned to the door.

'Julia, my darling.'

Jason stared at Julia in shock. Then horror.

Adrian grasped her arm.

Her face and wrists were badly bruised. She wore the same orange overalls as Jason. Her eyes were completely vacant.

'Julia!' Jason gasped.

'She won't recognize you, I'm afraid. A real little tigress – fought till the end. We had to sedate her.'

'Julia, it's *me, Jason*.'

She stared straight ahead with glassy eyes.

Jason fought the heaving sobs deep in his chest.

'You bastard!' he whispered through gritted teeth.

'A king needs a queen. She's being groomed. And, of course, she will take the Mark of Alexander.'

'It's a–'

'It will change her genetic code. She'll have fallen angels' DNA, Jason.'

'You bastard!' Jason screamed. 'You evil bastard!'

Adrian released his grip on Julia, and two guards led her from the cell.

'In less than forty-eight hours, her memory will be erased. All recollection of Jason De Vere will cease to exist.'

He hesitated at the door.

'She'll be a *monster*, Jason.'

The cell door slammed.

Jason's anguished wail echoed beyond the cramped cell.

Beyond the walls of the prison.

Beyond the Wailing Wall.

Into the brooding Jerusalem skies.

Underground Base
Petra
3 a.m.

Alex tossed and turned in his sweat-drenched sheets. He rose in frustration, his entire body shaking from the panic attacks that had dogged him since his captivity by Guber.

'Damn PTSD,' he muttered, fumbling for the hip flask on his nightstand.

He swallowed his Librium, slugged down the gin, and frowned. He walked into the deserted hallway.

Voices. Several voices were coming from further down the corridor.

He pulled on his jeans and a T-shirt, then padded out across the corridor and slowly opened Lily's door. She was tossing and turning but very much asleep.

He quietly closed the door and walked down the hallway to Lawrence St Cartier's door. Lawrence's battered leather suitcase lay open on the bed. The professor had returned.

Alex slipped out of the back corridor, and made his way stealthily in the direction of the voices. They were coming from the kitchen. The door was slightly ajar.

He placed his head against it, listening.

The voice had to be Lawrence's.

Alex stood listening intently. His grandfather, Lawrence, King Jibril, and the general were talking in hushed tones.

'We have a weapon that De Vere and his minions know nothing of,' General Mahmoud said. 'The most elite, highly trained group of special forces and intelligence networks

231

on the planet today. They live undercover in a thousand different stations throughout the Middle East. Moving. Always moving.'

'Undercover?' David Weiss asked.

'All we know is that when amassed, their total number is a 144,000. They are divided into twelve elite battalions of twelve thousand, each battalion representing a tribe of Israel.'

'They're Israeli,' Alex murmured in wonder.

'Alex,' Lawrence called. His voice was stern. 'Alexander Lane-Fox, show yourself.' The door slid open. 'Your insatiable curiosity never fails to impress me.'

Jibril shook his head and smiled. 'I told you, danger calls you, even from your bed.'

He embraced Alex and pulled out a chair next to his. 'You are welcome, my dear friend.'

He nodded to an aide, who poured fresh lemonade into the empty glass in front of Alex.

Alex looked suspiciously at Lawrence, who had a napkin around his neck and was tucking ravenously into his beloved poached eggs. He wore an air of triumph.

'Professor, where have you been?'

'Ah, Alex, my boy.' Lawrence dabbed at his mouth with a second napkin. 'I had pressing matters to attend to: tidying up a long-running court case, one might say.'

'Were you successful?'

He gave Alex a satisfied smile. 'Oh, extremely.' Lawrence poured his Earl Grey tea. 'Successful beyond imagining. We won, hands down. The case is settled and beyond appeal. But back to the present.'

'You're talking about nearly a 150,000 elite soldiers that no one knows exist?' Alex asked. 'Not even Interpol?'

Jibril nodded. 'Their existence registers nowhere. They appear on no databases. They are ferocious, highly disciplined,

232

and trained Israelis – commandos of Shayetet Thirteen, the naval commando unit; Unit 269, Sayeret Matkal, strategic intelligence; Unit 5101, Shaldag, forward air control, aerial and special reconnaissance; Unit 217, Duvdevan, counterterrorism unit with undercover operational abilities; Unit 621, Egoz, counterguerrilla warfare; Unit 845, Rimon, desert warfare.'

He handed Alex a document.

'Airforce . . . Shayetet 7,' Alex muttered, scanning the document. 'Submarine flotilla . . . human intelligence gathering . . . Unit 8200.'

He looked up from the document to Jibril.

'But their records *must* be held by the Israeli Defence Force, which is now totally under De Vere's command.'

General Mahmoud shook his head. 'Every soldier in the Resistance movement is registered as dead or missing in action. After the massacre of the Russians by the Israelis in World War Three, it was the perfect cover.'

'Clever. Who's their leader?'

There was a long silence.

Then, softly, Jibril said, 'They call him the Ghost. He's never been seen, not even by his men. A loner. Never sleeps in the same place twice. Moves three hundred and sixty-five days a year. Uses burn aliases.'

'Burn aliases?' David Weiss frowned.

'They're like burn phones, *Zayde*. You use them once then discard them.'

'There are rumours that each commando bears some strange supernatural seal and cannot be killed,' said Jibril.

'The Ghost? A seal?' Alex exchanged a strange look with Jibril.

Lawrence studied the general, then Alex. He was silent.

'Well, why are they going to help us?'

'*Because*, my dear Alex,' Lawrence finally said, 'Jason is

not the only one marked for public execution. The High Priest of the Third Temple is being executed first.'

'Ah,' said David Weiss. 'So they will come out of hiding to rescue their High Priest.'

'Precisely.'

General Mahmoud turned to the young king. 'The colonel is here.'

'Escort him in.'

A tanned, handsome young man, his head wrapped in a black and white kaffiyeh, entered, escorted by two Jordanian soldiers. He bowed deeply to King Jibril.

'Colonel Zawahri, *salaam*,' said Jibril. 'We are honoured.'

'The honour is mine, Your Majesty,' the colonel replied.

Alex frowned.

The man's accent was not Arabic, but Israeli.

'The Ghost relays to His Majesty, with honour and respect, that he alone is in total command of the operation. Or there will be no operation.'

King Jibril nodded. 'Tell him I accept his terms.'

The colonel bowed deeply. 'He sends his honourable tidings to His Majesty as always, with deep gratitude to Jordan for its part in the Resistance.'

'I send my deep respect and warm tidings in return. It is Jordan's privilege. My forebear Aretas the Great would expect nothing less of his kingdom.'

Lawrence recited from Daniel 11: 41: 'He shall enter also into the glorious land, and many countries shall be overthrown: but these shall escape out of his hand, even Edom, and Moab, and the chief of the children of Ammon.'

Jibril leaned toward him. 'What does that mean, learned Professor?'

'Edom, present-day southern Jordan; Moab, central western Jordan; and Ammon, present-day Amman. You see, Your Majesty,' he said softly, 'thousands of years ago, long before your esteemed forebear King Aretas was born, the Archangel Gabriel appeared to the Hebrew seer Daniel. In the scrolls of the Revelation of Daniel, Gabriel revealed to him that not only would Jordan escape the Antichrist's armies, but Bozrah – specifically, the very land we stand upon now, Petra – would be a refuge in the time of the very end, especially to the Israelis. You are fulfilling the prophecy before our very eyes, Your Majesty.'

The colonel removed his kaffiyeh.

'Indeed, Professor,' he said. 'We revere our prophet Daniel deeply.'

'Ari, my long-time companion.'

Jibril clasped the young Israeli to him in a fierce embrace.

'We attended Eton together. Ari's family and mine go back many decades. The trust between us is unbreakable.'

Alex watched in fascination. 'So you know the Ghost?'

Ari gazed back impassively. 'No one knows the Ghost.'

Alex noticed the brief look between Lawrence and Jibril.

Jibril nodded. 'It is the only way.'

Ari turned to Lawrence.

'Professor, time is our enemy. De Vere has already stopped the daily sacrifices our people perform. His forces have incarcerated our President, Prime Minister, and the Israeli Cabinet, as well as thousands of our people who refuse to worship his abomination of a statue. They are all marked for execution.'

Lawrence looked at Ari with compassion.

'*And from the time that the daily sacrifice shall be taken away, and the abomination that maketh desolate set up, there shall be a thousand two hundred and ninety days.* Gentlemen, our Maker's clock is now winding down. We have precisely 1,290 days.' He hesitated.

'That's three and a half years,' Alex interjected.

'Three years, six months, one week, five days, eight hours,

nine minutes and fifty-nine seconds, to be precise,' Lawrence said softly.

'Until *what*, learned Professor?' Jibril looked into Lawrence's eyes intently.

'Until the day that was scribed in the Apocopalypse of Saint John – Armageddon.'

Ari bowed to Lawrence, then embraced Jibril again.

'Operation *Kontsa Dney* has begun,' the young Israeli said. And donning his kaffiyeh, he disappeared.

Alex frowned. '*Kontsa Dney*? What does it mean?'

Jibril turned to him. 'It's Russian.

He hesitated.

'It means *End of Days*.'

Black Site
Undisclosed Location
Israel

Jason lay facedown in a restless slumber on the thin urine-stained mattress. Tossing in frustration, he opened his eyes. Someone was in his cell.

He struggled to sit up, but it was as if his entire body were paralyzed. Finally, he managed to turn his head.

In the far corner of his cell stood a priest, his face covered by a cowl. He faced the wall, praying.

'Come to give me the last rites? Your god–' He stared with undisguised hatred at the priest. 'Your god is nothing but a vicious, vengeful tyrant; a weak, cowardly charlatan. Get *out*!' Jason screamed, half blinded by tears of rage. 'Get out of my cell.'

Slowly the priest turned, his face still shadowed by the cowl of his cassock.

'Where can I find your god?' Jason rasped, his fists raised to the ceiling. 'Have it out with me, man to man.'

The priest remained silent.

With great effort, Jason managed to raise his head a few inches off the mattress.

The priest came towards him and said, 'Who is more afraid, Jason de Vere?' The beautiful tones reverberated through Jason's body. 'The child who is afraid of the dark?' There was a long silence. 'Or the man who is afraid of the light?'

'Get out!' Jason cried. He stared blindly at the sandalled feet before him. 'Didn't you hear me?' he rasped, his fingers clawing at the concrete floor. 'I said *get out*!'

'The agonizing pain of loss is almost too deep to articulate.'

'Loss?' Jason muttered. 'How could you ever understand loss?' Jason drew himself up to his knees, his face contorted with bitterness. 'Loss of the only person I ever really loved.'

The priest was silent for what seemed an eternity. He gently took Jason's hand in his. Blood dripped onto Jason's hands.

'It was in a garden,' the priest's voice sounded wistful, filled with the understanding of suffering, with immense sorrow, 'not far from where I stand now, where I, too, knew what it was to lose the greatest love of my entire being. To experience such intense loss and abandonment is indescribable. The agony, the utter torment.'

'Jesus Christ!' Jason shouted, sobbing with rage. 'Who *is* this god – this vengeful, merciless tyrant who torments us with his rage? How can you *serve* him?'

He rose unsteadily to his feet, his fists clenched, but some strange force pulled him back onto the thin, grimy mattress.

'I will find him, this god,' he hissed through clenched teeth.' And I will *fight* him.'

The priest moved into the moonlight.

Jason stared at him, suddenly disorientated. The figure seemed somehow familiar, yet not familiar at all. He gazed upon Jason with overwhelming love, with what seemed to be the understanding of the ages, and with immense sorrow.

'Then fight me.' The priest reached down with his hand, to where Jason lay. 'If you must.'

Jason gazed up, transfixed, at an inch-long wound in the priest's palm. His gaze dropped to the sandalled feet. They bore the same grotesque scars.

His entire body began to tremble in a mixture of rage, a strange wonder, and dread. And as though magnetized by some strange supernatural force, against his own will he raised his face, inch by inch, to the stranger's.

'You are no priest,' Jason stammered.

The stranger pushed back his cowl, and the moonlight falling through the sliver of a cell window illuminated his face fleetingly.

He was young. Very young. About his brother Nick's age. His countenance shone with a luminosity so intense that his features were hidden from Jason's view.

The brightness gradually faded until the priest's face was fully visible. Jason stared, mesmerized by the noble countenance, the high cheekbones, and regal aquiline nose, the gleaming shoulder-length dark hair.

But it was the stranger's eyes that captivated him. Jason tried to shield his own eyes from the consuming waves of love, compassion, and tenderness.

Then the waves became deep understanding and authority. And Jason De Vere knew, from a place beyond his own earthly comprehension, that he was staring into the eyes of a king.

The king.

A new and fierce fire felt as if it were burning in his heart.

Then, his entire body trembling, he collapsed back onto the thin mat on the concrete floor.

The stranger stood perfectly still. In his eyes Jason saw love and understanding he could not fathom.

'Jason, you have fought me all your life.' He smiled straight into Jason's eyes. 'Follow me now, Jason De Vere.'

Jesus knelt and held Jason tightly to his chest.

Jason clung to him in a mixture of sheer desperation and wonder. He could not keep the racking sobs from coming.

An hour then two . . . How long the stranger held him, he would never know. Only that the storm that had raged in his chest for forty-seven years was finally stilled.

He was finally home.

CHAPTER TWENTY-FIVE

Petra

Jibril's aide entered quietly and handed him a note. Jibril read it, looked at Alex, and then handed it to Lawrence.

Lawrence scanned it, bowed his head, and crossed himself. 'They have taken her, as we knew they would,' he said softly.

Jibril nodded. 'Activate the nano-camera immediately. Wake Weaver from his slumber.'

Alex stood up. 'Who have they taken?'

Lawrence looked grim. 'Julia.' He took a deep breath. 'I'm so sorry, Alex. They just murdered your grandmother.'

Secret Surveillance Operations Chamber
Petra

'Where is my grandfather?' Alex asked.

'Your grandfather is resting,' Lawrence said quietly.

'No, he's not.' David Weiss's voice came from behind them. '*Bubelah.*'

David embraced Alex fiercely. His eyes were red-rimmed.

'Alex, do not grieve. It is the only way your grandmother would have wanted to go.'

He smiled weakly.

'She shot four of her assailants and wounded Guber before he murdered her. She died as she always lived – a hero. My Rebekah.'

'I'm not grieving.' Alec's voice shook with rage. 'I want *revenge*.'

Gathering himself, he asked, 'Where's Lily?'

'She cannot know the danger her mother is in,' Lawrence replied. 'I instructed King Jibril to deliberately distract her.'

'Rebekah sensed this would happen,' David said softly. 'Avi Cohen just spoke to me. It seems he gave Rebekah the latest nano-camera that Mossad's technology department had just developed – completely undetectable by any tracking device. Rebekah surgically implanted the tracking device into the cornea of Julia's right eye. We will see what she sees.'

He gestured to the wall of blank screens in front of them.

'Activate the nano-camera,' Von Bechstein instructed.

'Microphone activated,' Weaver answered. 'Camera activated.'

Instantly every screen on the wall came alive.

'She's walking down steps,' Weaver muttered. 'Must be coming off a plane. Looks like a Gulfstream. Stepping onto tarmac.'

'Oh, my god, look who's waiting for Aunt Jules!' Alex exclaimed.

'My, my. Xavier Chessler,' Lawrence murmured.

'She's walking with him to a limousine. Where's he taking her?' Alex said.

'Damn!' Weaver hit the console with his chubby fingers. 'The microphone's stopped working. Let me work on it.'

'It's *got* to be Babel.' Alex stayed riveted to the screen.

'It is Babel,' Lawrence said quietly.

They watched, transfixed, as Julia got out of the limousine. She was gazing up at a soaring structure.

'The Tower of Alexander,' said Lawrence. 'We're the first ones apart from the Fallen to see it.'

'She's going inside,' Alex murmured.

Tower of Alexander
Babel

Julia's hair was swept back into a long ponytail. Now dressed in black Armani jeans and a chic leather jacket, and clutching a Balenciaga handbag, she was being escorted through the soaring golden doors of the Tower of Alexander.

The drugs were slowly wearing off.

'Where am I?'

She turned to Xavier Chessler. 'Uncle Xavier,' she said groggily.

He put out his arms, and Julia fell into his embrace.

'Xavier, where am I? What's going on?'

'You're in a safe place, Julia, my dear.'

'Jason.' She felt a surge of panic. 'Where's Jason?'

'My dear, there are certain matters . . . hard matters for you to accept. We have had to wait till you regained your strength.'

Chessler led Julia through the soaring marble foyer to a palatial breakfast room reminiscent of the Ritz in London. He pulled out a chair for Julia. She sank slowly into it.

Coffee for three, he mouthed to the concealed waiter at the door.

Petra

'Damn! Microphone's just not activating!' Weaver slammed the console in frustration.

Chessler's face appeared on the screen. Everyone watched, riveted.

'Come *on*, Weaver!' Alex stood over him. 'We *have* to hear what they're saying.'

Tower of Alexander

'Unfortunately, Jason has lost his faculties, my dear. It's tragic. He views everyone as his enemy. We have to keep you safe.'

From Jason? Julia stared at him in confusion.

The waiter returned, cafetière in hand, and deftly poured the aromatic Turkish blend into three china cups.

The enormous mahogany doors opened amid a flurry of activity.

Petra

'Oh my god! It's Adrian!' Alex exclaimed.

'Got it!' Weaver exclaimed. 'Microphone activated!'

Tower of Alexander

Adrian walked through the breakfast room, straight toward Julia, embracing her.

'Julia, my darling, you're safe now.'

He sat down opposite her and gently took her hand in his.

'I'm *so* sorry for all the trauma you've been through.'

She put her hands to her head. 'My head, Adrian . . . it feels so groggy. I'm struggling to remember things.'

'The truth is,' Adrian placed a single lump of brown sugar in his cup and stirred it slowly, 'Jason has been mentally ill for a very long time. Lilian, Nick – the whole family tried to keep the facts from you. It finally resulted in his shooting me, his own brother, in cold blood.'

Julia put her head in her hands. 'Yes, I only found out a few days ago. I . . . I still can't believe it. It's horrific.'

'Julia,' Adrian pulled his chair closer, 'Jason has been through multiple batteries of psychological tests. He has been diagnosed by the leading psychiatrists in the world as psychotic.'

Psychotic? Julia reeled.

'His brain chemistry and neurotransmitters have been permanently affected by the post-traumatic stress of having murdered his own brother. The incident was simply too much for his brain to assimilate. We have done everything we possibly can, but he is trapped in an impaired reality. He has retreated into a dark world of delusion. He believes that his family and friends are his enemies, and his enemies are his allies. He believes that you, Lily, and Alex, and all your family are enemies to be ruthlessly exterminated.'

'But Rebekah – she got me better. They were protecting me . . . hiding me.'

'No, Julia, my dear. Jason and Rebekah Weiss were kidnapping you, with full intent to use you as collateral to save their own skins. We had no option but to rescue you and bring you safely here to Babel. You're safe here.'

'But . . . but Lily . . .'

'Lily will join you as soon as possible.'

Petra

'Goddamn liars!' Alex clenched his fist. 'He murdered my grandmother. Now they want Lily. Over my dead body.'

David Weiss gently laid his hand on Alex's shoulder.

'We will protect Lily, Alex. My beloved Rebekah knew

the risks. She died doing what she has always done: fighting to protect the truth. You will continue her legacy, Alex.

'Turn the volume up, Weaver.'

Tower of Alexander

'But I thought you were . . .'

'Dead? Evil?' Adrian sipped his coffee, then dabbed his mouth with a monogrammed napkin. He shook his head. 'More psychotic fantasies of Jason De Vere, my darling Julia.'

Julia's hands trembled as she lifted her cup. She studied Adrian. This was the boy she had known since he was nineteen years old.

Her mind raced back to Nick. Adrian had looked after Nick faithfully. Paid for his medications.

When Nick was cut off from his trust fund, Jason hadn't even taken his calls. Adrian, by contrast, had given him hundreds of thousands of dollars, purchased his South Bank apartment for him. He had always been there.

She brushed her blonde hair back off her face. Adrian had always been so good to her: bridged the loan to secure her fledgling PR business a few years earlier; introduced her to her most influential client – the England Football Team.

Adrian rose. He held out his arm to Julia. 'You've been through enough stress and trauma for one lifetime,' he said as he guided her through the palatial lobby.

He brought his eye to the gold elevator.

'Julia, let me introduce you to the Tower of Alexander.'

Julia drew a deep breath as the elevator opened onto the most stunning architectural garden she had ever seen.

She started to walk along a marble path, stopping to smell the jasmine and the endless roses. At every corner were huge crystal conservatories filled with orange, lemon, and lime trees, olive and cypress trees.

She looked back at Adrian in wonder. 'Oh, Adrian, it's heavenly!'

Adrian smiled and took her hand. 'And now, Julia St Cartier, my pièce de résistance, constructed especially for you.'

They rounded a corner. Facing Julia was a large infinity swimming pool, its waters the colour of the Mediterranean, pouring downward in a waterfall to a sea below. Pale-pink and cream fabric cushions covered twelve gold-plated chaises longues. A swing seat with a canopy in the softest gold and cream stripe, with pale aqua cushions, swung gently to and fro in the mild breeze.

Books of every description lined the outside tables: fashion and beauty, Chanel, Lagerfeld, art . . . A white scalloped French dining table with matching chairs stood to the right, set exquisitely with Limoges china and crystal glass.

'Oh, Adrian,' Julia murmured, 'it's exquisite.'

'It's *yours*, Julia,' he said, and kissed her hand. 'All yours. This is your private garden, for you to recuperate from all you've been through. Your suite is through the orange grove.'

Julia moved nearer the waterfall and looked below. 'Who are those people?' She frowned. 'They look like they're shackled.'

'Don't worry your pretty head over our resisters. Follow me.'

Julia followed Adrian, her senses overwhelmed by the sensual fragrances all around her. They stopped at a dwelling of pure crystal.

Adrian pushed open the doors. 'It is a small palace, created by my architects to suit your every taste.'

Julia gasped. The entire open-plan living room was in shades of azure, robin's-egg blue, the palest pinks, gold leaf, and silver. Aubusson and Savonnerie rugs covered the floors.

There was a library with a reading area, and a relaxing area with sofas.

'To the right, you have your own personal spa. Swedish massage, facials, body wraps. Your sleeping chambers.' They walked into a vast bedchamber with an enormous white French antique bed, with a silver and white canopy.

Adrian pushed the crystal doors leading to a vast dressing room. Julia sifted through the left side of the wardrobe. There were suits, blouses, dresses, all in her favourite colours, and all somehow tailored to her exact measurements.

'Oscar de la Renta, Stella McCartney, Vera Wang, Vivienne Westwood. All your size.'

Adrian led her through to a closet off the main dressing room. Julia stared in wonder at the ball gowns of silk and tulle and organza. She gazed up at the crystal ceilings.

'Light. Oh, you remembered how much I love light!'

'At night,' Adrian said tenderly, 'you can see the stars.'

A nun stood in the doorway, holding a tray. Only her eyes and the lower half of her pasty face showed beneath her wimple, yet somehow even this betrayed her deep Teutonic origins. A long habit was draped over her thick-set frame. Below it, dark stockings covered a pair of calves like tree trunks.

'Abbess Helewis Vghtred will look after you. You can trust her implicitly. She has been with our family for years. She tutored me when I was a boy, and she is here to meet your every need.' He looked at his watch. 'It's time for Madam Julia's medicine, Abbess.'

Julia frowned.

'You were *very* ill when we found you, Julia. Rebekah had been drugging you every day. We need Dr Gravenstein to examine you. He is my own personal physician – nothing less than the best for you, darling Julia. You'll be sedated to calm you. It will take less than an hour.

'Madam Julia is to be at Dr Gravenstein's surgery tomorrow evening at six.'

'We have to get you strong,' the abbess said softly in a strong Germanic accent.

'Rest, my beautiful Julia.' Adrian smiled. 'I have my duties to attend to, but I will be there with you. I promise.'

Julia smiled weakly. 'You're so good to me, Adrian.' She kissed him on the cheek and embraced him. 'You promise.'

'I promise.'

Petra

'He's going to sedate her; then Adrian's ghoul Gravenstein will give her the Mark,' said Alex. 'Julia doesn't have a clue who she's dealing with. She's like a lamb to the slaughter.'

David Weiss said, 'If she doesn't get the antidote within a six-hour window after receiving the Mark, her DNA will be permanently changed into Nephilim DNA. She'll . . .'

Alex finished the sentence. 'Aunt Jules will be a monster.'

CHAPTER TWENTY-SIX

Two Hundred Metres Underground

Petra

'My god!' Dylan Weaver stopped and turned to Storm, who was looking pale. They both turned to Dr Von Bechstein.

'It can't be,' Storm mumbled.

Weaver nodded slowly, shaken to the core. 'It is, isn't it, Professor Von Bechstein?'

Von Bechstein nodded gravely. 'Yes. We have been working on it for over eight years. It is the Resistance's supercollider. It lies in a massive underground ring over two hundred metres beneath Petra and measures more than fifty kilometres in circumference. From a magnetic perspective, this device acts like a wormhole, as if the magnetic field were transferred through an extra dimension.'

'Einstein-Rosen,' said Maxim.

Von Bechstein gave him a curious look.

Maxim continued. 'In 1935 Einstein and Rosen discovered what they believed was the existence of certain bridges that would be able to link two different points in space-time. The Einstein-Rosen bridges – call them portals or wormholes if you will – could theoretically allow something to travel instantly across huge distances.'

Von Bechstein ran a hand through his thick silvering hair. 'Common knowledge in our field: the "wormhole from Jordan", in layman's terms. It should in theory connect straight to the Fallen's collider in Babylon.'

Maxim coughed. 'Has any form of matter been *proved* to have materialized from here to the Babylon portal?'

Von Bechstein shook his head. 'The challenge is: how do we turn the theoretical into an actual working practical solution? We've approached the challenge from *every* angle. We're missing something – some logarithm, some component. It continually eludes us.' He raised his hands in frustration.

Maxim said, 'Can I have a tinker?'

Von Bechstein frowned coldly.' Is this, as you British say, a *joke*?' He turned to Weaver and Storm. 'He's a *butler*.'

Dylan Weaver took him aside. 'I'd watch your manners, Professor. The gentleman you see before you, mate, is one of the world's foremost experts on wormholes. Astrophysicist and particle physicist extraordinaire.'

Maxim was already studying every aspect of the collider. Then, as Von Bechstein looked on, utter disbelief written on his face, Maxim transformed into Xacheriel, eight feet tall, his white corkscrew hair awry, his voluminous robes askew.

'Blueprints!' Xacheriel commanded, fierce authority in his voice.

Half-stupefied, Von Bechstein walked to the far side of the laboratory and came back laden with three huge bound manuals. Then he went back and returned with three more.

Xacheriel grabbed one and started reading. Von Bechstein watched in shock as the being he had known as Maxim the butler speed-read all six manuals in just over a minute.

'You just downloaded the information *straight* into your cerebral cortex,' Von Bechstein said softly.

Xacheriel gave him an impatient look. 'Kindergarten stuff, Bechstein.'

Weaver rubbed his hands in glee. '*Told* you.'

'I need a cat,' Xacheriel said. 'Or a chimpanzee.'

Bechstein pressed a buzzer, 'Bring Atlas immediately.'

'Give me two hours,' Xacheriel barked. 'Alone. I will have your answer.

'Oh,' he added, 'I need to contact your counterpart in the Resistance working on the collider in Babylon.'

Bechstein, for some strange reason that defied his logical brain, wrote down a name and a series of logarithms. 'Von Lowenstein is our contact. You can communicate with him through our secret communications system that links directly to the Resistance in Babylon.'

The door slid open, and Atlas the chimpanzee's cage was wheeled in. Xacheriel looked deeply into the creature's eyes.

'Atlas, you are going on a trip to Babylon,' he declared dramatically.

He continued to converse with the chimpanzee, making strange simian noises, which Atlas seemed to understand and respond to.

'Ha!' Xacheriel clapped his hands. 'Atlas says he will travel through the wormhole on two conditions: one, that he is no longer forced to live incarcerated in that cage; and two, that he is given a supply of ripe bananas each day. He tells me that the bananas supplied to him are too green. Is that accepted?'

Von Bechstein was by now as white as the pages that Xacheriel had just read through. 'Yes, yes. Ripe bananas, no cage.'

'I shall convey the message,' said Xacheriel. He whispered in Atlas's ear, and the chimp jumped up and down, screeching.

Xacheriel flapped his large hands, waving everyone out. Go, go,' he commanded. '*Go*! Now, Weaver, Storm, as my younglings are absent, I will need your hands.'

'Two hours,' Von Bechstein said.

Xacheriel grunted.

Two Hours Later

Von Bechstein entered the supercollider to find Xacheriel dancing around the centrifuge, his large hands raised in ecstasy.

'Lowenstein tells me Atlas arrived in Babylon twenty minutes ago. And if my calculations are correct, which they *always* are' – this with a glare at Von Bechstein – 'he should be arriving back with us in perfect shape . . . any minute now.'

Lightning and loud thunder began to erupt from the centrifuge. When the noise finally stilled, Xacheriel carefully opened the door of the collider and walked into the embrace of an exhilarated chimpanzee.

'Lady and gentlemen,' he declared triumphantly, 'we have an Einstein-Rosen bridge straight to Babylon. We can travel through the wormhole directly to the Fallen's portal there.'

When the astonished professor could speak, he said, 'Yes, it *works*!'

'And now,' Xacheriel said, 'someone has to deliver the antidote to Julia St Cartier.'

They all stared at one another in silence, the same thought in everyone's mind: *Who?*

King Jibril's Quarters
Petra

Jibril and Alex walked in silence. Jibril stopped mid-stride.

'Alex, I need your help.'

Alex frowned. 'Of course.'

Jibril shook his head. 'No. I have no right to expect you to embark on such a dangerous mission. But I have to lay it before you.'

'It's Aunt Jules, isn't it?'

Jibril nodded.

'Julia St Cartier. Alex, they've moved their plan forward. My intelligence alerted me that Dr Gravenstein will sedate her and implant her with the Mark in less than four hours. Her DNA will be transformed into Nephilim DNA. The so-called nuclear spill over Babylon was a complete hoax – a strategic plan by De Vere to eliminate all human contact: 150 square miles with no prying eyes. There is only one way to infiltrate it and get Julia the antidote,' Jibril said. 'Jordan's supercollider.'

'You already know my answer,' said Alex. 'I'll do anything for Julia and Jason. I'm like a son to them. My mother and Aunt Jules were inseparable. She'd want me to do this. It's a fait accompli, Jibril. I'm in.'

'It's extremely dangerous, Alex. Plus you'll have to pass an intensive physical with Dr Gustav Anders. He was chief medical officer for NASA; looked after the astronauts.'

'Jibril, promise me one thing – that you will protect Lily.'

'My promise in the name of my ancestor Aretas the Great.'

'Lily can't know that her mother is in any danger, Jibril. It will break her.'

Jibril put his hand on Alex's shoulder. 'She's in good hands. We'll look after her.' He studied Alex intently. 'I didn't realize you cared about her so deeply.'

'I do,' Alex murmured.

'I give you my word. As your brother-in-arms.'

Alex nodded. 'I'm Aunt Jules's only chance, Jibril.'

'Come,' Jibril said. 'There's no time to lose. Dr Anders, then the supercollider.'

Lily bent over the jasmine bush, inhaling the intoxicating scent. Alex studied her. She had changed this past year. She was twenty-one now. She had always been slightly built, but her strong features had softened. Her glossy dark hair framed the heart-shaped face. Lily had grown beautiful – not breathtaking like Polly, who could have been a supermodel, but she had a real, ethereal beauty.

'Lily,' Alex said, 'I came to tell you I have to leave for a while.'

Slowly she raised her face to his. 'You're leaving?'

'I have to complete a mission. It could be dangerous.'

Lily looked into Alex's eyes. 'How long will you be gone?'

He shook his head. 'I don't know, Lils.'

'When do you leave?'

'Tonight.'

'Can't you tell me *anything*?'

Again he shook his head. 'I'm so sorry, Lils. I just can't.'

'James Bond,' Lily said weakly. 'If you told me, you'd have to kill me.'

Alex smiled. 'Yes,' he said. 'Very James Bond, Lils.'

'Is it connected with Dad?'

'No. That much I can tell you. Jibril . . .'

Lily finished his sentence. 'Will look after me while you're gone.'

Alex moved a step nearer. 'Yes, I did come to tell you that. He's given me his promise.'

Lily turned away from the jasmine bush, her expression blank. 'When will Mum arrive, Alex? I miss her so much.'

Alex grasped Lily's hand. 'Soon, Lily. Very soon. They're working out her travel arrangements now, as we speak.'

Lily drew a deep sigh of relief. 'At least I know Mum's safe.' She looked up at Alex with trusting eyes.

'She's safe, Lily. You don't have to worry.'

'And Dad . . . Oh, Alex, they're going to execute Dad.'

Tears rolled down Lily's cheeks. She made a heroic but unsuccessful attempt to wipe the mascara from her cheeks.

'Here . . .' Alex took the tissue from her and tenderly wiped away the smudged make-up.

'No, they're not, Lils. There's a huge rescue operation under way. Elite forces. The very best. Your dad's going to be back with you in no time.'

'It's okay,' she sniffed. 'It's . . . it's just that I've never been so scared in my life, Alex.'

Alex held the sobbing Lily tightly.

'I'm so sorry, Lils.' He took a step back. 'I'm out of time. I have to go.'

He kissed her gently on her head, moved her gleaming black hair out of her eyes.

'Hey, Lils. I think Jibril's taken quite a shine to you. Imagine, you could be Queen Lily of the House of Jordan. Has quite a ring to it.'

'My heart's already taken,' she said softly.

Alex strode out of the garden, leaving her staring after him with tears of undisguised longing in her eyes.

CHAPTER TWENTY-SEVEN

Tower of Alexander

Babel

Julia wandered out into the palatial gardens. She was still groggy. Every day, it seemed her memories of Lily and Jason were weakening.

She walked to the edge of the waterfall, then stepped back. She was sure she heard the sound of sobbing.

She moved nearer the conservatory of orange, lime, and lemon trees. The old abbess had her apron over her face, her shoulders heaving.

Julia went to her and tentatively placed her hand on the abbess's shoulder.

The nun looked up in horror. 'Go,' she whispered. 'You cannot see me like this. There will be retribution. Now, go!' The abbess ran into the tower as fast as her heavy legs could take her.

Alex and Weaver threw on the olive-green coveralls of the Jordanian astrophysicists.

'Storm, you, too.'

Storm pulled the uniform on over her jeans.

Weaver threw two official-looking passes to Alex. They were of the highest-level security clearance.

Weaver opened the small administrative room door, looked left and right down the corridor.

'Follow me.'

Fifty metres later, they arrived at a desk manned by eight Jordanian soldiers.

Weaver bowed his head in deference.

'Mr Weaver,' the colonel acknowledged.

'We are here on Professor Von Bechstein's direct orders.' Weaver passed over an official document in triplicate.

'We have been expecting you,' the colonel said.

Weaver nodded. 'Thank you, Colonel Habib. You know the astrophysicist Storm Mackenzie, of course.'

The colonel nodded. 'I have had the honour. You are from CERN.'

'I was, Colonel, sir.'

'My guard will escort you to the collider. We go no farther.'

'Understood.' Weaver passed him Alex's documentation.

The colonel stamped Alex's papers.

'Rather you than me. Some strange things happening down there.'

He beckoned two guards armed with machine-guns.

'Escort them to the supercollider.'

Julia sat up in her palatial bed, leaning against the pillows, flipping through the latest fashion magazines flown in from New York.

There was a knock on her door.

'I'm awake.'

The abbess entered with a tray of steaming hot coffee in a cafetière, eggs Benedict, and the usual medications.

'Your breakfast, Madam.'

Julia put down the magazine. 'Please stay,' she said. 'It's so lonely here with no one to talk to.' She patted the bed.

The abbess shook her head vehemently. 'It is not my place.'

'Adrian's left,' Julia said. 'And Guber with him. No one's going to tell on us.'

The abbess put her fingers to her lips and walked to the far side of the room. She pointed to the ceiling, the two bedside lamps, and the television.

'Take my breakfast outside,' Julia said gaily.

The abbess nodded. They walked to the far side of the gardens.

'They cannot monitor us here,' the nun whispered.

'Why are you so scared?' Julia asked.

She studied Abbess Helewis. She was very old, maybe even in her nineties.

'In my youth my parents forced me to witness atrocities – child sacrifices – things an eight-year-old girl should never see.'

She motioned to Julia to remain quiet.

'My family were Illuminati, my father the chief Warlock for the entire Western hemisphere. I became Satan's bride when I was eleven years old, and sold my soul. I have done things of such wickedness, such evil . . .'

She started to tremble violently.

'I had a son. They murdered him for one act of disobedience on my part. I knew I was trapped forever.

'And yet, there was a day, the only day of freedom I have ever known. A strange, unforgettable day. I was in a church. A priest stood over me. He placed his hand on my shoulder. His eyes were so kind, so compassionate. I felt goodness surge through my entire being. That is when I determined to do the only good act in my life, despite great peril to myself.'

She stopped abruptly and whispered, 'We are being monitored.'

Then, like the wind, she was gone.

Julia was awake. She heard the sound of voices drifting down from Adrian's palace, directly above hers. She moved nearer, straining to hear, then stopped in horror.

Ten chariots raced along the walls surrounding the palace. But the creatures driving them were at least thirteen feet in height, with orange hair . . . and *wings*.

Suddenly, Julia felt an overwhelming sense of evil. She walked quietly to the waterfall's edge.

Far below were thousands of people, naked, carrying rocks, being beaten at every turn by monstrous figures with thigh-length black braids, laughing lewdly.

She watched in horror as two monsters grabbed one of the walking dead, threw him to the ground, and sodomized him.

Julia clung on to the fountain and vomited, then ran to her room in horror and locked the doors.

She rifled frantically through her belongings until she found it: the plain silver cross that Polly had given her.

She stood silently in the darkness, trembling violently, holding the cross to her lips.

The guards stepped back, saluted, and marched back down the corridor. 'We're in,' Alex said.

'No,' Weaver said. 'Not quite.' He took a minuscule glass container from his pocket. 'Professor Von Bechstein's exact iris duplication.'

He removed the slide and held it up to the iris scanner at the first entrance to the supercollider. The thick steel door slid open.

'Go,' Weaver whispered.

The three barged into the anteroom just before the steel door shut.

'Now what?' said Storm.

'Two more doors,' Alex replied. 'Then the wormhole.'

Weaver, Storm, and Alex stared into the holy of holies of the supercollider, shielding their eyes from the blue lightning flashes. Two figures walked toward them: King Jibril and Xacheriel.

'You are absolutely sure, my friend?' said Jibril, grasping his arm. 'You don't have to do this.'

Xacheriel passed Jibril a small vial in a refrigerated container.

Jibril looked long and hard into Alex's eyes. 'This is the antidote to the Mark,' he said. 'It is essential that Julia be injected with it no later than one hour after she is injected with the Mark of Alexander. And this is adrenaline. To wake her.

'Her life is now in your hands alone, Alex. When you transfer through the portal, the night shift in Babylon, headed by Dr Markowitz, will be there to meet you. They are Resistance. They will hide you.'

'Time! Time!' Xacheriel said, clapping his hands.

Alex stared at the huge blue police box standing next to the supercollider.

Xacheriel smiled in triumph. 'My Tardis. Atlas and I have just returned from Malta and the Bermuda Triangle.'

Alex grinned, then zipped up his yellow hazmat suit and put on the goggles. Storm led him into the centre of the collider cylinder, giving him a weak smile before she returned to the others.

'In five.'

'God be with you, Alex Lane-Fox,' Jibril said softly.

Xacheriel bowed his head, then flung down the steel lever.

Antimatter and atoms started to surge and interact until Alex was no longer visible through the tornado of particles.

Three minutes and thirty-two seconds later, the collider slowed to a calm. Alex Lane-Fox had vanished.

Babylon
Supercollider Portal

Alex was thrust out onto the ground. He raised his head, his mind still reeling. Looking down at him were six forms in purple jumpsuits and goggles.

'Get him up,' one said. He removed his goggles. 'Doctor Len Markowitz, chief astrophysicist. Resister.'

He smiled wryly. 'Welcome to Nightmare Hall, Babylon. Julia St Cartier is being taken to receive the Mark as we speak. You have precisely one hour.'

He motioned to two men behind him. 'Get him to the safe house.

'An old friend is waiting for you.' He threw a set of handcuff keys to Alex, who caught them in one hand.

'You'll need those.' He passed Alex a circular perspex container. 'And this. Replica of Guber's iris. Call it a master

261

key. We have five minutes before the monsters check on us again. Run.'

Laboratory
Babylon

'She is sedated and sleeping,' Dr Gravenstein said, and ready to receive the Mark.' Adrian studied the unconscious Julia.

'She will wake not even realizing she has received the Mark of Alexander,' Dr Gravenstein added.

'Then prepare her to be my bride. She shall be named Olympias, after my predecessor Alexander the Great's mother. I will propose to her tonight. The royal wedding is set for seventy-two hours' time. It will be broadcast globally.'

He checked his watch.

'I have a pressing appointment I must attend.'

And Adrian vanished.

Golgotha
Jerusalem
3 a.m.

Lorcan De Molay paced impatiently up and down outside the Damascus Gate. Lawrence St Cartier walked toward him.

'Golgotha.' De Molay threw his cigar onto the pavement and crushed it with his shoe. 'A telephone pole . . . a Muslim cemetery.' His tone was drenched in sarcasm.

Lawrence studied the burned and mangled features shadowed by De Molay's cowl.

'You are grateful, no doubt, that you can possess the body of your handsome Adrian De Vere clone. Your unparalleled vanity was always your intrinsic weakness, Lucifer, even when I was you mentor.'

'Those days are long gone,' De Molay replied.

He spread his arms dramatically out to the deserted area surrounding them.

'The greatest victory of the Nazarene, memorialized by a car park and a *bus station*. How singularly appropriate. This is how my father is honoured on this mewling planet.'

'And the place of your greatest defeat, Lucifer.'

'*Golgotha*!' De Molay spat. 'The Nazarene!'

'You summoned me,' said Lawrence, 'regarding the final battle.'

An icy wind blew from the north, whipping De Molay's black Jesuit robes. 'Megiddo,' he said. 'Armageddon. John the Revelator . . . his wishful–'

'Not *wishful*, Lucifer. The facts.'

'I require the deeds of Armageddon, my old mentor. The consequences of my victory, or defeat, at Armageddon.'

'Precise and to the point,' Lawrence replied. He took two sealed deeds from his inner coat pocket. 'The edicts of the Royal House of Yehovah, sealed by Yehovah himself.'

De Molay snatched them hungrily. He tore open the first. 'In event of the victory of the Fallen . . .'

Slowly he drew his cinquedea across the second. 'In event of our defeat, I will be incarcerated for one thousand years.'

'In the bottomless pit,' Lawrence added.

'Oh, how his great mercies and compassions touch my heart. Mercies for all mankind, but not for Lucifer.'

De Molay's face contorted in bitterness. 'Tell my father I am deeply overcome by his mercies for Lucifer, Son of the Morning, and the Fallen.'

De Molay took out his cigar lighter, lit the edicts, and casually watched them burn. He discarded the ashes on the

263

floor of the dirt road and ground them in with his heel. He raised his gaze to Lawrence in rage.

'Gabriel delivered my ultimatum to my father?'

'Gabriel relayed to him your diabolical ravings, yes.'

'My father does not respond,' Lucifer snarled. 'Well and good. Let the second holocaust lay at his door.'

'You, above all, Lucifer, will know Yehovah does not succumb to your manipulation.'

'Even when it involves the utter annihilation of his mewling pets? Why he chose this miserable tract of dust is beyond all comprehension. The unparalleled enchantments of the streets of Rome, of Paris, the insatiable throbbing power of Manhattan, of London . . . but no, he covets this innocuous unpalatable excuse for a city. Jerusalem!' Lucifer hissed.

'No matter. Jason De Vere will be dead, gassed with sarin in front of six billion viewers, who will exult in his death.'

He smiled, but his eyes were as hard as steel.

'Relay to my father. Then my holocaust begins. How he will weep and rend his garments, Jether the Just.'

Lucifer stared up at the Place of the Skull, hatred in his eyes.

Then vanished.

CHAPTER TWENTY-EIGHT

Sewers

Babylon

Alex ran for his life, following the two swarthy-looking men through a concrete sewage tunnel for at least a mile. The first stopped suddenly and slipped through a small door mounted in the concrete. He motioned to the others to follow him.

They sprinted another five hundred metres, down seemingly endless metal stairs. Finally, they reached a steel door. Alex doubled over, panting. The first put his eye to the scanner, trembling.

The door swung open.

'We go,' he said in Russian.

Two hands grasped Alex and pulled him in. The door slammed, locking him inside.

A lex's eyes slowly grew accustomed to the darkness. He took a step backwards, staring in shock at the form in the shadows.

Liam Mercer, ex-SAS and Jason's bodyguard, stood directly in front of him.

'How how long have you been here?'Alex stammered.

'Ten seconds before you,' Mercer grinned.

Alex scanned the room, or rather cell.

Grotesque monsters and disfigured fifteen-foot forms were shackled to the walls, their limbs stretched to the limit as if on a torture rack.

'Michael,' a voice rasped.

A nine-foot form in the shadows limped into the light. His face was burned and disfigured, his wings seared, and his arms and legs covered with seeping bleeding sores.

'Astaroth,' Mercer whispered in horror.

'Michael.'

Trembling, Mercer reached out his hands to the unrecognisable form before him.

Astaroth fell to his knees, his head bowed.

Mercer knelt, clutching the bleeding, tormented Astaroth to his chest.

'*This* is what he has done to you?'

'My punishment. For betraying him. This hellhole. Wounds that never heal.'

Alex's mouth opened and shut. 'He . . . he . . . he's an . . .'

Mercer looked up. 'Yes. He's Angelic.'

Mercer held out his hand. 'The keys Markowitz gave you.'

Alex passed the set of keys to Mercer, his mouth still open as he stared in fascination at Astaroth.

Mercer studied the shackles around Astaroth's wrists, sifted swiftly through the keys, and unlocked the shackles around Astaroth's blistered wrists and ankles.

'We have forty-five minutes to get to Julia St Cartier, Astaroth.'

Astaroth nodded. 'We prisoners built every square inch of these foundations. We can enter through her private spa. It has two entrances. One is from the sewers.'

'Do you have the blueprints?' Alex asked.

'In here.' Astaroth tapped his head.

Mercer helped Astaroth to his feet. 'You have the antidote?' he asked Alex.

Alex held out the vial.

Mercer nodded. 'Let's go.'

Underground Sewers
Babylon

The three followed the underground sewers, almost gagging from the stench. Alex grimaced. 'How much longer?'

Astaroth checked the angelic writings on a steel door embedded in the tunnel.

'Thirty-five,' he said. 'The spa.'

He held his hand out. 'Keys.'

Mercer handed Astaroth the keys from Dr Markowitz.

Astaroth turned the first lock right, then a second directly underneath it to the left.

'Iris scan.'

Alex unscrewed the cylindrical jar. Mercer held the precise replica of Guber's right iris to the scanner. Another gift from Markowitz.

The door sprang open.

'We're in.'

The spa was empty and silent, but there were muffled voices coming from Julia's suite.

Mercer clicked a small device. The voices amplified.

'She will sleep for another hour.'

'Take your lunchbreak, Abbess, and after that do not leave her side.'

There was the sound of doors closing and a lock turning.

Astaroth motioned to Mercer, who swiftly placed a small device on each camera in the spa.

He signed the all-clear, then slowly opened the connecting door to Julia's private suite.

Julia lay on the bed in a deep, anaesthetized sleep.

Mercer signed to the others to stay back. He held up a bug scanner.

Five cameras, four audio transmitters, he mouthed.

And he vanished.

'Wha–?' Alex gasped.

'He's changed the frequency of his DNA, become invisible,' said Astaroth. 'He's adjusting the cameras and audio transmitters. All that anyone monitoring will see and hear will be precisely as before. I'll stay back. They won't see or hear you.'

Mercer rematerialized.

'We have thirty-five minutes precisely. Hurry.'

Alex walked towards Julia, who lay on her bed, seemingly dead to the world.

Mercer looked to Alex. 'You know how to deliver the antidote?'

Alex nodded. He took out the antidote, pressed the top, and a needle appeared.

He rubbed Julia's arm with an antiseptic swab, pricked her shoulder muscle with the needle, and pressed the plunger until the contents were fully discharged.

'We need to wake her,' said Mercer.

Alex held up the second phial. 'Adrenaline.'

Mercer grabbed the vial and the antiseptic swab from Alex and injected the second needle deftly into Julia's thigh.

'Quicker absorption.'

A few seconds later, Julia drew a long, gasping breath. She sat up abruptly.

Alex put his hand gently over her mouth. 'Aunt Jules, it's me, Alex!'

Julia stared at Alex and Mercer in sheer bewilderment.

Mercer swiftly emptied the entire contents of the pillbox on her nightstand into a plastic bag and filled it up with exact replicas of her tablets.

'They've been drugging you systematically, Aunt Jules,' said Alex.

Finally Julia managed to speak. 'But . . . they said Jason was psychotic; that he was trying to kill me.'

'All Adrian's lies.'

Julia started to cry in confusion.

A form materialized at her bedside. Now it was Alex's turn to stare in disbelief.

'Time travel, my dear boy,' said Lawrence St Cartier crisply. 'The simplest exercise in the world.'

He nodded to Astaroth and Mercer in acknowledgement, then turned to Julia

'Unc– Uncle Lawrence,' she stammered.

Lawrence held her hand gently.

'Julia, my dear,' he said softly. 'Listen to me very carefully. Your life depends on it.'

Ten Minutes Later

'Rebekah Weiss saved your life,' Lawrence explained. 'Jason was forced to leave you there. Adrian organized the greatest manhunt the world has ever seen – his retribution.'

'So . . . so . . . Jason *isn't* psychotic?'

'Stubborn and, in the words of your late mother, *bloody awkward*, but psychotic? Never! Indeed, Jason De Vere is the most pragmatic, grounded man I know. He loves you, Julia. He always has.

'Adrian, on the other hand, is not who he seems. In less than seventy-two hours, Adrian De Vere will execute Jason in cold blood.'

Julia swayed in shock, tears running down her cheeks.

'Sarin gas,' Lawrence continued. 'He is a monster – nothing less. It is not the time to reveal anything further, only to say that your life lies in the hands of the most evil, demonic being that exists. Believe *nothing* they tell you. They expect you to be compliant now that you have taken the Mark of Alexander.

'It's a matter of life and death: *your* life or *your* death. Be a good girl. Are you paying attention?'

Julia nodded, her eyes locked on to Lawrence.

'You will accept Adrian De Vere's proposal of marriage when he returns tonight. You have only one request.'

Julia nodded.

'Not a demand. A request.'

'What if Adrian refuses?' she asked.

'Then you feign complete hysteria. You have to do this one thing, Julia.'

'I have to request,' she said, 'that in proxy for my late father, Lawrence St Cartier, my uncle and only living male relative, gives me away.'

'Good girl.'

'But he'll never agree to that.'

'Oh, but he *will*, my dear. He will indeed. You have your mother's genes.'

Tears welled up in Julia's eyes. She held them back.

'Yes, she was the ultimate performer.' She smiled weakly.

270

'Lola was strong. Tenacious. Courageous. You are so like her. You have to play their sinister game every step of the way. You falter once, make *one* mistake, they *will* kill you.'

He kissed her tenderly on her head.

'Julia St Cartier, give the performance of a lifetime. You're a brave woman. You always have been.'

They embraced.

'I'm so proud of you,' he said. 'Now, remember, once the ceremony is over, Adrian will return straight to Jerusalem. You will follow.'

'And the wedding night?' Julia shook with revulsion.

Lawrence placed gentle hands on her shoulders and looked into her eyes. 'I have it in hand. Trust me, he will be in no state to consummate your marriage. Be brave. Be strong. The nightmare is almost at an end.

'Now, remember,' he urged, 'take the placebos in the pillbox. They are magnesium citrate. Here are herbal sedatives that will give you the appearance of being drugged, but they will not impair your thought process. I will be there to protect you.'

He looked up at the others. 'We have to leave.'

Thirty seconds later, Julia lay alone in her room. Steeling herself for the arrival of the monster who would propose to her that night.

Resistance Safe House
Babylon

'Alex, stay back a moment. I will escort you back to Doctor Markowitz. I have business to attend. Michael and Astaroth have minutes to escape.'

Alex stood back in the sewers, then succumbed to the overwhelming urge to turn around at the precise moment that Lawrence transformed into Jether. He rubbed his eyes.

Liam Mercer was literally morphing into a nine-foot angelic being, massive seraph wings protruding from his spine.

'You – you . . . I – I'm hallucinating.'

Michael looked over to Alex, laughing, his dimples showing.

'Alexander Lane Fox, son of courage. Yes, I'm angelic.'

'You, Alex,' said Jether, 'are looking into the face of Chief Prince Michael, Archangel, Commander of the Royal Armies of the Royal House of Yehovah.'

Alex picked up his Xphone.

'No photographs, Alex,' Jether declared in a voice like steel. 'Now stay back.'

'Jether.' Michael embraced him fiercely.

'Michael the Valiant. Yehovah be with you.'

'Astaroth,' Jether said.

Astaroth looked down at the floor. Jether walked over to him, and slowly Astaroth raised his gaze.

'You were once Michael's second-in-command.'

He took out a bottle of liniment and rubbed it on Astaroth's open sores. Instantly, Astaroth became whole.

Jether put his hand in the folds of his robes and took out a golden ring with the seal of the Royal House of Yehovah embossed on it. 'By the authority of the Royal House of Yehovah, you are to be reinstated, Astaroth.'

Slowly he placed the ring on Astaroth's ring finger. 'You will return with Michael to the First Heaven.'

'I can't . . .' Tears ran down Astaroth's cheeks. 'I entered the Portal of Shinar. I am earthbound for eternity.'

Jether smiled and removed a handkerchief from his robes and carefully unwrapped it. In the centre of the cloth lay a burning, fiery ruby some three inches in diameter.

Michael gasped.

Jether nodded.

'It is from Yehovah's ephod. Michael, use it only in times of direst need.'

Jether held the blazing ruby to Astaroth's heart.

Instantly, a shimmering blue arc of lightnings enveloped Astaroth's entire body.

Astaroth fell to his knees, unable to stand, as the intense lightning surged through every cell of his being.

'Your DNA frequencies are restored to their pre-banishment angelic state.' Jether leaned over and anointed Astaroth on the forehead.

'Your nightmare is finally over. Arise, Prince Astaroth of the Royal House of Yehovah. Serve your commander well. Now, go, before the dawn.'

'Alex,' Lawrence said, 'we have twenty minutes to get back to the supercollider.'

'I'm not going back, Professor. I can't. I *have* to document what's going on underground. The world has to see what monsters they are. It's the least I can do for my grandmother. You can't *make* me.'

Lawrence sighed deeply.

'Like your mother, like your grandmother.' Lawrence sighed.

'Alex Lane-Fox, do you think I didn't *know* when we sent you here that you wouldn't be going back? Dr Anders surgically implanted a nano-camera transmitter – the same that Julia wears – when you were under sedation during your brief physical examination in Jordan. Weaver will activate the camera and microphone in precisely forty minutes from now. We will see and hear exactly what you see.

'Stay close to the Resisters. The Ghost will come for you. Be vigilant. Be circumspect. This is like nothing you've ever experienced before. These are *not* the Turks, Alex.'

Lawrence looked intensely into Alex's eyes.

'You are dealing with supernatural beings of untold power

273

and aeons of evil. You are in far over your brilliant, intrepid head.'

Lawrence sighed deeply and turned to his right.

'You can come out now. He's staying, as we both knew he would.'

A figure walked out of the shadows.

It was Nick.

CHAPTER TWENTY-NINE

Adrian De Vere's Suite

Tower of Alexander

Charsoc stood silently at the window. Adrian De Vere lay deeply asleep on the four-poster bed. Suddenly, his body started to oscillate, and an angelic form rose up from it, hovering directly above the sleeping form.

Lucifer stood to his full nine feet of height. His face, arms, and thighs were still horrifically burned from the Stones of Fire, but his ebony hair and black seraph wings had grown back.

He thrust his long fingers through his hair and smiled.

'Matter,' he hissed, looking disdainfully at the inert form on the bed.

'The High Council is prepared,' Charsoc said. 'They await you in the vortex, Your Excellency.'

Vortex
Tower of Alexander

Lucifer stood, his six black seraph wings outstretched, facing the High Council.

He studied the Fallen before him: the Warlocks of the West, the Twins of Malfecium, the Witches of Ishtar, the Shaman Kings.

Lucifer paced the room. 'The Tower of Alexander is erected in the exact place where the Tower of Babel stood. Above us lies the very reason that the Tower of Babel was destroyed. The Portal of Shinar; one of the major portals with access to the First Heaven. The only portal that is vulnerable – its force field between the land of men and the Second Heaven ruptured, torn' – Lucifer sat on his throne, stroking his new wolf's coarse white fur – 'in the Tower of Babel–Nephilim fiasco.'

A faint smile flickered on his lips. 'Yehovah confused their languages by day.' He held out his hand to his cupbearer. 'By night, Michael and his armies overthrew our battalions, took control of Shinar, and sealed the portal.'

He winced at the memory of his defeat, then snatched the golden goblet from his trembling cupbearer. 'The inter-dimensional force field was permanently ruptured in the battle.' His fingers caressed the rim of the goblet.

'We reversed the restructuring process once before, from the Second Heaven down to Earth. Now we shall endeavour to do the same, this time from Earth to the Second Heaven, and make our entry through the rupture in the field.'

'But our frequencies are permanently changed, your Majesty.' Charsoc whispered. 'We have no ability to travel beyond the Kármán Line.'

'Am I a *simpleton*, Charsoc?' Lucifer hissed.

Lucifer gestured to the Twins of Malfecium.

'Maelageor!' Charsoc bowed low. 'The frequencies, Your Excellency. His Majesty summons Maelageor, first twin of Malfecium.'

Maelageor bowed deeply to Lucifer. 'Your Majesty, as you are well aware, there has been a fundamental shift in

276

the Fallen's DNA since our banishment to this planet.' He bowed again. 'Whereas our frequencies previously were set to access the First and Second Heavens, our DNA has been reprogrammed by the Nazarene. We, the Fallen, no longer possess the capacity to rise above the atmosphere of Earth. However, if we can gain access to *unfallen* angelic DNA, it is entirely feasible that we could duplicate the Mark of Alexander . . .'

Lucifer's eyes gleamed with the revelation.

'But in *reverse*.' Lucifer finished Maelageor's sentence.

'Indeed, Your Excellency. Instead of inserted Nephilim DNA to rewrite the human genetic code – the process we used in the Mark of Alexander – if we use DNA originating from a *perfect angelic code*, we can isolate the frequency gene and then programme it to rewrite *our* fallen genetic code. The challenge we face is obtaining access to *unfallen* angelic DNA.'

Marduk slunk towards the throne. He held out a missive to Lucifer.

Lucifer tore it open, scanned it, and then walked slowly to the monstrous crystal dome that housed the Bells of Limbo. Staring out over the fortress of Babel, he caressed the missive in his hands.

He turned to the Council.

'I am almost tempted to convert.'

He held the missive high.

'It seems today that even *Lucifer's* prayers are answered. We have a visitor. A trespasser; one who is the bearer of unfallen angelic DNA, here in Babel.'

His lips curled in a malevolent smile.

'Search every inch of Babel for my brother. Find him. Then bring him directly to me!'

He swung around to Charsoc, his eyes blazing with fervour.

'Chief Prince Michael is here!'

Julia sat staring with dead eyes at her reflection in the ornate French mirror. She ran her hand lightly over the enormous bouquet of exquisite pale-pink and coral peonies – her wedding bouquet, flown in from Regent Street in London that morning.

Methodically she put on her primer, then her foundation, touched up her brows and eyeliner, and placed the finishing touches of pale-pink blusher onto her high cheekbones. She steeled herself. She had to get through the ceremony without giving Adrian the slightest indication that she was fully *compos mentis*.

The abbess entered, holding her freshly steamed wedding dress.

'Oh, Madam Julia,' she gasped, 'it is so beautiful!'

Julia rose and walked over to the abbess. Her wedding dress was exquisite, classical – white satin, taffeta, and silk chiffon, with a low-cut back.

The sweeping skirt of tiers of ruffles and lace fell to the floor; boleros, capes, and veils draped themselves over a bustier with an off-the-shoulder cut. Sewn with silk and platinum thread, it was timeless.

'I'm ready,' Julia said softly.

The abbess helped her into the white creation and arranged the long train.

Julia stared at herself in the mirror.

The classic fairy-tale bride – about to be wedded to consummate evil.

The monster.

'I need to be alone, Abbess.'

With a nod, the abbess checked that the medication dose was gone.

'You've had your medication. Good. You have twenty minutes before the carriage arrives to take you to the shore.' The abbess smiled almost tenderly. 'You look exquisitely beautiful, Madam Julia.'

And with that, the abbess left, softly closing the doors to the palatial suite behind her.

Julia breathed in and took out two of the herbal sedatives Lawrence had given her. She drank them down with the Perrier water on her right.

They would give her the appearance of still being heavily drugged.

'C'mon, girl,' she murmured to herself. 'You were the lead in the college plays.'

She put on her lipstick, spritzed her face with setting spray.

She placed the veil with the glittering diamond tiara on her head, then covered her face with the veil.

Royal Wedding
Tiberias

The silver-and-white-striped pavilion stretched along the shores of Galilee for fully half a mile to cater for the five thousand dignitaries who had flown in on twenty-four hours' notice from every corner of the Axis Ten kingdom.

Inside the pavilion was a vast expanse of white tables and blue Tiffany Parisian tablecloths, adorned with the finest crystal stemware and Limoges china. No expense had been spared. Blossoming peonies in silver urns were the centrepiece for each table. It was a sight worthy of a Hans Christian Andersen fairy tale.

Julia couldn't help recalling her own tiny wedding to Jason.

They had been so young. Jason wasn't eligible for his trust fund at the time and was supremely independent of his family, as always. They had been married at a Justice of the Peace's office in New Jersey, then gone out to party with their few closest friends.

Their wedding night was spent with giggles and laughter, trying to fit in a three-quarter-size bed, with six-foot Jason complaining the whole time.

But they were finally together. And that was their joy.

Julia disembarked from the golden carriage pulled by eight white Arab stallions and walked toward the Garden of Ceremony, her train carried by six eight-year-old bridesmaids.

Xavier Chessler, dapper as always, hurried over to her side.

'I have the rings.' Chessler beamed. 'Highest viewing statistics in the history of broadcasting, my dear. Are you ready?'

Julia nodded. 'Where's Uncle Lawrence?'

Chessler's mouth tightened. 'Your uncle is waiting for you.'

Julia turned, and her whole body relaxed.

There stood Lawrence St Cartier, immaculately attired in an ivory suit and paisley cravat, with a white Panama hat and cane.

'Ah, my beautiful niece. You look divine.'

Adrian stood twenty metres down the garden aisle, in deep conversation with Kester Von Slagel.

Julia studied Adrian. *The monster*.

Handsome as always, his ebony hair in an elegant cut. Well preserved tan. Perfectly veneered teeth.

Today he wore a soft-grey morning suit of wool, cashmere, and diamonds, with a silver cravat, an Audemars Piguet watch, and a pair of elegant men's dress shoes studded with full-cut round white diamonds. The embodiment of modern royalty.

He caught her eye and smiled.

The monster, Julia thought, smiling back.

280

Tomorrow, he would execute his own brother.

She was about to become the Bride of Frankenstein.

The hundred-piece orchestra, flown in from Vienna, began to play.

'Take my arm.' Lawrence sneezed, then sneezed again. 'Mandragora,' he muttered. 'He must have showered in it just to rile me.'

Julia frowned. Kester Von Slagel was wearing an electric-pink tuxedo with a fuchsia cravat under a voluminous cerise- and saffron-striped robe, and a turban to match. She caught Lawrence's eye, and they erupted in laughter.

'How does he hold his hands up with the weight of those jewels?' Julia whispered.

'With great difficulty, my dear,' Lawrence remarked drily.

Lawrence took Julia's elbow and started to walk her up the aisle.

'To your right, the kings and queens of Norway, Belgium, and Denmark, the Prime Minister of the United Kingdom; to your left, the President and First Lady of the United States. The row behind them is entirely Secret Service, I might add. Charles and Diana's wedding pales by comparison. We've had to keep over a thousand press photographers fifty metres away, and the paparazzi even further.'

They walked slowly up the aisle.

Towards the monster.

Julia stopped mid-step.

'Courage, dear heart. Ten minutes, and the ceremony's over and the champagne starts flowing. Which, I might add, was flown in at dawn from the Rhône. The plan to rescue you, and Jason, is in motion. Give the performance of your life.'

Julia was now only five steps away from Adrian.

Lawrence took both Julia's hands in his and kissed them, then delivered her into his strong grasp.

'Professor Lawrence St Cartier,' Adrian said icily.

'Your Excellency.'

'You look beautiful, Julia.' Adrian smiled. 'You make me proud.' He turned to Chessler.

'Chessler, you have the rings?'

'I have the rings unless Liberace here has them.'

Von Slagel gave Chessler an icy stare and continued to polish his vermilion index-finger ring with vigour.

'Well, let's get on with it,' Adrian declared. 'We've an intense schedule tomorrow.'

An execution, Julia thought silently.

She caught herself though, and smiled softly through her veil at Adrian.

'Let's get this over, Julia, darling.' Lawrence kissed her again, then moved to the front row and sat down beside Von Slagel. He held his handkerchief to his nostrils.

'Did you have to *shower* in it, Charsoc?'

Charsoc smiled. 'Mandragora. I like to be extremely clean, Jether.'

'Clean, and quite dashing in pink, I must say. There's so much material, you must have cleaned out the whole of southern England's Oxfam charity shops.'

Charsoc glared at him from under newly waxed eyebrows.

'It's Turkish. Expensive,' he hissed. 'Anyway, you look as if you've just arrived back from Kenya in the fifties.' He gave a self-satisfied smirk. 'What are you doing here?'

'I would think it quite evident. My niece is betrothed and about to be married. Now, could you please move your carpetbag?'

Charsoc took out a handful of chocolate toffees, put four in his mouth, and sucked loudly on them.

'Couldn't you wait till the ceremony is finished?' said Lawrence.

'My mouth is dry. I detest this heat. This parched tract

of dust sends my blood pressure spiralling.' Charsoc uncapped a green bottle and threw three tablets into his mouth.

'I have it on good account that Xacheriel has now built his own Tardis,' he said.

'Why? Do *you* want it? For your carpetbag?' Lawrence studied Charsoc's attire. 'Although you *could* fit it under that monstrosity of a turban you're wearing.'

'Why did you come, Jether?' Charsoc hissed. 'You do *nothing* without an agenda.'

'My agenda is solely the well-being of my niece.' Jether stared out at the Sea of Galilee. 'And one other, Charsoc the Dark.'

Charsoc turned, impeded by his voluminous robes.

He gave Jether an icy stare.

Black Site
Undisclosed Location
Israel

Jason was shackled to the wall, his eyes taped open, while guards brought in a digital screen. 'A gift from your brother,' one of the guards laughed. 'Your ex-wife's going to get her comeuppance tonight, alright.'

He flipped a switch. 'Just in time for the holy nuptials.'

Jason watched the screen as a Jesuit priest stepped forward.

'I, Adrian De Vere, take you, Julia Lola St Cartier, to be my wife. I promise to be true to you in good times and in bad, in sickness and in health. I will love you and honour you all the days of my life.'

Adrian lifted Julia's veil and kissed her perfunctorily on the mouth. He turned her to the audience.

'I present my royal bride, Queen Olympias II.'

283

The guard ripped the tape from Jason's eyes.

'Sweet dreams, De Vere.'

Tiberias

There was a dazzling flurry of light as hundreds of photographers' cameras flashed simultaneously. The band struck up Mendelssohn's *Wedding March* as Adrian's Secret Service minders escorted Adrian and Julia down a path littered with fresh peach and pink peonies, and confetti, through the marquee over to the head table that lay under the pavilion.

Xavier Chessler picked up the microphone.

'Ahem.'

Almost instantly the thousands of attendees fell silent.

'It is my great honour, having known the groom since he was a babe in arms, to witness today the joining of a unique man and a unique woman in matrimony.'

He turned to the couple.

'His Royal Majesty Alexander the Great and his bride, Queen Olympias II.'

He raised a glass of champagne.

The sound of champagne bottles popping filled the marquee.

'A toast to the royal bridal couple.'

Immediately, the thousands of dignitaries rose, lifting their glasses, toasting the bridal couple.

'As His Majesty is without doubt far more well versed in addressing his subjects,' Chessler continued, 'it is my great honour and privilege to hand over the proceedings directly to His Royal Majesty, King Alexander the Great.'

Adrian rose. The guests gave a standing ovation. Adrian raised both his hands, but the ovation continued.

Finally, he spoke. 'Thank you.' He raised his hands higher

to quieten the applause. 'Thank you. Today, Julia St Cartier and I came together in matrimony to celebrate our love.'

He raised a glass of champagne to Julia.

'I have known Julia St Cartier for twenty-five years.' He smiled his charming smile and looked down tenderly at Julia.

A titter of polite laughter broke out among the tables.

'. . . as she knew me when I was a boy of nineteen. My sorrow at the loss of my first wife, Melissa Vane Templar, cannot be expressed in words. But today I have a second chance at happiness.'

Adrian leaned over and kissed Julia full on the lips.

'Julia St Cartier, a woman I have admired from up close and afar for over two decades. A woman of unique spirit, kindness, generosity, intelligence, and creative genius. That she accepted my marriage proposal and . . .'

Adrian hesitated and started to unknot his tie. 'It is warm in here, isn't it?'

Julia watched, perplexed, as perspiration poured from his forehead. He coughed, then turned to Chessler.

'The air-conditioning, please.'

Chessler frowned. It was already cool, verging on chilly, in the pavilion.

'We have postponed our honeymoon and will be travelling back to Jerusalem to conclude business at hand. But first, I have a gift for my bride.'

Chessler handed him a large pale-pink box. Adrian opened it slowly.

Gasps of wonder came from all around the pavilion as he held up an exquisite tiara – five huge aquamarines in an ornate diamond surround.

Julia removed her veil, and Adrian placed the stunning tiara on her gleaming blond hair.

'Ladies and gentlemen, my queen, Olympias II.'

Adrian started to cough. Chessler passed him a handkerchief, and he wiped the perspiration from his forehead. His eyes were glazed.

Van Slagel frowned as Adrian started to gasp.

'Remove the crowd,' Von Slagel hissed to Chessler. 'Any excuse – *now*!'

Chessler grabbed the microphone. 'I apologize, ladies and gentlemen. We have just received news of an imminent terrorist attack on the pavilion. We need you to evacuate immediately.'

Security in black militia uniforms swarmed between the tables, escorting the alarmed royalty and politicians out onto the helipads.

Julia stared at Adrian, transfixed. His eyes looked drugged. He flung off his morning jacket and wove unsteadily through the crowds rushing out of the pavilion. He stumbled towards the shore of Galilee, retching.

She rose as though to go after him, but Lawrence lightly took her elbow. He shook his head.

'Abbess Helewis, please escort Her Royal Highness to her quarters immediately.'

The pavilion was almost emptied.

Charsoc stood to his full height.

'What have you *done*, Jether?' he spat. 'What sordid magic is being spun?'

'It is no magic, Charsoc the Dark. These are the shores the Nazarene walked for years.'

Charsoc watched as Adrian stumbled to his knees on the sand of Galilee, clawing at his tie, pulling it off, then tearing his shirt off his torso, gasping for breath as his face hit the sand.

Von Slagel rushed over.

'Baron, the ambulance helicopter is two minutes away,' said Charsoc, then snarled, 'This is no *heart attack*.'

'No,' Jether said softly. 'There was an addendum in the

title deeds you witnessed all those aeons ago. More small print. Ninety-two weeks. The Great Tribulation started today.'

'It is the Nazarene,' Charsoc hissed, starting to choke. 'His presence.'

'Your choice of venue was somewhat lacking in foresight, don't you think?'

'The prophet Daniel!' Charsoc hissed. 'What is the date?'

'Three-and-a-half years since the beginning of the seven-year Tribulation scribed in the Apocalypse of St John began. Today heralds the Great Tribulation. From this day onward, the Nazarene walks the Earth once more.'

Jether studied his watch.

'I'd say your master has about eight minutes before full impact.'

Jether walked toward the shore, watching Adrian writhe dementedly in the sand.

Charsoc started to retch, his head on the table. Chessler stared at Lawrence with unveiled hatred as he stumbled to his knees.

Lawrence stood, bowed to both, and vanished.

Adrian lay on the shore, clutching his chest, still retching as he was placed on a stretcher and whisked away to the ambulance helicopter.

Six Hours Later

Julia tossed and turned in a restless sleep. A soft light flashed through the window. She slid out of the silk sheets, placed her wrap over her shoulders, and opened the windows to catch the sea breeze.

She frowned.

About forty metres away, a figure appeared on the water.

She rubbed her eyes. It had been such a tense, exhausting day.

Julia opened both windows. Suddenly, the light in her room turned on.

The abbess slammed the windows shut and drew the curtains. She raised both hands, trembling in terror.

'Go back to bed, Your Highness.' Her voice rose in pitch. 'Go back to bed. Now. I beg you.'

Julia allowed the abbess to tuck her into bed like a little girl. Then the abbess turned off the lights and locked the door.

Julia lay in the darkness, terrified, yet strangely magnetized by something . . . someone. She *had* to go to the shore.

She pulled her silk robe around her, climbed out through the full-length window, and walked past the pavilion, over the rocks, until she stood beside the rippling waters of the Sea of Galilee.

She surveyed the horizon. Far away in the distance, she saw the white figure standing on the water.

Julia rubbed her eyes again. She must be hallucinating from the medications she had been given. The figure was walking across the water, heading straight towards her.

She tried to turn back, but it was as though a heavy, warm liniment were being poured from the crown of her head through every fibre of her body. She fell to her knees as an overwhelming peace filled her entire being. It was as though every part of her was being cushioned in the softest bed of chamomile and jasmine. Her eyes felt so heavy.

She sank onto the sand, breathing out the trauma of the past months, breathing in a peace that was unfathomable.

Her eyes were almost closed. The white figure was only a few paces away from her.

She stared, drawn by the young man's features. Shoulder-length dark hair. High cheekbones. His face radiated a warm, unearthly light.

Gradually, the light began to fade.

'Julia.' The tones reverberated through her. 'Julia St Cartier.'

And then he smiled. Her heart started to well up with a joy that she'd long forgotten. She smiled back up at him, knowing somehow that he wanted her to reach out her hand. Slowly, she held out her hand to him as the young man knelt beside her.

'These are for you.' He placed a small bunch of flowers in her hand. The rose of Sharon. Then he laid his hand softly on her head.

'Who are you?' Julia murmured.

His eyes seemed filled with limitless understanding, with overwhelming love.

As she felt herself falling into a strange twilight between sleeping and waking, she could faintly hear his whisper.

'I am the Prince of Peace.'

CHAPTER THIRTY

Tiberias

Dawn

Julia woke up with a start. There was a loud, insistent knocking on her door. She looked at the time – 5 a.m. The helicopter was flying her to Jerusalem in an hour. To watch the execution of Jason De Vere by the monster.

Panic started to flood her chest.

What strange dreams in the night . . .

She turned her face to the bedside table . . . and stared in shock. The bunch of purple flowers lay beautiful, fragrant, and untouched.

'Your Highness!' The abbess entered.

Julia shook her head groggily as the abbess looked over to the flowers.

'What are they, Abbess?'

'They are the rose of Sharon,' the abbess answered softly.

Julia bit her lip in ecstasy. That same overwhelming peace flooded her entire being. The young man who was Peace – it hadn't been just a dream.

She caressed the flowers with her hands and drank in their fragrance.

'Your Highness's dress is freshly pressed, awaiting you in your dressing suite. We leave for Jerusalem in an hour.'

Holy of Holies, Third Temple
Jerusalem
2.50 p.m.

The thrones were all filled. Xavier Chessler sat to Alexander's left. Julia, now Queen Olympias II, sat to his right. Her blonde hair was swept into a chignon. She wore a pared-down pink dress of pure silk that fell to mid-calf. Her face was an impassive mask.

The Temple fell silent as five militiamen entered, dragging the High Priest. Though emaciated, he was still clothed in his Temple regalia.

Directly after him followed more militiamen, shoving Jason ahead of them. He was now freshly shaven, his hair washed and cut, and dressed in an Armani suit with white shirt and silver cufflinks.

Jason . . . Oh, Jason! Julia closed her eyes, holding back her stinging tears with sheer tenacity, her heart pounding with such intensity that she thought she would faint.

Jason stopped mid-stride to stare in shock and horror at Julia.

'Julia!' he cried.

Julia willed herself to stare straight ahead, as though in a drugged stupor. This had to be the performance of her life.

'*You've drugged her, you bastard*!' Jason screamed at Adrian.

'No, brother, she is one of us now. She has taken the Mark.' Adrian smiled, relishing Jason's pain. 'Escort my brother to the dais.'

Julia watched, her face as impassive as a Madame Tussaud's wax effigy as the High Priest and Jason were taken unceremoniously to the dais and seated, in full view of the thrones, and the worldwide television and internet audience.

Adrian turned to Chessler. 'Give them our *hors d'oeuvre*,' he said.

Chessler nodded to Guber. Guber disappeared and returned with a prisoner in shackles.

The prisoner was stripped naked and hauled savagely into the glass containment area.

The doors slid closed.

Julia leaned over to Adrian. The Monster.

'Feel faint,' she whispered.

The Monster laid his hand on hers.

'Close your eyes, darling.'

Julia bowed her head and closed her eyes in relief.

An unseen, colourless gas started to fill the glass cell.

The man started to shake in paroxysms. Then green and yellow vomit erupted from his mouth and nostrils.

Jason leaned over and he, too, vomited. He clenched his fists. The High Priest laid a frail hand on his arm.

'They can kill our bodies, my son,' he whispered, 'but not our souls.'

He raised his noble face to the ceiling and started to pray in Hebrew under his breath.

'How are you so calm?' Jason said in an undertone. 'There must be some way we can fight them.'

'Ah, my son, it is not our way.'

'Didn't you learn *anything* from the Holocaust? *Fight*!'

Jason punched the first militiamen in the face with his shackled hands, then kicked the second in the groin.

Adrian sighed theatrically. 'Tut-tut, big brother. Chain him to the chair and force him to watch.'

A third soldier put Jason in a headlock.

Jason watched as the naked man behind the glass urinated and defecated uncontrollably. Screaming noiselessly in agony, he clawed in desperation at the glass.

Minutes went by, and the prisoner's entire body went limp. Adrian nodded, and a soldier pressed a remote. Four soldiers in hazmat gear wrapped the body in foil and carried it out on a stretcher.

Adrian lifted his sceptre, then walked over and kissed Jason on both cheeks. He turned to the television cameras.

'I would show my magnanimity even now that I forgive my brother. But unfortunately, justice and world opinion demands his death.'

The militiamen started to manhandle the High Priest toward the glass cell.

He looked at them with immense pity. 'It is not necessary.'

He turned back to Jason and looked at him with intense compassion. 'Courage, my son,' he said.

The High Priest walked onto the steps, holding his noble head high, his hands trembling. He paused and steadied himself.

He looked back at Jason, then stepped in. The glass doors slid shut.

Jason gripped the hands of the chair in sheer rage, staring at Julia, who was white as a sheet.

'*He's a priest, God damn you*!' he screamed at Adrian. 'What have you done to Julia?'

Instantly his mouth was taped.

Suddenly, there was an ear-splitting crashing sound as the Temple's enormous glass windows shattered. Blinding lights and smoke flashed from hundreds of deafening stun grenades and EG18X military smoke grenades. Through the intense fog of smoke, militiamen rappelled from the soaring glass windows, light flashing from their sub-machine-guns.

Not one or ten or fifty, but hundreds of commandos in

black uniforms unclipped from their lines. Adrian stared in horror as another wave of militia rappelled down. Then another.

They yelled as one in Russian: '*Kontsa Dney*.'

'Mercenaries!' Chessler whispered in horror.

'Where are our security?' Adrian yelled as the militia hauled Kurt Guber to his feet, disarmed him and handcuffed his hands behind his back at gunpoint.

One of the commandos stood directly in front of Adrian, his head covered in a black balaclava, his weapon trained on Chessler.

'Dead,' he said in a Hebrew accent. 'All dead.'

He shouted in Hebrew to a commando, who ran towards Julia, hauled her to her feet, and ran, pulling her after him towards the Temple's eastern entrance.

Chessler reached for his revolver and fired a shot straight through the head of the man in the balaclava. Then another.

'You can't kill a ghost,' the commando in front of Adrian said softly. 'We are all sealed.'

He pointed to the glass dome. Militiamen in hazmat suits had broken through the glass, placed the High Priest on a gurney, and were running him out through the eastern entrance.

Adrian started to transform into his angelic form, his limbs trembling violently. Chessler and the dignitaries stared mesmerized as Adrian transformed into a nine-foot being with frightful burn scars covering much of his skin.

His black wings spread. His ebony hair fell past his waist. His scarred and mangled face began to burn from the inside.

'The Seal,' Lucifer whispered in agony. 'You wear the Seal. The Revelator!' he hissed at the Ghost.

'Yes. We are the 144,000 sealed in the Apocalypse of St John the Revelator.' The Ghost stood unafraid. 'You have no power over me, Son of Perdition.'

A soldier removed a rubber clasp from his shoelace and opened it, revealing a handcuff key. He swiftly removed the tape from Jason's mouth and undid the handcuffs.

'We're Resistance. There's a van waiting for you.'

Four militiamen grabbed Jason and ran him through the stunned crowd, out into the streets of Jerusalem. They bundled him and Julia into a black van. Its tyres screeched as it accelerated into a back road, heading straight for the main Jerusalem–Tel Aviv road with a roar and a squeal of tyres.

Van
Jerusalem

'Close shave, Jason, my boy,' Lawrence said, grinning. 'Operation End of Days went without a hitch.'

He kissed Julia on both cheeks.

'Julia, my beloved niece. Superb performance, my dear.'

'Oh god, you're alive, Julia!' Jason stared at her in wonder.

He kissed her passionately on the mouth.

'Oh god,' he uttered in wonder. '*I'm* alive.'

'Of course you're alive, Jason.' Lawrence lit his pipe. 'You didn't think we'd leave you both there, did you?'

Jason's and Julia's fingers intertwined.

'But Adrian said you – you'd received the Mark.'

Julia shook her head.

'Alex saved my life. He injected me with the antidote.'

'*Alex?*'

Lawrence held out a hip flask and a mobile phone.

'Isle of Islay; thought you might need it.'

Jason grabbed the phone, then the hip flask, and took a swig, followed by a longer one. 'Where are we going?'

'We have to get you lovebirds out of Israel. But first, there is someone you need to meet.'

295

Jason frowned. 'We've no time.'

'Trust me, Jason.'

The van stopped with a jolt.

Two men in militia uniforms opened the back doors of the van. Seven other black vans were lined up on the top ridge of Mevaseret Zion. The men pulled their balaclavas off their heads, revealing handsome Israeli features. Both had cropped dark hair.

Jason, Julia, and the Professor climbed out onto the tarmac.

The first soldier grinned and wrapped Lawrence in a bear hug.

'Professor,' he said in a thick Hebrew accent. 'Welcome to our world. Look at the view.'

They stood on the mountain ridge, staring at the vast expanse of Jerusalem before them in the far distance.

'Jerusalem will always be ours.'

'Where are we?' Jason asked.

'Mevaserat Zion; ten kilometres from Jerusalem,' Lawrence answered. He turned to the young Israeli.

'He is here?' asked Lawrence.

The young man nodded.

'He is here. Waiting for him.' He gestured to Jason, then turned to him.

'The Ghost awaits your company, Mr De Vere.'

'The – the Ghost?' his companion stammered. 'But *no one* ever meets the Ghost.'

The Israeli soldier slapped his companion's head affectionately.

'Have *you* ever seen his face?'

The soldier grinned again. 'No one knows the Ghost's identity. It's safer for him and us that way.'

'I need to thank him,' said Jason. Lawrence turned to Jason.

'Everything you are about to hear is the truth, Jason. I

296

have known the *Ghost* intimately since his birth. You can trust him. With your life.'

'You're not coming?'

Lawrence smiled in compassion at Jason and shook his head.

'Follow me. Just him.' The soldier pointed to Jason.

He marched them past five of the vans, then stopped.

'I can go no further. He waits for you. In there.'

The back doors of the van slowly opened. Hidden in the shadows was a man in a black militia uniform, with a black balaclava over his face.

'The Ghost,' the young Israeli whispered in awe.

The doors closed behind Jason. The van lit up. Inside was a vast communications system.

'I have waited a long time.' The Ghost put out his hand. Jason grasped it with both his hands.

'Thank you. *Thank you* for saving our lives.'

They both stood silent.

'May I ask you a question?'

The Ghost nodded.

'Would you have saved us if . . . if you hadn't needed to rescue the High Prie–'

Jason froze, his gaze riveted to the gold signet ring on the Ghost's little finger. He looked up at the Ghost, bewildered.

'Your – your ring . . .'

There was a long silence.

Very slowly, with trembling hands, the Ghost removed his balaclava.

'Hello, Jason,' he said softly.

Jason stared in amazement. The resemblance was not only uncanny; it was staggering. The elegant features. Dirty blonde hair. Piercing grey eyes. Strong jawline. Except for the two-inch scar splayed across his chin.

The Ghost holstered the SIG Sauer semi-automatic pistol he'd been holding. 'We don't have much time.'

'Who *are* you?'

'Can't you *guess*, Jason?' The Hebrew inflection had totally disappeared. The Ghost spoke with a London W1 accent.

The man standing in front of him was the spitting image of his father, James De Vere, from photographs when he was in his early forties.

'You . . . you look like . . .'

'Your father, James De Vere?' He took off the signet ring and held it up to Jason. 'I visited our father the night before he was murdered. He gave me this.'

Jason stared dumbfounded at the familiar ring with the De Vere Crest embossed onto it.

'He told me about our mother. Her Jewish heritage. I became the Ghost. I'm the infant that was swapped with the clone in the hospital.'

Tears welled up in his eyes.

'I'm your blood brother, Jason. I'm the *real* Adrian De Vere.'

The story continues in a future release.

THE CHARACTERS

Earth: 2021

The De Vere Dynasty

Jason De Vere – eldest brother, De Vere dynasty. Place of birth: New York, USA. US media tycoon. Chairman, owner, and CEO of multi-billion-dollar media corporation Vox Entertainment. Owns a third of the Western world's television and newspaper empires. Married to Julia St Cartier for twenty years. One daughter, Lily De Vere. Divorced.

Adrian De Vere – middle brother, De Vere dynasty. Place of (recorded) birth: London, England. Former Prime Minister of the United Kingdom (Labour, two terms), ex-President of the European Union (ten-year term). Nobel Peace Prize nominee. Negotiated the Ishtar Accord – the Third World War peace treaty. Married to Melissa Vane Templar for five years. Melissa deceased in childbirth. One son, Gabriel, deceased.

Julia St Cartier – former editor of *Cosmopolitan*. Present, founder/CEO of Lola PR. Married to Jason De Vere for twenty years. Mother to Lily De Vere. Divorced.

Lily De Vere – Julia and Jason De Vere's daughter.

Maxim – James and Lilian De Vere's butler.

Lawrence St Cartier – Jesuit priest; retired CIA; antiquities dealer. Julia St Cartier's uncle.

Alex Lane-Fox – son of Rachel Lane-Fox. Investigative journalist. Close family friend of Julia, Jason, and Lily De Vere.

Rachel Lane-Fox – supermodel. Julia's best pal. Killed aboard aircraft in 9/11 attack.

Rebekah and David Weiss – Rachel Lane-Fox's parents.

Charles Xavier Chessler – warlock. Former chairman of Chase Manhattan Bank. President of World Bank. Retired. Jason De Vere's godfather.

Dylan Weaver – genius IT specialist. Nick De Vere's old school friend.

Kurt Guber – first head of security at Downing Street, now director of EU Special Services Security Operations. Exotic-weapons specialist.

Neil Travis – former SAS, chief of security for Adrian De Vere.

Frau Vghtred Meeling – Austrian employee of De Vere household. Nanny to Jason, Adrian, and Nick. Also, Abbess Helewis Vghtred.

The Brotherhood
(Illuminati)

His Excellency Lorcan De Molay – former superior general of the Jesuit order. Supreme high priest of the Brotherhood, Jesuit priest. Birthplace: indeterminate. Current age: indeterminate.

Kester Von Slagel (Baron) – Lorcan De Molay's emissary.

Charles Xavier Chessler

The Royal House of Jordan

Jibril – King of Jordan.

First Heaven

Jesus – Christos, the Nazarene.
Michael – chief prince of the royal household of Yehovah; commander-in-chief, First Heaven's armies; President of the Warring Councils.
Gabriel – chief prince of the royal house of Yehovah, Lord Chief Justice of Angelic Revelators.
Jether – imperial warrior and ruler of the twenty-four ancient monarchs of the First Heaven and High Council. Chief Steward of Yehovah's sacred mysteries.
Xacheriel – Ancient of Days' Curator of the Sciences and Universes, one of the twenty-four kings under Jether's governance.
Lamaliel – member of the Ruling Council of Angelic Elders.
Issachar – member of the Ruling Council of Angelic Elders.
Obadiah, Dimnah – *younglings* – an ancient angelic race with characteristics of eternal youth and a remarkable inquisitiveness.
Zadkiel – Gabriel's general.

The Fallen

Lucifer – *Satan,* king of Perdition. Tempter; adversary; sovereign ruler of the race of men, Earth, and the nether regions.
Charsoc – dark apostle, Chief High Priest of the Fallen. Governor of the Grand Wizards of the Black Court and the dreaded Warlock Kings of the West.
Marduk – head of the Darkened Councils and Lucifer's chief-of-staff.

The Twin Wizards of Malfecium – the grand wizard of Phaegos and the grand wizard of Maelageor. The super-scientists.

Astaroth – commander-in-chief of the Black Horde. Michael's former general.

Nephilim – A hybrid between the angelic and the race of men.